AWAKENING

Book 1 of the Homecoming Saga

JOE HERRICK

ISBN: 1974433498
ISBN 13: 9781974433490

DEDICATION

This is for my mom.
As far back as I can remember, you were always encouraging my creativity
and telling me that if I worked hard enough, I could do anything. You've
been more than just a mom on this journey. You've worn many hats:
cheerleader, editor, creative consultant and even investor. Thank you so much.
This book wouldn't have happened without you, that much is certain.

PROLOGUE

It had been a long time. No, not just a long time, an impossibly long time. Hundreds of years had passed and nothing had moved in the room. Not one footfall, not one breath, not even one speck of dust had moved from its original resting spot. It was in many respects, a tomb. Darkness was everywhere. Light had not touched a single object inside the room for centuries. The chamber had remained sealed for nearly a millennia, but its purpose was finally at hand.

The walls, floor and ceiling were all made of a tough, non-corrosive metal. Not that it mattered, though. There had been no oxygen present inside the room to oxidize anything. Small circular bolts, made of the same metallic material, lined down walls and across the floor in precise, box-like patterns. They seemed to coalesce at a central point in one of the walls. Of course, in the utter blackness in the room, one would not be able to tell that any of these things even existed... until a small red light suddenly flashed on.

The entire room was now awash in a red glow. The first light this room had seen in ages illuminated everything that was contained within the thick metal walls. Then, just as abruptly, darkness again. Then red light once more. On and off, the small light blinked, indicating the beginning of a complex, but well-orchestrated cycle of events. Events, that once completed, would, quite possibly, save the human race from extinction.

A screen along the far wall that had stayed hidden until now popped on and displayed a series of status read-outs. A light-blue hue overpowered any semblance of flashing red that had existed before. Numbers clicked by on the screen faster than any human could read, not that there was anyone standing there to read them. The computer concluded, as hoped, that everything had remained intact and was ready for the upcoming procedure.

Once the computer had finished its analysis, a small beep sounded. After a slight pause, a piece of the floor fell away where it met the center of the wall. As if attached to some kind of string that was being pulled, a cylinder slowly rose up from the floor until it was standing tall against the wall like a pillar.

While most of the cylinder had the same metallic surface as the rest of the room, the midsection were made almost completely out of a transparent material. As soon as the cylinder was in place, the clear surface began to glow. It was subtle at first, but after a few moments it was shining a bright blue. Then, in a flash the blue glow vanished, and with it, the transparent material. Now a thick, grey gas was pouring into the room from inside the large canister. As the grey cloud grew larger, it became clear that the gas had not just exited from within the cylinder itself, but must be pumping in from somewhere else as well, perhaps from another room behind the wall on which the cylinder was attached.

When the greyness finally began to dissipate and only wisps of it hung around the floor like the mists of an early morning, the naked body of what appeared to be a human male, possibly in his mid- to early-thirties, was revealed inside the cylinder's hold. Small, metal braces held his wrists and ankles in place. Tubes about a millimeter thick snaked out of his neck and into the inner workings of the capsule behind his head. With a giant *boom* the tubes fluctuated. The man's mouth flew open, exhaling. A light blue liquid splashed out onto the floor. A light cough... a short, hesitant breath... and then, finally, he took a long, deep inhalation.

The coughs came more frequently now as he attempted to control his breathing. More blue liquid found its way onto the floor. His eyes flashed open. Almost as quickly, they closed again. Even the relatively small amount of light emitted from the tiny computer screen on the far wall was still a bit too much for his sensitive eyes. Much like his breathing, his eyes had a few false starts, but eventually they adjusted themselves to their environment.

As if they somehow knew he was ready, the clamps opened up from his wrists and ankles. There was a slight drop as his feet fell down onto the padded floor of the metallic cocoon. He gingerly lifted his right foot up and off of the cylinder's floor, balancing himself somewhat on his left foot, forcing his right hand to shoot out against the edge of the capsule, stopping himself from toppling over.

As he steadied himself, he took his first tentative step out of the cylinder. Much to his surprise, his foot slipped out from under him on some of the blue liquid he had coughed out only moments before. Luckily, his hands were still gripping the inside of the capsule, so he did not fall. After kicking off as much blue goo as he could from his foot, he took another step, careful to avoid any of the multiple pools dotting the floor. Once he had advanced far enough away, the tubes connecting him to the capsule detached from his neck, creating faint popping noises as they did so. The holes left behind immediately sealed themselves, blending in with the rest of his skin.

After stepping on his tip-toes, careful to avoid any more liquid on the floor, our young male, still very naked, made his way to the computer. He touched a few icons on the screen, pulling up an aerial view map, which included topography. In all of the low-lying areas on the screen there were hundreds of small circles, pulsing white. A dozen or so additional circles were an ashen grey.

Hmmm... Not too bad, he thought.

He would have expected worse, considering how long it had been. Touching one of the pulsing circles, he pulled up a database containing a variety of information, including mean temperature, barometric pressure, O2 levels and population density. Each data point contained a link to even more thorough and detailed statistics. This was going to take too long.

"To hell with it," he muttered.

He scratched near his right wrist, where a tiny hole opened. He pinched inside with his fingertips and pulled out a razor thin cord with what looked like a needle on the end. Finding a miniscule hole beneath the screen, he pushed the pin into the nearly microscopic port. The entire screen dimmed and a status bar appeared. In 1.62 seconds the download was complete.

I'll try to start acting like an actual human later. Right now, I don't have the time, he thought.

He pulled the pin out of the port and squeezed his wrist gently with his thumb and forefinger. The cord and pin shot back into his body like a tape measure. The processing of the data took only a little bit longer than the download, 2.14 seconds. He had the first candidate. They were a bit of a ways away from his current location. Unless he found some mode of transportation it would take him months to get there.

Perhaps he could just find someone a little bit closer, but no, his mission parameters were clear: go with the most qualified candidate first and then work your way down the list. He wondered how this blasted machine even came up with its results. He knew of course. It was all one gigantic algorithm that consisted of a series of biometric scans, looking for genetic precursors or some such nonsense. It was the most accurate system they had, but that didn't mean he trusted it, especially when it meant he had to take a hike across that dead wilderness.

No time like the present, might as well get to it, he thought bitterly.

He walked half a dozen steps to the far wall. He pushed a button with his thumb that was about the size of a small coin. Part of the wall opened sideways to reveal a closet loaded with gear. He threw on a black jumpsuit, complete with boots, a pair of goggles and a breathing mask. With those winds out there, one would need to be prepared. He thumbed the closet closed and walked over to the wall furthest from where he had awoken. There was another coin-sized button on this wall. He pressed it.

It was like a supernova exploding in his face. Sunlight screamed into the small space, illuminating every nook, cranny and crevice. His eyes watered madly, even though they had been protected somewhat by the goggles he now wore. That wasn't even the worst of it, however. Winds carrying millions of grains of red dust poured into the not-so-large room, covering everything just after the hatch opened. He knew that this was what he'd have to deal with for most of this little "adventure", and it didn't make the anticipation of it any more enjoyable.

"Well, time to hit the road," he said to no one in particular. "It's been fun."

He stepped out into the storm.

The following is an excerpt from *The Book of the Founders:*

"In the beginning, the sky was a blackened void. There was no ground below. All was darkness. Then, the Founders came. The first of these was the Great Orb, the giver of all life. It exploded into the heavens, streaming its light in all directions. It gave birth to all of the other Founders: much smaller, but no less brilliant. Over time, hundreds and then thousands and then tens of thousands appeared in the sky. Twinkling their divine light, they looked out upon the emptiness before them. When the Great Orb became tired and began its descent into sleep, the other Founders would appear to keep watch in its stead. Even though their kind was spread out through every corner of the cosmos, they still felt strangely alone, isolated.

"Before long, a decision was made to fill the emptiness with something new. And from that decision, the world was made. Rocks, trees, water, grass, mountains and sand- all and much more were combined to form a world that was pleasing to the Founders. Now instead of just themselves and the void, the Founders had something new to look upon. Winds blew, rivers flowed and plants grew. A great tapestry had been laid out before them in all its beauty. Over time, however, they grew sad, for the world they had created was still more or less unchanging. Something else was needed.

"Soon, one of the Founders envisioned filling the world with creatures: living beings that would populate this wondrous work of art. And so, life was created. Birds, horses, fish, lions, deer, snakes and all manner of other creatures were brought forth. They moved about, interacting with one another, living and dying. The picture now had motion. It was no longer stagnant. The Founders could watch with joy as their created beings interacted with one another. These new beings were living out their own stories as they went along.

"Once again, however, the Founders grew restless. Something was still missing. Then, the answer came to them and the decision was made to form a new creature, one to lord over all others. It would be imbibed with the knowledge and capabilities to decide its own fate and path. With this new revelation, the Founders were overjoyed. Finally, there would be something that they could not predict, something building a history as it lived and breathed. Would this new creation fail and die out, or would it transcend even the Founders' wildest expectations? They did not know, and in that came the excitement.

"And so, man was born. As before, the Founders were proud of themselves and their new accomplishment. And for a time, man did not disappoint in dazzling them with his ingenuity, creativity, resourcefulness and passion. The human race prospered and multiplied. Their seed spread to every corner of the lands of creation. For thousands of generations, the Founders looked upon man with pride.

"But this did not last.

"After a long period of prosperity, human beings began to turn on one another. The Founders were confused. They had not expected this. Man became greedy, self-indulgent. Some declared themselves greater than the Founders themselves. Others even began to question the Founders' very existence! Wars were fought between neighboring tribes. Many were killed for no more reason than for one man to appear superior over another. But that was only the beginning. Humans not only destroyed one another, but soon they began to destroy their world as well.

"The Founders looked on in dismay as man began to tear apart their beloved creation, bit by bit. Trees were chopped down, rivers dried up, whole species of living things were wiped out of existence, all in the name of humanity's greed. Great machines were developed and constructed, simply for the purpose of destroying the environment and other living things more efficiently. Before long, the whole of creation was in danger of

being completely destroyed. The world had been stripped of so much that it had in essence become unlivable.

"The Founders had reached an impass. Would they allow their creation to be destroyed or would they intervene? If they did nothing, it seemed inevitable that their great experiment was doomed for failure; the humans would destroy themselves and the rest of their world with them. This was the moment of The Great Miracle. Through the everlasting grace of the Founders, humanity was given a second chance. Only a few were selected. These were those whom the Founders favored above all others, those that the Founders felt they could trust. It was these chosen ones that the Founders believed could begin again and not descend into chaos, as their brothers and sisters had. The rest were decimated by the Founders' wrath: snuffed out of existence and turned to dust in a single stroke of fury. Only the chosen ones remained, though the world was still teetering towards its demise.

"In order to save the chosen ones from certain death, the Founders sealed them in a protective barrier. Inside was plenty: food, water and shelter: everything they needed to start again. Outside was a reminder of what had been: a wasteland of death and despair. Forever would humanity's future generations look out and see what their ancestors had reaped for themselves and their world. It served as a stern reminder not to repeat the mistakes of the past. Humanity now had an opportunity to learn from their history and take a more enlightened path."

Chapter 1

The air that had filled the small bar was rank. It was always rank. This wasn't the kind of place where one would take their family. People came to Joe's to get drunk, it was as simple as that. Most of the clientele there were workers from the mine, which had been by design when the place was built. When the workers filed out of the mining complex, a sizable number of them filed right in through the entrance to Joe's. Jake was no different.

He stopped for a moment inside the doorway. He had to duck slightly to avoid hitting his head. In most cases being slightly taller than the average man had its advantages, but not always. He brushed his hand through his short, brown hair, throwing up a cloud of grey smoke. He still had his work clothes on from the mine, which were nothing more than a tan-colored, one-size-fits-all jumpsuit that zipped closed from the crotch up to the neck and a pair of thick-soled work boots. Dark streaks of dirt and dust still clung to them. Most of the miners that entered Joe's didn't bother changing clothes. The place was so filthy itself that it hardly seemed to matter.

Jake surveyed the bar. Large cracks could be seen working their way down the course, stone interior. Pebbles were scattered all over the floor. He had long since assumed that the place would probably cave in at some point. There were no games; no darts, no pool, no card tables. Those were for the more upscale joints that were not to be found anywhere in New Salem. The tables were made of the same rocky material as everything else in the bar, sprouting out of the floor like mushrooms. A small candle was set on each one, strictly for lighting purposes, not for any kind ambiance. For additional lighting, torches lined the walls. Smoke from the torches combined with the fumes from cigaras and the dust flying off of the dirty miners, making breathing difficult. Fights were common. There had been a few serious ones that had ended in death, but it had been a while since any of that unpleasantness. Most people turned a blind eye to any disruption that might occur. It wasn't their business.

He finished his scan of Joe's interior and furrowed him brow in frustration. Tom was late. This wasn't like Tom. He stepped inside and slowly made his way towards the long table in the back of the room. This is where all manner of dangerous beverages could be found lining the back wall, most of which hardly ever tried by Jake himself. There had been rumors that a man had died from only one shot of something appropriately named "The Devil's Nectar". Jake smartly chose to stick mostly just to beer. The back table was also where Joe himself could be found, usually dressed in his signature beer-stained apron, which ballooned out from his midsection like some grotesque pumpkin. If anyone here knew where Tom was, it would be Joe. There was very little that got past that man's eyes. He knew everyone in New Salem quite well. Some even better than they knew themselves.

Jake had lived in the small town of New Salem all of his twenty-two year (or eleven cycle) life and had worked in its mine nearly half of that time. It had always seemed peculiar to Jake that people's ages were determined by twelve-month "years" instead of the twenty-four-month cycles the sun took through the sky. Sometimes the reasoning behind society's seemingly illogical choices baffled Jake. People said that using years made it easier to differentiate between people, plus it was what had been done for generations. This made little sense to him, but who was he to argue?

New Salem was the kind of place people ended up when they were all out of options in life. If opportunity and career advancement were on your mind, New Salem was the place you ran *from*, not *to*. The mine itself was basically your only option as far as work was concerned. Sure, there was the Golden Inn (why it was called that, Jake never knew- the place was more the shade of excrement, in his opinion), the school, the stables, the med clinic, a few shops that dotted Main Street, and of course, Joe's bar. The shops in town sold only the most essential items to get by in the rocky, arid climate surrounding the town: food, protective clothing, maybe a few bars of soap if they were lucky. Only a handful of people worked those jobs, but every one of them still had at least one family member that was a miner. For all intents and purposes, the mine *was* the town of New Salem.

He had once thought he would escape the maw of New Salem and run off to parts of Magella yet unknown to him. Perhaps Hope City in the forests of the Southwest Quarter (the name was encouraging enough) or Waterville, on the shores of Grand Lake in the Southeast Quarter. There was always the capital city of Apex, of course. That was probably too much to hope for. It was located in the exact center of the circular footprint of Magella, for either logistical or aesthetical reasons. Probably both. Only the wealthiest and best-connected people lived there. Jake didn't count himself in with that particular group.

He had been young when thoughts of affluence and prestige danced around in his young and blossoming imagination, but reality had struck its forceful blow not long after. Within the timespan of six weeks, both of his parents were dead and he had been orphaned. He had been twelve years old at the time. Had he been ten or even eleven, maybe he would have been placed in an orphanage, most likely not in New Salem. However, the town magistrate deemed him old enough to begin making his own living. So, while all of Jake's friends continued to work on their studies, Jake worked on breaking what precious metals he could out of walls of black and grey rock.

Jake's father had also been a miner. Ten years ago, there had been a cave-in, trapping over a dozen workers. It was all over the local papers and had caused quite a stir. Everyone seemed to be talking about it as Morzellano, the mine's operator, and his "consultants" worked to figure out a way to get the men out. It had taken them weeks before they finally came up with a plan. They had decided to dig down next to the open space where the collapse had occurred and then tunnel in sideways. Though they had broken through without any further cave-ins, all of the trapped workers had died from the noxious fumes that had built up inside the cavern. Jake's father had been one of them.

If Morzellano was tough with the workers before that, he was an absolute tyrant afterwards. Not a single inch of that cavern was excavated without his knowledge and approval ahead of time. If a worker was even suspected of some dereliction of duty, they were dragged into his office to explain themselves. If Morzellano didn't like the answer, they were booted out of the operation for life. Most workers lived in fear of this. If they lost their position working for the mining operation, they were hard-pressed to find any other kind of employment. Morzellano knew this all too well and exploited it.

The death of Jake's mother was remarkably similar to that of his father's. No one had seen the particular rockslide happen, but it didn't take long for people to notice. The pile had blocked a roadway, stopping the small amount of horse-bound traffic that passed by each day. Later, when Jake had heard about the rockslide during one of his classes, his heart began to race. The area was exactly where he and his mom walked to take him to school. Almost immediately he ran off in the direction of the rock pile, leaving all of his school supplies scattered around his study area. Someone should have stopped him. Someone should have put two and two together and realized what he was running towards... but no one did.

Now at twenty-two years old, most of Jake's schoolyard friends were long gone, off to lives of purpose and meaning. Not every child made it, of course. A few years after Jake had began his work in the mine, a few of his classmates had joined him. These kinds of drop-outs were common and Morzellano was more than happy to give their young lives a new direction. For Jake, the reason had not been grades (he actually did quite well in school), but it was the lack of a solid parental situation at home. He was too old for new parents, or to be considered a case worth fighting for. He was a lost cause, thrown to the side of the road and discarded.

There were plenty of other students anyways, as far as the government of Magella was concerned. In fact, there were so *many* young people coming up through the educational system, that many older citizens were worried what was to become of them. Higher-level jobs like medical technicians, law officials and government workers were sparse at best, even outside of New Salem. A few students who had earned their Certificate of Completion even ended up down in the mines anyways. The looks on their faces told the other workers that this was *not* what they had planned for.

According to Apex and its leaders, all should be happy with whatever job they may end up with, for all serve the whole of Magella, no matter what their trade may be. "For The Greater Good" was a phrase that everyone had known since birth. Everyone had a purpose and a way to serve Magella. Schooling just helped siphon out people along the way. Those that showed an aptitude for a certain area were directed towards a career in that field. The rest were placed "elsewhere". The mine was one of many "elsewheres" throughout Magella, and not even one of the best on the list. Jake wondered whose "greater good" he was really serving as he toiled down in those mines, day after day.

Going to Joe's afterwards was usually the sole bright spot in his tiresome routine. The run-down, dirty stick-hole of a bar, its walls physically crumbling away, was a sort of chaotic sanctuary for him.

"Hey Jake, where are you going?"

Jake looked down at the sound of the voice and saw his friend Tom smiling up at him.

How did I miss him? Jake thought to himself. Had he been there the entire time? Surely not. Someone like Tom stuck out like a sore thumb in a place like Joe's.

Tom was dressed in the same dirt-caked jumpsuit as the rest of the miners, but for some reason he always seemed a bit less disgusting... even a bit less miserable, too. Perhaps the man actually enjoyed the job. There had to be somebody somewhere that liked this kind of stuff, Jake supposed. Tom had a face that didn't seem fit for this type of work, though. He looked more like a performer who should be on stage or a dignitary off having his portrait done somewhere. His bright blue eyes sparkled out from within his grey-streaked face. His perfectly straight, bright white teeth made absolutely no sense, once one took a moment to look at the chompers of everyone else at Joe's. His blonde hair seemed to almost hang there, suspended a bit over his head and dammit if the dust from the mine didn't seem to just bounce right off of it, as if there was some kind of invisible shield there keeping its color that natural golden yellow.

They had met only a few months before. Tom was a new worker at the mine, sent over from the town of Westing, on the far side of Magella. It didn't make sense to Jake at the time why someone from Westing would ever want to come to a dusty, worn town like New Salem. Westing was such a colorful, vibrant place, full of culture and excitement and new opportunities. All New Salem had going for it was the bar. Hell, it wasn't even *that good* of a bar.

On the day Tom arrived, he had joined Jake's team, despite there not being a vacancy amongst them. No one had quit or been injured in the group. But Jake relished in the extra help and invited Tom to the operation with open arms. It was quite unlike the treatment Tom had received from everyone else on the team.

It was quite commonplace in the mine for a new hire to get the cold shoulder from their fellow workers until they had proven themselves. Jake could care less about this convention, so, quite naturally, he had befriended Tom, much like other newcomers in the past. However, as time went on, the bridges of camaraderie would burn away in some way or another. Once the new worker had been there long enough to gain the acceptance of the rest of the gang. Jake would be left, forgotten. So far, that hadn't been the case with Tom. In the back of his mind, Jake was sure that it was only a matter of time, but for now, he was glad that he had someone that he could talk to.

Even though Jake had spent weeks working with him, Tom still seemed to be a bit of a mystery. Morzellano hadn't told them much of his story when he had joined, just that he came from the town of Westing. When they first met, Jake had asked Tom all kinds of questions about his life back in Westing, but all questions had been politely declined. That was fine. Tom liked to keep a lot of his past to himself, which Jake respected. All men have their secrets. If Tom ever wanted to share them, Jake would be willing to listen, but for now, he was content with his friend either way.

Founders knew why anyone would ever want to leave a place like Westing and come to New Salem. New Salem was literally a dusty old hole in the ground, surrounded by a few modest homes and shops. In Westing, there was life: rivers, woods, rich farmland, and if the stories were true, fields of some of the most beautiful flowers in all of Magella. One thing was for sure: there was not a single mine to be found in Westing. Jake would have done anything to get out of that miserable town and move to Westing, if he could.

Jake pulled out the chair across from Tom, sat down and set a small coin down on the table's surface. Sometimes if one of them was feeling especially generous, the other would end up having quite a night. The night before had been Tom's night to buy. So, seeing as it was now Jake's turn, he was set on knocking his friend off his chair by the night's end. The bar maids knew them both well. They enjoyed the pair, mainly because Tom and Jake's drinking added up to some nice extra coin in the bar maids' pockets. It definitely wasn't their charming personalities. Frankly, most of the servers thought the two of them were a little weird.

Jake had tried to charm the young ladies there a few times, but he always came off as nervous, unsure or awkward. Most of the time it was a combination of all three. Jake's mother had been a server at Joe's before she died. Although most of the ladies hadn't worked with her when she had been a server, it was just a little strange for them to be getting her son drunk. They felt sorry for him. They knew his past. They knew that his mother had toiled here, like they all did every night, to keep her family afloat. That knowledge, coupled with Jake tripping over his own words constantly, made the decision easy: they were friendly with the boy, but not THAT kind of friendly.

"What'll it be, boys?" their new friend but not THAT kind of friend asked as she approached their table, a small smirk riding the edge of her lips.

"How's the brew?" Tom inquired.

"Well, we just opened up a new barrel not ten minutes ago. It is a little bit on the bitter side, but otherwise I hear it's a good one."

"Alright, sounds wonderful."

"And you, hon?"

Jake looked up and asked, "How's the whisky?"

"Always the same: hard."

"I'll start with a double-shot." It had been a long day. Plus, he was not relishing the conversation that was about to take place. Hopefully this gulp of firewater would help calm his nerves.

"Startin' strong. My kind of man."

She turned and headed off towards the bar. Jake was not her kind of man. He knew it. She knew it. The whole bar knew it. The game for a little extra money at the end of the night was on. Although Jake knew nothing would ever come of it, he enjoyed being wooed, if just for a little while as he drank with his friend. This would be the closest he would ever get to being in a real relationship. He had come to terms with this fact a while ago, when it became obvious that his techniques at charming the ladies were not effective. Women just didn't seem to see much in him. He had kissed a girl back when he was ten years old, but in reality, the girl was just curious what a kiss would be like. Once she had found out, she had moved on, not really giving Jake any further thought. He bet she wouldn't even remember him if she saw him again.

"Maybe this will be the night!" Tom bellowed as if he were giving some sort of speech.

"The night for what?" Jake asked, a little worried at what his friend was playing at.

"The night you get to take one of these fine barmaids home with you!"

"Ok, now you are just being mean."

"There's always hope."

"Not with me. Not with this. Thanks, though."

"You never know, things change."

"Time to change the *topic*, my friend. I've had a hard enough day as it is. I don't need to be reminded of my ineptitude with women as well."

Tom just laughed. Shortly thereafter, their drinks arrived. Almost as soon as the small glass had hit the table, it was up again, Jake throwing its burning contents down his throat. Tom laughed again. He sipped his beer, trying out the new flavor. The look on his face told Jake that their server had been right. It wasn't bad.

"Alright, my friend. Let me tell you what is really on my mind," Tom said, now in a slightly more serious tone.

Here we go, Jake thought.

"I think we have an opportunity here." Tom continued.

"The new cave?" Jake replied. "No, absolutely not."

Only a few hours earlier, Jake and his team had discovered a new cavern, untouched by mining hands. The news had traveled quickly. Morzellano had been called down as he always was in situations such as those. The pudgy old man had taken no more than a few seconds' glance when he turned around and declared, "too close to quittin' time. I'll check it out tomorrow." And that was it. He instantly began his slow ascent back up out of the cave, muttering as he went, "hardly worth sloggin' all the way down into this Founders-forsaken pit..."

Jake shuffled nervously in his chair.

"Tonight's the night, Jake," Tom said. "If we wait for tomorrow, Morzellano will get his greedy little hands on everything."

"I know, but-"

"This is the kind of opportunity we've talked about before and now it's here, ready for us to take advantage of it! Look, it's simple: we slip in tonight and take a look around. Nobody needs to be the wiser. If we find something of real value, we grab it. We need to be selective, though. Don't go for the cheap stuff. We need high value items, here. Gold, platinum... that kind of stuff. It needs to be something we can cram into a couple of packs and carry out the same night."

"You know what will happen to us if we are caught, right?"

"Sure, they'll probably hang us by our toes out on Main Street or something."

"Tom, in the eyes of the Council of Elders, this is taking from The Greater Good. That is punishable by death."

"Only in extreme cases."

"And this isn't?"

"Probably not. I guess it would be up to the town magistrate... but listen, we are not *going* to get caught, ok? Nobody keeps an eye on that place at night. It is laughably easy! We sneak in, dig around for a few hours, and sneak back out. Nobody will know we were ever down there!"

Tom was right there. Morzellano had hardly any security after hours at the mine. Maybe it was a simple case of overconfidence? More than likely, Morzellano knew the place was so dangerous that only fools would try to break in after the crews were gone for the night... fools like Jake and Tom, apparently.

"And you are sure that if we *do* find something, that you have a buyer for us?" Jake asked.

"Absolutely. I have my contact with The Underground."

The Underground. It was a risky proposition. Jake had heard stories about the organization, everyone had. They worked in secret, dealing in stolen goods and redistributing wealth to those with whom they did business. To many who saw the government of "The Greater Good" as tyrannical and unfair, The Underground was viewed as freedom fighters and patriots, fighting a corrupt system. But, cross them or not follow through on a deal? That was bad news. There were many citizens of Magella that had done business with The Underground and then one day they were just gone. Poof. Never to be seen again.

"Do you think dealing with them is wise?" Jake asked.

JOE HERRICK

"I have already in the past, Jake," Tom said, lowering his voice, "I have a good rapport with them. Besides, think of it, Jake! No longer just living off of the few coins Morzellano throws at us each week for doing this dirty and dangerous job! The Underground... that is where the *real* wealth comes from! Your days of digging out a few precious metals from the ground so that some well-to-do snob from Apex can have another piece of jewelry she'll only wear once will be over! You and I both know that you deserve a better life than what has been handed to you."

Tom knew right where to turn the screws.

"Ok, if we do try this, I need your word that we are going to be careful. The last thing we need is to get caught or injured before we ever find anything. And if we don't find anything..."

"We simply head on back to work like nothing happened and look just as shocked as everyone else on the team when the cavern turns out to be a dud."

"Do you really think Morzellano will go down there tomorrow on his own? It is Founders Day, tomorrow, after all. That's a day off."

"True, but you know Morzellano. He'll still be there at the mine tomorrow, no matter what day it is. For him, that damned mine IS his religion."

"Yeah, I suppose you're right."

"So, does that mean you are in?"

"Yeah," Jake sighed. "It's a deal. I'm in."

12

CHAPTER 2

"Only that which is made by the hand is
worthy. All else is an abomination."

-*The Book of the Founders*

The tunnel Jake was standing in was a little bit wider than two meters and just tall enough that he didn't have to slouch over, but only just barely. For most miners, the ceiling would never even get close to hitting their heads. Jake, however, had knocked his head into a low-hanging chunk of rock more than once. The tunnels throughout the mine were small enough to make most men claustrophobic, but Jake had gotten used to it. He had spent enough years working in the tunnels of the mine that it was not even a passing thought anymore.

Jake was dressed in his workday jumpsuit, even though he was now in the mine during off hours. A few loops were outfitted to carry all manner of mining tools. This evening he had kept things simple, selecting only a pickaxe and his small chiseling tool for more delicate rock removal. Jake's hair was already turning grey from all of the dust that had been picked up by his movements inside the mine. He could have worn a mask to cover his mouth and keep out some of the dust particles, but he didn't. After a while, it just didn't seem like it made any difference anymore.

Dust puffed up and around Jake's gloved hands as he rubbed them together. The little cloud materialized directly in front of his nose. In an instant it was gone again, much like his confidence for this fool's errand. How could he have allowed himself to be talked into this ridiculous idea? Jake liked to think of himself as a fairly reasonable guy who didn't take on any substantial risk unless there was a fairly good reason for doing so.

Dammit if Tom wasn't persuasive, though.

Where did that come from? What was it about Tom that seemed to pull out all of the sense from Jake's brain? Jake had to remind himself that in all likelihood, there would be few, if any, items of real value down there in that cave. He had worked in this mine long enough to know that one could go for days before even a scrap of good copper popped up. No, he had to stay logical here. The most likely outcome was probably just a pair of empty hands.

Tom's face materialized out of the darkness, his blond hair flopping side to side. In one hand was his torch and in the other was a small tan pack, about the size of an average housecat. He panted a few times, briskly. He may have been a little out of breath but it didn't seem to be bothering him too much. The smile on his face said it all. He was excited, ready to go. No worries or second thoughts here. Those perfect pearly whites of his blazed in the dark cavern. He clapped Jake on the shoulder as he passed him and bent over to peer down into the small hole near the floor.

"Are you sure we can fit through there?" Jake asked.

Tom just gave him a look as if to say, "yeah, of course we can."

Jake just nodded.

"Here, hold this," Tom said as he handed Jake his torch. Jake had to react quickly, nearly dropping it. Tom then placed his pack on the ground, unzipped it and began rummaging around. He removed a hammer, a couple of metal spikes and a length of rope. As he inched closer to the opening, he felt around on the ground with his gloved hands. After seeming somewhat satisfied that he had found the correct spot, he began hammering one of the spikes into the ground. Soon, there were three stakes firmly planted in the rocky floor, each tied tightly to the rope. Tom took what was left of the rope and threw it into the opening by their feet. He gave it a few quick, hard tugs and smiled up at Jake, approvingly.

Jake walked up and snatched the rope out of Tom's grasp before he had a chance to offer it to Jake. He then sat down on the ground and inched forward until his feet were dangling out of the opening and into the newly discovered cavern. He leaned forward, careful not to hit his head, and peered through, torch extended out into the void. He saw only blackness. He dared to hope for a moment. He allowed himself to believe that Tom was right- that there was some rich vein of ore down there that they could sell to The Underground for a new lease on life.

He ducked his head further in through the opening, tightened his grip on the rope, and pushed off from the wall. Tom was not far behind. After working the rest of the way down the wall, the two men took a look around. Even with Tom's torch, it was difficult to see much of anything. The pair decided it would be best to go separate directions and maximize their efficiency. Jake pulled a second torch out from their pack and lit it. He turned to his left and walked about 20 meters until he came upon a wall. After a brief scan of things, he wasn't encouraged: just black rock everywhere. He traced his hands along the jagged wall, continuing to scan. The telltale sign of an expensive find was the shine or the sparkle of the reflection of light. So far, nothing. Just, drab, boring, plain old rock. He hoped that his friend was having better luck.

"Tom, you got anything?" Jake yelled out into the dark. He had no clue of Tom's whereabouts at this point.

"I was just going to ask you the same thing," Jake heard a disembodied voice say back from deep within the blackness.

We had better find something down here, Tom, Jake thought to himself, *or I may just have to start looking for a new friend.*

Friends had been hard to come by for Jake, even at a young age. Growing up, most of the other kids had politely avoided conversations with him. Jake was a quiet kid and found it hard to find the words to begin a conversation with someone. So, in order to keep things from possibly getting uncomfortable, he just kept his mouth shut. A lot of the other children took this as him being rude so they avoided him when they could. Some even shot him concerned glances as they passed him between classes. Their looks seemed to say, "why are you so quiet?" or "what's wrong with you?" or "what's really going on inside that head of yours that you aren't telling us?"

The only person that ever seemed to understand Jake had been his father. Many nights, after a long day of work in the mine, Jake's father would join him up on the roof of their modest home. They would lay down together and stare up at the sky. They didn't have a lot of things that they did together since Jake's dad always seemed to be at work, but looking at the evening sky together was one and it was by far Jake's favorite. He remembered vividly the last time they had been up there. As usual, his imagination was on overdrive.

"Do you think the stories are true, dad?"

"About what, son?"

"About the Founders… that they are up there, keeping watch over us."

"Well, that's what our faith teaches us. What do *you* think?"

"I think they are. They are constantly keeping a vigil, every night, to make sure we are safe."

"You seem pretty convinced."

"I know they are there. They won't let anything bad happen to us."

"Jake?" his father said, sitting up.

"Yeah, dad?" Jake replied, doing the same.

"I want to apologize."

"For what?" Jake could see the look of strain on his father's face.

"For not being here for you and your mom as much as I should be. I know it has been hard on the both of you, me being away so much."

"It's ok, dad. We know it's not your fault. You are doing what you can to keep the family going."

Jake always felt that his father was way too hard on himself. The man was only doing the best he could to keep food on the table and clothes on their backs. Both Jake and his mother understood this and appreciated it. Whenever they could, they tried to be as strong for him as they knew he was for them. Still, the man seemed to constantly beat himself up over it, as if there was something he could do differently.

"I want to show you something," Jake's father said, scooting closer and placing his arm around his son. "You see that bright blue star?"

"Where?" Jake was scanning the sky in all directions. Finally, his father pointed, helping him zero in on the target.

"Right there, near the horizon. It can be kind of easy to miss, since it is so close."

Jake looked carefully, even squinting a little bit. "Oh yeah! I see it!"

"That is our special star. Whenever I'm away, you can look at this star and know I am with you. Since it is so close to the horizon, most people miss it and don't even realize that it is there. That one is just for us."

Jake looked up at his father with tears in his eyes, but with a face that was still trying to be strong. "Ok, dad."

The following day, his father had been trapped in the cave-in.

Jake's memories of his parents were both some of his most joyous and yet sorrow-filled thoughts. How he wished he could touch them again, if only for a brief moment.

Snap out of it!

Jake realized that he had no idea how long he had been standing there, wasting time. He guessed that he and Tom had been down in the cave for probably around three hours now. Still not one speck of anything valuable had been seen by either of them. Jake had first made a quick sweep of his side of the cavern, hoping to stumble across something substantial. Now, he was back, retracing his steps, looking more closely at the finer details. Still, he knew it in his gut: this was a lost cause. He had to believe that even Tom would be losing hope by now.

"I found something!" came Tom's excited voice from his side of the cave.

Well, scratch that.

"What is it?" Jake shouted back.

"It's… ah… well, to be honest, I'm not really sure," Tom replied. His voice sounded almost a little bit scared.

"Is it gold?"

"No."

"Silver?"

"Um, maybe… Listen, just come over here and take a look. It will be a lot easier than me tying to explain."

"Alright, hold on…"

Jake got up from his crouched position and felt half a dozen different joints all crack in unison. He hadn't realized just how long he had been bent over, examining the rocky surface of the cavern wall. He felt a slight ache in his back, like someone had been pressing the pointy end of a stick into his lower spine. Bending from side to side, he tried to stretch his muscles a bit, but it didn't seem to do much good. Looking deep into the long stretch of nothingness, he could barely make out Tom's torch. The tiny flicker of light was moving side-to-side and bouncing up and down slightly, like a lightning bug off in the distance. Jake pointed his own torch in Tom's direction and cautiously began to make his way toward his companion. The last thing he needed to do right now was to roll an ankle.

After a couple of minutes, Jake finally arrived at Tom's side. Tom had a look of awe mixed with confusion. His picture-perfect smile was gone. Jake wasn't exactly sure how to react. He didn't know what Tom had found, but it seemed unclear whether or not it was the huge payday both of them had been looking for.

"What is it?" Jake asked again.

Tom didn't answer, but shifted his gaze from Jake's eyes to the wall of rock next to him. Down near where the wall met the floor, a small shiny object was sticking out from the rock. Only about half of it was visible, but even that was enough for Jake to know instantly that this object was unlike anything he had ever seen before. He crouched down and held his torch close to it for a more detailed inspection. It looked as if someone had flung a discus right into the rock wall, where it had become stuck.

Based on what was visible, Jake guessed it was a little bit wider than his fist. It was also quite flat, perhaps a tad bit thicker than his hand, from top to bottom. It was probably made out of platinum or silver, or perhaps a combination of the two. The rays of light from both torches sparkled and danced atop its surface. Whatever it was, he hoped that it would be worth *something* to *someone*.

He let his fingertips slide across its silvery surface, finding not a single blemish or rough edge. That was strange. All of the metals that were mined in the caves down in Morzellano's mine were as jagged as the rocks they were imbedded in. This thing was not natural. Someone had *made* this, someone with extremely sophisticated tools and craftsmanship. No one in Magella that Jake knew of had the means to craft something this perfectly smooth. It was impossible.

A few quick tugs proved just how firmly it was implanted in the rock. How had it gotten into the wall like that? It was an unnatural item found in a very natural place. Something didn't fit here, like they had stumbled upon some great secret they were not meant to discover. And yet, he was inexplicably drawn to it, as if he were in some kind of trance. A part of him deep down felt as if he were *meant* to find it. He shook the thought away, breaking the spell.

"Ok," Jake said to Tom, "I'm stumped. Do you have any ideas?"

"None," Tom said.

"Well, I say we dig it the rest of the way out," Jake said.

"Are you sure that's wise?" Tom cautioned, "We don't even know what in the world it is."

"I know, I know. But, we'll never figure that out if we just leave it here! We came all this way. There's still a chance we could get in trouble for this. I'm not going to leave here empty handed."

Tom sighed, "Alright, Jake. I'll trust you on this one. Thankfully it isn't all that big so we should be able to get it out without too much difficulty. I have to be honest though, you are kind of giving me the willies."

"The who's?"

"Nevermind."

Must be a Westing thing, Jake thought to himself.

"Let's get started," Tom said.

Jake responded by getting out his small chiseling tool and chipping at the rock around the metallic disc. Within seconds, Tom had his own chisel out and had joined him. While they were working, each one of them accidentally hit the little saucer a number of times, but not a single nick or scratch appeared on its surface. Whatever it was made of, it was clearly tough stuff. The tougher the metal, the more it was probably worth to The Underground. Jake smiled inside.

The prospect of making some real money from this little venture of theirs seemed to be going up.

With the two of them working together, they were able to get their strange little discovery dislodged in a matter of minutes. It fell out of its resting place and hit the ground with a clang. Jake knelt down, picked it up and dusted it off. As he had suspected, it was a perfectly circular disc. It was lighter than he had expected. Maybe it wasn't platinum or silver. How could something this light be so resistant to their tools? Had they found some kind of new metal down here? This could be an even bigger find than he thought! Still, its perfectly smooth and geometrically exact shape was troubling.

Jake knelt down and gently placed the disc and their chiseling tools inside of Tom's bag and zipped it up. When he looked up, he peered inside the hole from which the disc had been removed. He couldn't help thinking once again, *how did you get there? Where did you come from?* When Tom bent down to pick up the bag, Jake nabbed it first and sprang up to his feet almost instantly. He made a slightly apologetic face at Tom, then turned and made for the rope they had climbed down.

The climb back up the rope was more difficult than Jake had been expecting. He had to remind himself that although he was energized by their new find, it was still the middle of the night and he had already worked a full day in the mine before their little scavenger hunt. He now had the bag draped across his back like a hunter's quiver. He could feel and hear its contents jostling around inside. Part of him was worried that the disc might be getting damaged, but the logical portion of his brain reminded him just how durable it had been when they had removed it from the wall. Nothing short of an explosion would probably damage that thing.

Working one hand at a time and concentrating hard as to not lose his grip, he eventually made it to the top of the rope and through the small opening where they had originally entered. Tom wasn't far behind. Jake extended his hand and helped his friend back into the tunnel, dragging Tom's body unceremoniously through the dust and rock that littered its floor. As soon as Jake saw Tom's feet come into view, he let go and collapsed on the ground. They had first entered the mine around 24:30, only 30 minutes before the end of the 25-hour day. It was now 3:45. The new workday didn't start until 6:00. A few more minutes weren't going to hurt.

After a brief respite, Tom and Jake slowly got to their feet and made their way down the side tunnel until it connected with the main artery of the mining system. Jake looked to his left and saw the enormous tunnel make its slow arc up and to the right until it disappeared completely. Like the threads on a screw, it would continue along the arc for another five and a half revolutions until finally arriving at the mouth of the cavern. Along the way, dozens of side tunnels spat out like twigs on a tree branch.

About halfway back up the main tunnel, Jake suddenly stopped. He checked the bag. The disc was still there. Phew. He felt strangely like a mother who was afraid of losing her small child at the local market. Tom looked down at Jake's hand and then up at his face.

"Everything alright?" Tom asked.

"Yup, everything's fine," Jake said. They then continued their long march towards the exit of the mine.

CHAPTER 3

"Fear not the outside world, for the Founders
have placed their yoke of protection upon you.
Within this yoke is the realm of man. Without
this yoke is the realm of the Founders."

-*The Book of the Founders*

The following morning, Jake lay in his hammock, staring into the ceiling, mind racing. He was exhausted. It had been a late night to begin with and he had hardly slept even when he had been back in his hammock again. His thoughts kept returning to the small bag, lying on the floor just below him. When Tom had departed the previous night, he had allowed Jake to take the bag with him. Jake was a little concerned that Tom might not trust him with it. Would he risk Jake possibly running off with it? No, most likely not. Tom had proven to be a trusting fellow and even if Jake *had* chosen to run off, Tom still had those connections with The Underground. It wasn't a risk Jake was willing to take and Tom knew it.

Jake eyed the dust-covered bag as he leapt down from his hammock. Even though he knew the bag wasn't going anywhere, he still had a small irrational fear that it might go missing.

His residence was one of hundreds of small apartments, spread out, side to side and stacked atop one another in a giant grid. Aside from the bathroom, the entire apartment was just one open space. In one corner was his hammock, the other, a small kitchenette. There was also a table with two chairs, a couch along one wall and a handful of slightly rotted and scraped up dressers for his clothes and various small personal possessions. That was about it.

His shoes crunching on a couple of overturned bugs, Jake approached the front door. *Maybe if this deal works out, I wouldn't have so many deceased roommates,* Jake thought to himself, wryly. He turned the handle and opened it wide. He closed his eyes as the sunlight fell over his face. This was his favorite part of the day. It was Founders Day today, which meant he would have to be on his way to the temple soon... but not just yet. There was still time.

As he stepped outside, doors identical to his own seemed to go on forever in all directions: left, right, up and down. There were no windows. Each level had its own rickety, metal walkway attached to it, wide enough for two or three people to walk upon it abreast. Even though it was probably frowned upon, he had placed a small, fold-out chair on the walkway in front of his apartment.

Each morning, Jake would take a few moments and stare in wondrous amazement at the structure before him. It was his daily ritual. He couldn't help it. He sat down in his chair and allowed his eyes to stare straight into (straight through!) the mysterious object that had drawn him in by its wonder nearly his entire life. Jake couldn't quite explain it, but he had always felt mystically connected to it somehow. People often said he was crazy and that he should spend his free time (which, of course, he had very little of in his workaday life) doing something more constructive than just sitting there and staring at it. But it was too seductive... too unbelievably exciting and mysterious.

It was a gigantic glass wall that marked the edge of the known world for all who lived in Magella. On the other side: red desolation. It was about a meter thick, as one could see by the indentation it made in the ground. One could walk up to it and see right through it, but it was harder than the heaviest metal mined from the ground. This particular morning, Jake mused whether or not his newly discovered object might actually be able to do the job, but he quickly dismissed it. In his gut, he already knew the answer: it was impenetrable.

Absolutely NOTHING had ever been able to break through the clear shield around Magella. Nothing had even *scratched* it. If one put their hands up against it, no fingerprints would remain when they removed them. No matter how hard someone tried, no marks of any kind had ever been made on its crystal clear surface. The only thing that suggested it was even there was the dim reflection (and sometimes refraction) of light that shone upon its surface.

Calling it a wall was actually a bit of a misnomer. Technically, it was curved, but only slightly. To someone standing nearby, it really did look flat. However, if their eyes followed the surface of the wall up into the air, they would notice that eventually it would begin to curve in, little by little. If your eyes continued their motion upward, it would never actually end. As it curved in further, the highest point would often be obscured by clouds, a few kilometers up in the air. When there were no clouds present, one could see the very top. It would then fall back down the other side again, creating a surface that had no end: a gigantic dome.

Centuries earlier, the people of Magella had attempted to measure the diameter of the dome and found it to be about one hundred kilometers. The edge of the dome cut through the ground in a perfect circle. Once again using their primitive mathematical skills, the earlier generations of Magella had calculated that there was over 7,800 square kilometers of land under the dome. It was also calculated that the monstrous and awe-inspiring structure rose around 50 kilometers into the air at its highest point. Needless to say, no one had ever been able to reach the top. It was impractical to try and besides, everyone knew what to expect if they ever reached it: just the same mysterious clear surface that covered the rest of their world. Attempts had been made to dig under it, of course. None were successful. Whenever someone had dug into the ground along the edge of the dome, the clear barrier had just followed them, further and further down as they dug. One particularly adventurous man, who was convinced there was a way under, actually got a team of men to dig nearly a kilometer down into the ground in an attempt to circumvent the gigantic, clear barrier. When the team had reached that particular goal depth and still found the invisible wall there, most had quit and gone home right then and there. No other major attempts had been made since. Looking back at the event, the most fervent of religious figures had deemed the entire enterprise as blasphemy, anyways.

The dome was home for everyone who lived in Magella. It was actually more accurate to think that the dome *was* Magella. They were one and the same, for all intents and purposes. No one had ever been outside the dome, and few showed any desire to do so: it was a barren wasteland of red sand and grey boulders that stretched as far as one's eyes could see in all directions.

No living thing had ever been seen outside of the dome. Well, nothing *substantiated,* anyways. There were always a few people who swore they saw some wild creature off in the distance, or another human just like them, staring back through the dome's glassy surface, or a strange craft of some sort, flying around near the horizon. Most people didn't pay them much attention. It was commonly thought that these were just people looking for attention. They were written off as crazy folk and everyone else carried on as they always had, content to ignore the ravings of lunatics. In the end, most people just didn't care. Most people were quite content where they were and had no desire to get themselves worked up about what was or was not outside of the dome. Here they had safety and security; out there was the great unknown and danger. Most people were scared of what might happen to them out there, but Jake wasn't most people.

Jake spent numerous nights sitting out on the walkway in front of his apartment, usually enjoying a warm cup of tea. He would stare out through the clear shield, dreaming of what life would be like outside of it. The red landscape just outside of his corner of Magella had been carved into his memory forever and yet, he longed for the chance to actually *touch* that landscape, to reach down and feel it with his own hands.

And then there were the things he could not see. Over the years his mind would dream up strange worlds beyond the horizon. Were there people just like him out there? Were there completely alien beings instead? Maybe both? Were there societies more advanced than this, watching them from afar? His mind danced in and out of these musings until his eyes were too heavy to stay awake.

Since he was a child, Jake felt the pull of the unexplored land before him. It was like a woman trying to seduce him. He felt somehow drawn to that giant open, empty space beyond the dome. Whenever he tried to explain it to others, they always seemed quite confused.

"Why would you want to go out there? It's just empty space, nothing of value," they would say. "We have everything we need right here, inside the dome."

He knew they were right, of course. Logically, if he thought about it, it made sense. Why would he want to go out and get hurt or die when there was nothing but worthless junk out there? Besides, the Founders had put the dome here for a reason, hadn't they? They had known it wasn't safe out in the great beyond so they had created a home that was livable and sustainable for humanity. While Jake knew all of this to be true, he couldn't ignore the wanderlust that he felt inside.

After about ten minutes of staring and dreaming, Jake got up from his chair and made his way down the rickety walkway attached to his level of the apartment building. He soon came to the spiraling staircase that would lead him down to the ground. As he placed his hand on the railing to the staircase, he felt his heart race for half a second. He quickly turned around, ran back down the walkway and back into his apartment. He bounded over to the dusty bag, still sitting nonchalantly in the corner under his hammock. He unzipped it, found the small disc, and quickly stuffed it into his pocket. Almost immediately upon doing this, he felt his heart begin to slow.

Once Jake was on main street, he could begin to see the top of the temple behind the buildings along the way. A gigantic stone spire shot up from the ground and rose nearly 350 meters high. Being a Starseeker temple, it was constructed to "reach up" to the stars, in an effort to be as close to the Founders as possible. Inside the temple was a winding staircase that would take you all the way up to the top. It was the exact center of New Salem and the crown jewel of the town, dwarfing nearly everything that surrounded it. Each Founder's Day, every member of the temple would get an opportunity to climb the tight, winding staircase and sit up in the small room to meditate for a time, sharing a communion with the Founders. In order to accommodate each person, a schedule of sorts had been developed. The oldest members of the congregation got first pick, of course. Everyone who went to the temple got an equal amount of time, however.

After his parents had died, Jake had snuck up to the top of the spire on regular, "non-Founders" days and had spent hours up there, thinking of them. This was strict blasphemy as far as the Starseeker faith was concerned, but their temple's priest hadn't tried to stop him. Jake's parents were now up with the Founders in the stars and all he wanted to do was be near them. He had had a lot of days filled with hurt and pain after his parents had left him, but his days up in the spire were not among them.

The rest of the temple was almost as fantastic. If one thing could be said about the Starseekers, it was that they did not shy away from grandiose artistic displays. Almost every inch of the outer wall of the temple had beautiful depictions etched into the stone. This was all done in an effort to portray as close as possible, the glory and wonder of the Founders.

The main focus of the etchings was strictly on the beauty of the work. Starseekers believed very strongly that the Founders appreciated beauty in all its forms. Some were depictions of handsome men and women in flattering poses. Others were of flowers, trees, and many other plants. Still some others depicted different beautiful creatures, such as deer, birds and horses. The best works of art, however, were saved for the roof. Only the most honored artists were allowed to create art for the roof. Those works were the ones that directly faced the Founders, glittering up in the sky, in an effort to please them. Anyone down on the ground would not be able to see them. They were placed in such a way that the only way anyone could really appreciate them was if they were up in the spire. Jake had never been to see it before, but he had been told that the roof of the largest Starseeker temple in Apex was considered by many to be the greatest work of art in all of Magella.

When Jake made it to the front gate of the temple, he craned his neck back and looked up to the top of the spire... and then onward all the way to the top of the dome. He always got a little hint of vertigo whenever he did this, but he didn't really mind. It was his way of reminding himself just how small he was in the big scheme of things. As his eyes worked their way up into the sky, he felt another person's shoulder run right into his chest.

"Oooph! Sorry!" Jake said.

"Hi, Jake. Taking it all in, huh?" an elderly woman said with a warm smile.

It was old Miss Marla.

"Oh, hi," Jake said, a little embarrassed. "Yeah, I guess so."

Marla smiled and continued on her way into the temple. Jake slowly followed, along with the rest of the mass of people who had been milling around outside. They were about five minutes away from the beginning of the service. Starseekers enjoyed their social time before their worship, but tardiness was something not tolerated in their religion. If you were late for worship, then you were disrespecting the Founders.

As Jake followed the steady stream of people into the temple, his hand instinctively moved into his pocket and felt the small, metallic disc. He wasn't sure, but he thought that it actually felt a little bit warmer now than it had before. He shrugged off the thought and made his way through the two massive stone doors and into the structure. Each door had a figure carved into it. The left door had a muscular, bare-chested man wielding a sword, depicting conflict. The other had a woman draped in a gown and holding a small flower, depicting peace. They served as a constant reminder that the two would always be intertwined in one's life.

In contrast to the grandiose exterior, the inside of the temple was fairly simple. From their vantage point in the sky, the Founders would have no way of seeing within the temple, and therefore its design was not as big of a concern as the outside. The main gate led into a massive gathering place that was one large square room. The spire was placed on top of this. A door on one side of the room led to the upward staircase for the spire and a door on the other side was the exit for the staircase that led down from the spire. The two sets of stairs were critical for the steady flow of people up and down from the top. As soon as the room was vacated from one worshiper, another could enter right behind them.

The inside of the gathering room was warm and inviting. It had an embroidered carpet (which was a high commodity in New Salem) and beautiful, yet simple, polished silver chandeliers that hung low from the high ceiling. The walls contained all manner of artistic patterns engraved in them, although quite plain when compared to what was on the outside of the building. On the far side of the gathering room was a door that led to the worship area.

The worshipping space could be described as a miniature version of the dome itself, except made out of stone. The worshippers would sit on the floor in an area that surrounded the main altar, which was located in the exact center of the circle. The curved ceiling contained a depiction of the nighttime star field, chiseled into the stone with excruciating detail. Each star was depicted by six slashes, painted bright yellow and all intersecting each other at their center. The larger the star in the night sky, the longer the slashes. Since the placement of the stars changed throughout the year, the particular alignment chosen was that of the day of "Rebirth", the day known to all as the first day of a new 24-month cycle.

Jake took his seat on the floor. There were no assigned seats. Everyone just filled in the space outside of the altar's designated circle. The altar itself was nothing more than an extremely small but tall stone table. It was about chest-high, but only about half a meter wide in all directions, creating a perfect square on top. Here, different items could be placed, depending on the time of year. Along its legs and sides were carvings very much like those in the gathering space. Jake had been told what they all meant at some point, but he had since forgotten. On top of the table sat a bowl with water in it. This particular Founders Day was during the time of Great Cleansing.

The priest entered by means of a winding stone staircase that led directly out of the floor right next to the highly decorated stone altar. It was a pretty dramatic way to enter, Jake had to admit, giving the priest more of a dignified and holy aura. The tenants of the Starseeker faith were taught that the priest had a special connection to the Founders. When one priest died, another was elected. It was said that the newly elected priest would then be given "new eyes to see" and open up a direct spiritual pathway with the Founders. When the time came, elders of the temple would fight like mad to be chosen.

As the priest entered, the crowd of worshippers stood up. Jake followed suit. Some dismissed all of the pomp and circumstance of worship as silly and unnecessary, but not Jake. There was a distinct understanding (or was it fear?) that if they did away with their ancient traditions, they would lose their connection with the Founders, the beings responsible for humanity's very existence. Some even said that those who went against the Founders in life would spend their afterlife outside of the dome, choking on dirt and dust forever.

The priest was wearing long, black flowing robes. In the dimly lit room, it appeared almost as if he was just a floating head. The priest was a slightly portly figure, but the black robes helped to cover that up nicely. The hair on top of his head was shaved down nearly down to the scalp, but he sported a full beard, as was the custom for Starseeker priests. He gave the room a meaningful scan and then placed his hand on the altar.

"You may be seated, followers of the stars," he proclaimed in his deep basso-profundo voice.

The crowd of people lowered themselves back down to the floor. Some of the more elderly members of the congregation were assisted by their younger counterparts. All eyes were locked on the priest. All eyes, except for Jake's. His eyes looked up at the stars in the ceiling. The light from the flickering torches that lined the wall reflected off of them, making them appear almost alive, as if they were trying to communicate with him. Jake often thought of his parents while here. It wasn't quite like the time he spent up in the spire, but it was close.

"Welcome to all on this great day of cleansing," the priest said. "On this Founder's Day, we give thanks to the Founders for providing us with our home, our place of refuge. We thank them for life itself. Without the Founders, we would be cast out into the wilderness to suffer and die. The Founders have brought us protection. They have brought us security. Like a mother who cares for her child, they have held us close and kept us from harm. We honor them today with our hearts, with our minds, with our spirits."

With this, the priest raised both of his arms straight up towards the ceiling, fingers stretched out as far as they could go. Everyone else in the congregation followed his example. All eyes turned skyward.

"Oh great Founders," the priest spoke, now in a much more declarative and forceful tone, "we seek you. We seek your guidance. We seek your continued support. We seek to do your will. We seek to join you someday among the stars."

All of the hands slowly fell back down to people's sides. After a few seconds' pause for added reverence, the priest looked upon his followers. For the first time since he arrived, a smile crossed his lips.

"Welcome all! Today is the Day of Cleansing! Let us rejoice!"

The Day of Cleansing was a day in which one's past misdeeds were "washed away". Each of the worshippers would approach the alter one at a time and receive a droplet of water. The priest would dip his finger into the bowl and allow one drop to fall on the head of each person. From that point forward, they were "clean" in the eyes of the Founders. The timing of this particular event was not lost on Jake. What he had done the previous evening had been wrong in the eyes of the law, and most likely in the eyes of the Founders, as well.

The priest continued with his speech. "Before we begin the cleansing ritual, let us take a moment to meditate on how the Founders have affected our lives since we last gathered here."

Everyone closed their eyes and once again lifted their arms to the heavens. As soon as Jake's arms were almost fully extended, he heard a rather strange noise come from his pocket. It was like nothing he had ever heard before, but it was high in pitch and shrill in tone. At first he wasn't sure if it had come from him or someone near him. A man seated next to Jake opened one eye and looked at him for a brief moment before closing it again. Ok, it had been him.

It chirped again, this time a bit louder. Another worshipper broke their meditative trance to look in Jake's direction.

Jake's hand fumbled around inside his pocket, found the foreign object and pulled it out. It was glowing bright neon blue! Its temperature was rising, feeling almost hot enough to burn his skin. It was hard to tell for sure, but Jake thought he felt slight vibrations coming from it, too. Several more eyes opened and looked in his direction. Jake knew he had to get out of there before more people took notice. Much more of this and...

BEEEEEEEEP!!!!!!

Jake swallowed hard. Everyone in the room must have heard that one.

"What in the name of the stars was that?!?" the priest boomed.

Jake couldn't believe it. The priest NEVER interrupted a group meditation. It was absolute sacrilege! Everyone's arms fell and all eyes turned to Jake. He looked up to see the priest staring at him straight in the face. Just as quickly, he looked back down at the strange glowing object in his hand. He quickly tried to conceal it, but the damage had been done.

"What is that?" someone asked.

"Did you see that?" someone else whispered.

"It was glowing blue…" said another.

This was more than Jake could take. It was against everything he had been taught growing up as a Starseeker, but in the middle of a holy worship service, he awkwardly got to his feet and began to make a move for the exit. He had to be careful not step on all of the people sitting cross-legged on the floor. It was like a strange obstacle course. Jake could feel all eyes on him, burning into his soul, judging him. After quite a bit of bobbing and weaving (and stepping on at least one hand), Jake made it to the door. He turned for a brief moment to face the priest, who still had a look of shock and confusion on his face.

"I… I'm sorry…" Jake said simply, and left.

Once outside of the temple, Jake took a closer look at the strange object in his hand. It was incredibly hot now, but for some reason it still didn't burn his hand. The glow had died down somewhat, but there was still a faint blue hue to its surface. Whatever this was, it was not simply some object carved out of metal. This was something else entirely.

Chapter 4

*"Beware the false prophets. Their silver tongues will
speak words that sound like wisdom, but if you follow
them, you will be led down the path away from knowledge
and enlightenment... and into complete darkness."*

-*The Book of the Founders*

Jake moved as quickly as his legs would allow, gaining more and more
distance between himself and the Starseeker temple. The buildings, people and even the dome itself (still looming above as it always
did, like some gigantic hand pressing down on him) flew by in a
blur. The lack of sleep didn't seem to make a whole lot of difference.
Adrenaline was pouring into his system now. His heart was pounding in his chest like some giant aboriginal drum. He had one thought
only: *get home, get home, get home...*

Within minutes he was back inside the little cube he called home.
He slammed the door closed and lay against it with his arms outstretched to his sides, as if holding it shut against some impending
invader. The disc was still in his right hand, still glowing its strange
bright blue color. It took a few moments for his breathing to slow
and the drum in his chest began to play a decrescendo. Eventually,
he brought the glowing disc in front of his face for its first close

examination since he had left the Starseeker temple. Jake wasn't exactly sure what was creating its new color. Usually when objects would glow or create heat, it was because of some kind of fire that had been lit. That did not appear to be the case here.

"What the hell *are* you?" Jake exclaimed.

He brought the disc over to the table near the kitchenette to get a better look. It was at this moment that he first realized that the object was not the same on both sides. One was slightly curved, but the other was completely flat, kind of like the top portion of a hamburger bun. He placed it flat-side down on the table.

As soon as it touched the table's surface it let out that awful noise again.

BEEEEEEEEEEP!!!

Jake's pulse quickened. The Founders had specifically warned against this type of thing. Technology beyond simple tools or anything that could not be made by hand were outlawed. It was for everyone's own protection, of course, he knew this. They didn't want to repeat the awful mistakes of those that had come before them. Was this some kind of artifact, perhaps some remnant of a time long past? Would the Founders look poorly upon him for having this blasphemous thing in his possession? Was this some kind of punishment for his actions against "The Greater Good" last night?

"Oh Founders forgive me," Jake muttered. "I'm sorry. I didn't mean any harm."

He could hear the voice in his head with the comeback almost immediately: *It doesn't matter if you are sorry or not, Jake. It is done… and you are guilty.*

Almost at once, he tried to think of possible solutions to his current predicament. Maybe he could return it to where it had been found? No, that wouldn't work. One of the other miners would eventually find it. What if he found some place to bury it outside of the mine? No, that wouldn't work either. If it kept making this terrible sound, someone's ears would be led to it out of sheer curiosity. Then they would be in the same predicament that he was.

Jake thought that maybe he and Tom could just sell it off, like they had originally planned. They could take it to Westing that very same day and be rid of it. Founders knew that members of The Underground had no scruples or religious devotion. What would they care if this thing happened to be a cursed object? They'd gobble it up quick and find some way to make a profit off of it, sure enough. It could then be The Underground's problem and Tom and Jake could walk away, having nothing more to do with it.

Just as he was about pick it back up again, having decided that selling the strange glowing object as soon as possible was their only good option, something else happened that caused him to yank his hand back in shock and surprise.

Four tiny pieces folded down from the tip of the glowing rounded mound, like a blooming flower. A bright blue beam of light shot straight up and stopped only when it made contact with the ceiling of the apartment. At the base of the light, a small figure appeared. It was difficult for Jake to make it out at first, but after a few seconds it came into focus. A man about the size of Jake's thumb was standing at the foot of the blue beam, like… well, Jake had no idea what it was like. This was so far beyond anything he had ever experienced that it was hard to find a context for it.

The tiny man was dressed all in black and wore a white, trimmed beard. Beyond that, it was impossible to tell much more due to his miniscule size. Jake wasn't sure, but it looked as if he was taking a look around the room, getting a feel for his surroundings. After a few moments, he stopped and then smiled up at Jake. Then, he spoke.

"Hello, Conscript," the small figure said, still smiling, "it is a pleasure to meet you!"

Jake stumbled and nearly fell. Thankfully, there was a chair right behind him that he was able to grab ahold of. Slowly, he sat down without losing his balance too terribly.

The strangeness meter has just gone from four to ten, Jake thought to himself.

"Sorry if I startled you," the small man said. "I would expect that this whole production is more than likely a bit of a shock to you."

The man's voice sounded strange to Jake. It was almost as if he were speaking another language, even though Jake could understand what he was saying. The inflections were all in the wrong places. His "ayes" sounded more like "ahs" and his "ees" sounded more "ehs". It all sounded too, too... *proper.*

"Wh- what, who... what are you?" Jake managed to stagger out.

"Well, technically, I'm not really *anything.* I guess you could call me a representation of a man who once lived a long, long time ago. My assumption would be that I, er, *he*, has been dead for a while now."

"You mean you're not human?"

"Well, not anymore. Do I *look* much like a human to you? I mean, I'm about one one-hundredth the size!"

"You are not of this world..." Jake said rather softly.

"Obviously," the little man said matter-of-factly.

"You're, you're a demon!" Jake said, slowly getting up from his chair. "You've come to punish me, haven't you?" He took a few initial steps backwards, towards the door.

"No! No! Listen, sit down, um... I don't think I caught your name?"

"It's Jake..."

"Jake! Fantastic! Nice to meet you, Jake! Look, take a seat, my dear boy. I'm not a demon and you are not in any kind of trouble, I promise."

Still a bit fearful, Jake did as he was told. If this thing wasn't a demon and it wasn't a human, then what was it? *It is a demon, Jake. It is just lying to you. That is what they do, isn't it? Lie to you to lower your guard? Don't trust it!*

"I need you to trust me, Jake," it said.

Jake snorted at that comment. "How do I know you aren't just lying to me?"

"You don't, I guess," it replied. "Some things just require a leap of faith. That's what I need from you now, Jake."

"I gave you my name, but you still haven't told me yours," Jake said, trying his best to keep an open mind.

"True enough. Those who once knew me, or rather, the *old* me, called me the Overseer."

"The Overseer. What did you *oversee*, exactly?"

"Well, everything, I guess."

"You're not really making a whole lot of sense."

"I guess I am being a bit too vague and mystical, aren't I? My apologies. I'll try to get to the point here for you now, Jake. You have been quite patient with me. I appreciate you giving me a chance and hearing me out."

Don't jump ahead on me, Overseer, Jake thought, *I'm still debating whether or not I should take your little mushroom-shaped home and toss it out my front door.*

"I have come to you with a message," the Overseer continued. "Well, perhaps more of a task."

A task? Jake thought, *What task? Do you want me to take out your garbage or something?*

"I need you to do something for me," the Overseer said, "if you are up for it. In fact, one could argue that this is something not just for me, but for everybody."

"What do you mean 'everybody'?" Jake asked.

"Well, all of humanity, if you really want to know the truth," the Overseer said, once again sounding very laid back and relaxed about everything. "Jake, I'm asking you to save the human race from destruction."

Now Jake had had enough. Whatever this was, human or not, it was clearly messing with him. Save the human race? Riiight. Whatever you say, micro-man. The idea was preposterous for two reasons. First, why did the human race need saving? What from? Didn't the dome over Magella already do a pretty good job of protecting everyone? Wasn't that the whole point? Second, why him? Jake would be the first person to admit that he was nothing special.

"You don't believe me," the Overseer said, "I can tell by that look you are making. Jake, let me ask you a question, if I may. How many people live here?"

"Live where? This apartment? One. Me."

"No, no. How many people live under your shield, your barrier."

"In all of Magella?"

"Yes."

Jake really hadn't given it much thought. What had the latest statistics said? He wasn't quite sure.

"I don't know. Maybe two and a half million."

"Two and a half million," the Overseer repeated, "Okay. Let me take a guess here… I would bet that it is beginning to get a little bit cramped under here."

He wasn't completely wrong. As it turned out, when it came to population, New Salem was really more the exception than the rule. It was fairly small, by the standards set by the other cities in Magella. It was probably due to the fact the land wasn't all that desirable. Apex had somewhere around 700,000 residents alone, all densely packed in. Waterville had somewhere around 150,000, Lake Hope, 250,000. Westing, Magella's second-largest city was probably close to 450,000,

Jake surmised. Much of the rest of Magella's population was spread out all over the rest of the circular area under the dome.

In fact, now that Jake really thought about it, a lot of land that had once been farmland was being redistributed in order to make room for new housing. The lack of available farming space due to population growth was something the talking heads in Apex were often mentioning as a growing crisis. Jake had not paid all that much attention to it, really. His whole world was New Salem and the concerns of a few politicians in Apex didn't cause him to lose too much sleep.

"I guess you could say that things are a little tight," Jake agreed.

"What do you think is going to happen in say, twenty, thirty, or even forty years?" the Overseer asked.

"I don't know," Jake said, although deep down, he kind of did.

"Jake, your people are going to reach a point when they can no longer survive in here. The very thing that was created to protect them will be their destruction. You will run out of resources. Soon, people will have to make difficult choices. Not everyone will be able to live. Who will decide? It will be a very dark time, Jake. It could be the end of Magella as you know it.

Jake had never really considered that. He felt so stupid now, having it all laid out in front of him. Of course something like that was bound to happen. How could he have been so blind to it? How could all of them have been so blind? Destruction was inevitable. He suddenly felt very, very sick to his stomach.

"People often choose ignorance when confronted with unsettling facts," the Overseer said, as if reading Jake's mind.

"Many things have been attempted, historically, as a means of population control," the Overseer said, "but none of them have ever been affective. Laws have been passed declaring that a man and woman can have only a maximum of two children. But what happens if couples choose to ignore that? Is the third child killed? No, that would be barbaric. Any time an overpowering force has tried to control a human being's biological choices, it has always ended in chaos. Inevitably, the people turn against those attempting to make the choices for them.

"The best form of population control that we have seen has actually been disease. Like a brushfire, it thins out the forest and replenishes the soil so that new plants may grow. However, humanity has never been too keen to let such things happen. So, we go about developing newer and better medicines to stomp out such evils."

Jake paused for a moment, trying to contemplate everything the Overseer had just described.

"So, what is the solution?" Jake finally asked. "If humanity is ultimately doomed to grow too large, what really can be done about it?"

"Have you ever looked outside, beyond the barrier?"

Jake's mind quickly jumped to all of his evenings out in front of his apartment, sitting in his chair, sipping his tea, musing about the outside world.

"Have you ever wondered if you could get out there some day?" The Overseer continued. "Just look at it! So much empty space!"

"But it's ruined, rotten," Jake said. "Nothing can survive out there. There's not even a single tree, as far as I can see."

"Very true! But what if I told you that there was a place your people could go that wasn't just a rocky plain of nothingness? And it was so large that it could fit over a thousand Magella's in it? Would you be interested?"

"Of course, but-"

"Jake, that is what I would like you to do for me, for *us*. If you are willing, I would like you to find this new land for your people and eventually, lead them there."

"That's nice, but I think you've forgotten the fact that no one can get out from under the great barrier of the dome."

"Can't you, now?" the Overseer said with a slightly devious smile.

Wait, what? No, that was impossible! Thousands had tried. No one had ever stepped foot outside of the dome. However, a lot had already happened today that had challenged Jake's idea of what was impossible.

"How?" Jake asked.

"Believe that you can and it shall be possible," the Overseer said. "I believe in you, Jake. Do you?"

"What?"

"Do *you* believe… in *yourself?*"

Honestly, Jake wasn't sure.

"There are dangers beyond your borders, Jake, the likes of which you will not fully understand. Keep this device, this compass, with you at all times and you will be protected."

Jake noticed that the Overseer was clearly pointing with each hand, straight down along the sides of his body.

"Compass?" Jake asked. It sure didn't look like any compass he had ever seen. Other than the spectacular light show shooting out from its top, it still looked more or less like a hunk of metal.

"In time, it will show you where you need to go. You don't think I'd send you out into the wilderness without a map, do you?"

"And what about food, water, shelter?" Jake asked, perhaps a bit too incredulously.

"If you are resourceful, you'll be fine, I'm sure."

"And this," Jake said, pointing to the object on the table working as the Overseer's pedestal, "will lead me there? To this… this new land for humanity?"

"If you follow the path, yes."

"Ok, hang on a second," Jake said, really gaining steam now, "let's say I believe you. Let's say that I can venture outside of the great barrier and that indeed I will be led to some new, great paradise. That's all well and good but what about *everybody else?* Isn't the whole point of this to have all of humanity live in this wondrous new place? Just getting one person there isn't really going to do you much good, now is it?"

"As I mentioned before, Jake, you'll just have to have faith. Think of it this way: you are the one that holds the key that can open the door. Once it's open, all anyone else needs to do is walk through it. You have a decision to make, but you need to make it soon. Time is of the essence."

With that, the blue beam disappeared and with it, the Overseer.

Chapter 5

"Do not waste your time worrying about what may be. Keep your attention focused on what is."

-The Book of the Founders

Not long after the Overseer disappeared, the tiny pedals at the tip of the compass (he had said *compass*, right?) folded themselves back up and re-sealed the opening. Jake let his finger drag across its surface. Not one discernable seam could be found. The tiny metallic object just sat there, as innocuous as can be, as if saying, "what, little old *me* caused all of this trouble? You must be silly!"

Did I just imagine all of that? Jake thought to himself. *Like those stories you hear about people who think they hear the voice of their dead lover or think they see strange objects flying around in the sky, but in the end it is just all in their head? Is this just some psychosis digging its dirty little tentacles into my brain? Am I going crazy? Is it time to cart Jake Connelly off to the asylum in the Ashemore mountains to the south?*

Jake wasn't sure which reality he wished were true more. Either he was nuts, or he was responsible for the lives of every living thing in Magella. A dull ache began to rise up from the pit of his stomach. He felt as if a haze had slowly formed around his head, clouding his sight and his thoughts. He needed a fresh perspective. He needed clarity. He needed Tom.

Within fifteen minutes, his fist was pounding on the door to Tom's home. Jake probably would have gone there as soon as the disc had begun its color show, but Tom happened to live quite a bit farther away from the Starseeker temple than Jake did. Taking advantage of the distance between Tom's place and the temple, he wondered if any of his fellow worshippers were curious enough to follow him home. He had made quite the spectacle. It was probably best they didn't find him, or the compass, back at his cube.

Unlike Jake, Tom did not live in some multi-level apartment structure. Tom's home was located on the outskirts of town where there was a bit more room. Still, it did share walls with other residences. His was one of a long line of homes all made out of wood and connected to one another. It was as if someone had placed a gigantic piece of construction lumber on the ground and hollowed out dozens of little living spaces from it. There eight of these structures, all lined up perfectly with one another. In between each building was a small alley- it was too small to actually call it a *road*. Even though the whole complex still felt a little cramped, it was a far cry from Jake's living situation.

The door had a green awning over it that stuck out about a meter away from the wall. There was also a fat candle with a large wick attached to the side of the building just to the right of the door that was most likely used for nighttime illumination. Two small wooden chairs were also set out. Jake wondered if anyone had ever actually sat in them since Tom had arrived in New Salem. Hanging from the edge of the awning was a potted plant, and he could also see tidy, red curtains covering the back window. As he stepped back after knocking, Jake noticed a small mat that said, "welcome" on it. It all looked quite quaint. It was definitely nothing like Jake's place. There were no nice amenities like these; his place was strictly utilitarian. He didn't have the money to afford the niceties.

So how had Tom afforded all of this? Jake thought to himself. *It was probably due to his association with The Underground. He probably earned a little extra money on the side in return for a few "favors" or "deals".*

Jake's musings went away as soon as he heard footsteps approach the door. At first he heard the sliding of the lock and then a slight jiggle of the handle. Soon, this slight jiggle turned into an aggressive shaking, making the top half of the door wobble back and forth like some flimsy handsaw. Finally, with a loud *CRUNK,* the door was flung open and Jake saw the soft complexion of Tom's face smiling back at him.

"Rusty old doors that stick are the best home security," Tom said as he opened the door a bit further. It continued to creak as it swayed slowly back and forth a bit. "Most thieves move on after one try. Come on in!"

The door led directly into the kitchen. As Jake stepped through the doorframe, he gasped a little. The inside of Tom's place looked immaculate. There wasn't a single dish out on the counter. No little bits of food. No dust or dirt on the floor. The only food that was visible was a few canned goods, clearly organized on the shelves that hung from the wall just above the kitchen counter. The four chairs around Tom's kitchen table were all equidistant from the center.

It seemed kind of strange that they had been friends this long and Tom had never invited Jake over. But, Tom was a fairly secretive man. Jake had been embarrassed the couple of times when Tom had seen his unkempt kitchenette. The thing was, though, as far as kitchens went, nearly all were at least a little bit messy. The business of preparing food was hardly ever a clean one. Perhaps Tom just didn't prepare his own food all that often, choosing instead to eat out. Jake was more than a little bit confused how a man making a miner's wage could get away with such a luxury. Once again, his thoughts returned to The Underground.

"So, to what do I owe the pleasure?" Tom asked, "It seems a bit early for you to be away from worship, isn't it?"

"I ah, had a bit of an emergency," Jake muttered.

"Well, whatever it is, come on over and have a seat."

Jake pulled one of the chairs out from under the kitchen table and sat down. Tom did likewise.

"It has to do with our new discovery," Jake said as he pulled the... what? Object? Disc? Device? Compass? Thing? ...from his pocket and set it down on the table. "It's changed."

Once again, the little metallic blob just sat there, doing nothing. It reminded Jake of a story he was told when he was younger about a little dog that had learned to talk. Unfortunately, whenever the owner paraded it around to his friends and coworkers to show off this amazing feat, the dog just sat there, acting just like a normal dog should. The device seemed to say to Jake, "sorry, show's over, kid."

Tom palmed the top of it, as if feeling for a heartbeat. "Seems the same as when we found it," he said.

Playtime was over, it seemed. The bear had gone back into its cave to hibernate once more.

"It, um, well, it spoke to me," Jake said.

"It... what?" Tom replied, his eyes slowly rising up to meet with Jake's.

"It spoke with me. Well, not exactly, *it* per se, but the little man that lives inside of it."

Tom's expression was not helpful.

"Ok, I can't exactly explain it in a way that makes any kind of logical sense, but the thing kind of opened up and before I knew what I was looking at, this man about the size of a baby carrot was just standing there. And he spoke to me. He told me that I was supposed to save humanity."

This was going nowhere, fast. *Here come the nice men, ready to take you to Ashemore! We hope you enjoy your stay. You'll be well taken care of there!*

"Tom," Jake said desperately, "I know this sounds crazy, but you've got to believe me."

"It's alright, Jake," Tom said. "I do."

"Really?" Jake was shocked.

"Yeah, I do. This all sounds a little, eh, weird, I'll admit, but you've never struck me as the kind of person who would make up something like this."

"Thank you," Jake said, his chest visibly falling a bit.

"So, what else did this, ah, little person say?"

"Well, he was kind of vague, but I think the gist was that he wants me to leave Magella and find some new home for everybody."

"Wait, leave Magella? You can't just leave Magella, Jake. Nobody can! If you haven't noticed, there's this giant spherical thingy that kind of keeps everything in."

"I know, I know! I tried saying the same thing! He gave me some crap about how I just need to *believe in myself.*" The last part was said in as ridiculous a tone as Jake could muster.

"Well, where is this magical place?"

"I don't know. He said *that* would tell me," Jake said, pointing at the disc on the table. "He called it a compass."

"I'm no explorer, but don't most compasses at least have an east, west, north and south? This is just some hunk of metal. How is this possibly going to help us?"

Jake just lifted his eyebrows and pursed his lips, as if to say, "you got me."

"Well, that's... odd," Tom said. "So what's your next move?"

"I don't know, Tom," Jake said. "I'm scared."

He didn't realize it until the words had come out of his mouth, but he was. He was scared. *Really* scared. Scared for his own sanity.

Scared that the Overseer was right. He couldn't be, though, could he? This flew in the face of everything Jake believed as a follower of the Founders. Outside wasn't just impossible to reach, it was forbidden. Humans were not supposed to exist out there.

Of course, there was still the wanderlust. If the Overseer was telling the truth and Jake actually could go out there, this was his chance. This was his opportunity to do the thing he had dreamt of since childhood: to explore the great unknown, to finally see what lay beyond the horizon. The Starseeker elders had always just said, "there's nothing else out there but more rocks and dust", but were they right? Here was his chance to find out. Of course, if they *were* right, he would certainly perish, even if he had somehow found a way to leave Magella. Musings were one thing. The Book of the Founders was the foundation of humanity's knowledge of the world.

Jake knew he had a decision to make. It was either get rid of this thing (either by selling it or discarding it), cursing the day he found it, or attempt to follow the guidelines the Overseer had given him and use it to leave Magella. Tom was staring at him now, a knowing look on his face. Jake didn't have to ask. He knew Tom understood his dilemma.

"Ah hell," Jake said finally, "let's just sell the damn thing."

Jake felt somewhat relieved when he said it aloud. It was the logical, reasoned solution. The more he thought about it, the more he had himself convinced. How much sleep had he really had the night before, anyways? Not even one hour? He had been so tired. He was *still* tired! It was all in his head. Of course it was. Poor Tom. He had been forced to listen to the ravings of an exhausted lunatic.

"Sorry about all of that, Tom," Jake said. "I wasn't making a whole lot of sense, was I?"

"Are you sure this is what you want to do?" was Tom's reply.

"Yeah… yeah I'm sure. Let's just get this thing to Westing and find a buyer. The sooner we are rid of it, the better."

"Alright, if that is how you feel. Though, I have to tell you, I have absolutely no clue how much this will fetch us. It could be a lot, but then again, it might be nothing. It's rare, sure, but it is hard to say what practical value it might have for the person who buys it."

"Let's try to keep things positive, ok?"

"Sure, sure. I just don't want you to get your hopes up."

"When can we leave?"

"As soon as you want, I suppose. Westing is a good two days away by foot. If we leave yet this morning and really push it, we could probably be there by sun down tomorrow."

"Let's do it."

"Are you sure? You look pretty tired, Jake."

"I'll be alright. I just want to be rid of the damned thing as soon as possible."

"Gotcha. Give me a few minutes to gather some things and we can leave."

About an hour later, they were on the road, each with a small pack strapped to his back. Just a few necessities were inside of each: some dried food, water, clothing, an emergency med kit and some flint for fire making. The compass (or whatever it was) was tucked safely into a side pocket of Jake's pack. Tom still seemed content to let him hang on to it himself. In addition to his standard supplies, Tom had also grabbed his bow and arrow in case they found some small game along the way. Most of the path on the way to Westing was through the Dubline forest. A lot of creatures that could make for a tasty dinner called that forest home. Plus, it doubled as protection in case they ran into trouble. They were seeking out The Underground, after all.

The two largest streets in New Salem marked nearly the exact center of town. East-west was Main Street and north-south was Mine Road. As the name implied, Mine Road ran directly down to Morzellano's mine, the main source of survival for so many residents of New Salem. As the road ran north, it tilted up slightly, then curved to the west and dipped down out of sight. The mine was down in a small canyon, so it was impossible to see it from their current vantage point.

Jake found himself thinking that either way, his days working at Morzellano's mine were probably over. Whether or not this trip of theirs was successful, neither Jake nor Tom would be around for work the following day. That would be all the reason Morzellano would need to dismiss them. Even if they had explained that something had come up and they needed to be away for a few days, the grizzled old man wouldn't care. For Morzellano, human beings were no more than walking, talking profit machines, and when it came to "The Greater Good", he had a larger slice of the pie than just about anybody else in New Salem. Jake could see Morzellano's reaction the following morning: the man would just shrug his shoulders and then find two more men who were desperate for work. It wouldn't take him long in New Salem. There would be two new workers down in the mine before the end of the day.

That meant that Jake's days as a resident in New Salem were probably over, too. What else did anyone do in that town, anyway? Had he really thought this through? Was he ready for a completely new life? He looked over at Tom. His friend seemed perfectly content. Well, not completely. He did seem to have a slightly concerned look on his face, but nothing too out of the ordinary. He was probably already thinking about how to make contact with The Underground when they arrived in Westing.

Jake had to remind himself that Tom had already lived in Westing before he had come to New Salem. Perhaps he was used to moving around, from place to place. Maybe he had lived in other places before Westing? For Tom, this kind of thing might even be downright common, although, he was leaving behind a number of possessions and his home. For Jake, there was nothing back home worth caring about. It shocked him when he realized what kind of a sacrifice Tom had just made... and how quickly he had made it.

Jake was walking away from his old life and into a new one; that was the choice he had made. Was he prepared for it? Once again, Jake found himself doing something far more impulsive than he was accustomed to. He couldn't blame Tom this time, however. This had been his choice and his alone. Tom had simply been willing to come along for the journey. One thing did make Jake feel a little better, though. If things didn't work out, he was fairly certain that Tom would find a way to get back on his feet again. As long as Jake stuck close to Tom, he'd probably be alright. At least, he hoped so.

They continued down Main Street, passing Joe's bar, the Golden Inn, and even the Starseeker temple that Jake had been inside only a few hours ago. The worship services had now concluded and the building was nearly empty. Jake could only imagine what his poor congregation had thought of him. Oh well. There was probably another Starseeker temple in Westing, one that was a lot larger, too. In fact, Jake figured that he could take his pick from a handful of different temples, maybe as many as ten or even twenty!

Main Street ended when it reached Desperation Road. This cheerful little avenue ran along the edge of the dome, heading northwest around the mining cavern and into the Dubline forest. Once in the forest, Jake and Tom could then head directly west and make their way to Westing, which lay on the far side of the forest. As they marched further and further down Main Street, Jake saw less and less of his home and more and more of the strange world outside of Magella.

"Have you ever looked outside, beyond the barrier, Jake?"

The Overseer was in Jake's mind again, taunting him.

"Have you ever wondered if you could get out there some day?"

Before he had even realized it, Jake saw that he was now standing at the T-junction between Main Street and Desolation Road. Desolation's dusty path mimicked the world outside. There were no trees, no shrubs, no vegetation of any kind. There were no homes, no businesses, not even a small shack or two. It was empty, just like the lands beyond Magella, just like Jake's heart. What if he hadn't just dreamed up his conversation with the Overseer? What if he really did have an opportunity to save his people? Was he dooming them all to death and destruction by his own selfish actions?

"…but why me…?" Jake mumbled.

"What was that?" Tom asked.

Jake turned to his friend, whom he had forgotten was even there.

"Tom, I have to at least try," Jake said.

"Try what?" Tom asked.

Jake didn't answer. He simply pulled his pack off of his back, set it on the ground and removed the compass from the side pocket. He turned it over in his hands. He wasn't sure, but he thought that perhaps it felt a bit warmer again. He walked across the road and with a few more steps, his nose was almost touching the surface of the great barrier. He looked down. The compass was glowing a brilliant bright blue. Jake's eyes went wide. He no longer had any doubts.

He took a step forward.

The sensation was odd, to say the least. Jake felt a strange vibration building up from within his chest. It was as if someone was tickling him from the inside. Soon, his whole body felt it. He wasn't sure, but he thought maybe he smelled sulfur, like someone had just struck a match nearby. His vision blurred, but only for an instant. It seemed as if images in his periphery had turned a pale blue in color. His eyes shot down and he realized that it wasn't the world around him that was blue, it was *him*.

Everything, including his clothes, was glowing the same color as the compass now. It was as if he had become the compass himself. They were no longer two separate entities. They had combined. They were one.

A few more cautious steps forward and Jake stopped to process what had just happened. He looked up and out, scanning the world all around him. His heart began to race. His breathing quickened. This was impossible. His dream since he was a small boy had come true. This couldn't be real, could it? The Founders proclaimed it to be certain death, generations of men had tried and failed, but still, here he was. No more clear shield, no more barrier, no more protection.

He was outside of the dome.

Chapter 6

*"Good friends are a rare commodity, more precious
than the finest gold or the most perfect gem stones."*

-*The Book of the Founders*

Jake looked behind him and saw Tom, still standing back on the other
side of the clear wall. He had his arms to his sides, head cocked
slightly to the left. His eyes were a little wider than normal, his brow
furrowed. It looked as if he, too, was trying to make sense of the situation. It was so incredibly strange for Jake to see the dome from the
outside. It looked completely foreign to him now. Everything that he
saw inside of it still seemed familiar to him, but with a strange tilt to
it now, like he was in some odd alternate-reality. He didn't like it. He
didn't like it at all.

The worst thing was when he looked up above him. There was
nothing there. Absolutely nothing: just a strange pinkish-tan sky that
continued up and up and up forever. He had the weirdest feeling
inside of his gut: it was as if he were going to fall *upward*. He couldn't
quite explain it, but it made him feel like vomiting. A ringing sound
was building up in his ears. The sound of his heartbeat slowly faded
in as well. Jake could still see, but everything seemed fuzzy now.

What little food was in his stomach started to snake its way up to the back of his throat.

Jake immediately closed his eyes, which helped the queasiness in his gut subside a bit. There was still a strange sense that he was going to fly away into the sky, however. He tried his best to shake it off. If he was going to walk anywhere, he would have to eventually open his eyes. The trick was not to look up, he told himself. He kept his eyes focused squarely on the red, dusty ground. He just told himself that there was a dome overhead, protecting him, even though in his heart he knew that there was a cruel sky hanging there, waiting to gobble him up.

He took a couple of careful steps and nearly fell over. What was going on? It was as if the ground wasn't as hard as he was used to. No, that wasn't it. He took a few more steps, still stumbling, but as he continued to walk, he discovered that he was actually pushing himself up off of the ground a little bit, like each step was more of a mini jump. He felt almost... non-human. Jake began thinking that perhaps it would have been better to stay back inside the dome.

Suddenly, a gust of wind picked up behind him and tossed him up into the air, like a cork. Almost as quickly, he was slammed back down again, face-first into the ground. The small metallic device, still glowing blue, tumbled out of his hand and bounced across the rocky ground.

Ok, that hurt, Jake thought as he turned his body over.

Once again, Jake was at a loss. A wind gust that strong should not have lifted him off the ground! He may have had to steady his footing, sure, but it wasn't like it was strong enough to make him go airborne! Jake had always dreamed of being on this side of the dome. Now, he wasn't so sure. He was scared. Scared of the unknown, just like everyone else he had dismissed as being paranoid. Maybe they were the smart ones and he was just some stupid adventure-nut who had no real grasp on the real dangers in life.

Jake turned over so that he was facing back up. His eyes once again looked up into the sky above him… into that interminable void, that never-ending orangish-pink vortex from which there was no return. The feeling deep in his stomach returned with a vengeance. He covered his head with his arms and turned over onto his side, in the fetal position. He thought he might have shouted out, but he wasn't sure. His ears were ringing loudly now. Then, he thought he heard someone shouting… or at least some kind of muffled sound, far away.

"Jake! Jake! Are you alright?"

What was that? Did he really just hear that or was it all in his head?

"Jake!"

Soon he was being pulled back over, forced to face up once again, but this time instead of the deadly sky, he saw something that gave him a small bit of relief: Tom's face. Jake looked away from his friend's worried expression for a moment to see that Tom had snatched up the compass that had tumbled from Jake's grip earlier. It was an odd feeling to describe, but Jake was beginning to feel naked without the thing either in his pack or tucked away in his pants pocket. He found that he preferred keeping it in his pocket over the pack: it was closer that way.

"Jake, you ok, buddy?" Tom shouted.

"Yeah, I think so," was the best Jake could manage.

"What's wrong?"

"Just some adjustment problems with our new environment," Jake said, now gaining more confidence. He did his best to sit up, but it did require some help from Tom. He reminded himself to try and keep his eyes down as much as possible. He looked over at Tom, who was now crouching beside him. It took a moment to sink in: *Tom is out here with you, too.*

"I know, weird, huh?" Tom said, answering the unasked question. "When I saw that you were in trouble, I ran out after you. It was all purely on instinct. It took me a few seconds to realize what I had just done."

"So, can anyone leave Magella now?" Jake asked. Then, under his breath a bit, he added, "what did I do?"

"I don't know," Tom said, "I guess it is possible."

"Did anyone see us?"

"I don't think so, but it might be best to get out of sight. We don't exactly want to start a panic."

"You're probably right." *Tom was always probably right, it seemed.*

"If the dome is essentially gone now, it may not make any difference, but better to be safe than sorry."

Jake looked around and spotted a small, rocky outcropping that looked kind of like a fat finger, pointing up to the sky. It was about fifty meters away. He nodded his head in its general direction and said, "that'll work."

"Can you get up?" Tom asked.

"Yeah, I think so." *Don't look up, don't look up, don't look up...*

With Tom holding firmly to his right arm, Jake shakily got to his feet.

"Be careful, Tom," Jake said. "Things are... *weird* out here."

"I've noticed," Tom replied, "We'll take our time."

Before leaving, Tom placed the compass back in Jake's pack. It was no longer glowing, now. It had done what it was designed to do apparently, all of the magic now gone from it, at least for the time being. Tom slung both of their packs over his shoulder. Jake would have protested, but he was still feeling too unwell to protest all that much. As long as Tom was willing to carry the extra burden, he wasn't going to complain.

By the time they made it to the rocky mound, both were beginning to feel better about their footing. The outcropping was larger than Jake had first anticipated. He had remembered seeing it hundreds of times from the other side of the domed barrier. At the time, he had thought it was probably waist-high, no higher. In actuality, it was taller than either Jake or Tom. As they carefully walked around to its far side, Jake realized that he had never seen the backside of it before. It was silly, really. The thing was only a big chunk of rock, after all. But it had been a chunk of rock that had been a part of Jake's landscape for his whole life... and now that landscape was changing.

Jake sat down, Tom stayed up. He took a quick look around their surroundings and then eyed Jake with his trademark mischievous grin. Jake knew that look all too well. That was the look Tom gave when he was about to try something dangerous or stupid... or both.

"I have a theory, but I need to test it," Tom said.

"Like anything I am going to say is going to stop you," Jake replied.

"Right," Tom said and then vaulted himself straight up into the air. He landed on top of the outcropping.

Impossible! Jake thought. *That thing has to be at least two meters tall!*

Tom was standing tall, looking out across the wilderness. He was completely devoid of any fear, at least as far as Jake could tell. When he noticed Jake staring back up at him, he jumped back down, creating a sizable cloud of red dust. With a flick of the wrist, his perfect blonde hair was right back in place.

"How did you know you could do that?" Jake asked.

"I think I know why it feels so strange out here," Tom replied. "The pull of the ground isn't as strong as it is back inside. I felt it while we were walking just now. We can run faster and jump higher, hence all of the stumbling around when you first left the dome. Look!"

With that, Tom picked up a stone on the ground about the size of an apple and tossed it, up and away from the dome. It started out normal enough, but then it just kept going, up and out and up and out. Finally, it began its slow descent back down towards the ground and ended its journey with a small puff of red, no bigger than the size of Jake's pinky fingernail from their vantage point.

"I think I must have just set some kind of world record," Tom said with a smile.

"Two!" Jake said, remembering Tom's leap earlier.

"Want to try?" Tom asked, pointing up to the top of the rock mound. "Go ahead, try to jump up there!"

Jake's earlier fears were now almost completely dissolved, replaced by pure giddiness and excitement. Tom had that effect on people. Jake looked up. *No way,* a voice in his mind told him, *there is absolutely no way.* But then, a new voice spoke up. *There is a way,* it said. *Now, there are no more rules.* Jake crouched down and flexed his leg muscles. He allowed himself to smile for the first time in a long time. He pushed down on the ground hard.

His arms flailed as he ascended rapidly. Thankfully, he was able to steady himself as he reached the top height of his leap. His feet found the slightly curved but mostly flat surface atop the rock hill, one foot slipping on some pebbles, but he jutted one of his arms out quickly to help him find his balance. He looked out. For once, Jake's stomach didn't feel sick. He took a deep breath and unexpectedly, he let out a powerful yell.

"WOOOOOO-HOOOOOO!!"

The dome of Magella still dominated nearly his entire view. It was much like being inside it, but now instead of it encircling everything, it was just the opposite. The far edges slowly began to curve *away* from him. He knew that if they got further away, those inward curves would become more and more pronounced. Eventually, it would look like nothing more than a small ball, half-sticking out of the ground, as if some child had simply slammed it down, right there.

I can breathe! Jake thought to himself as he took more deep, tranquil breaths, *I can actually breathe! We were always told that we would choke to death out in this, but here I am, breathing, surviving, living! Why would the Founders lie to us?*

Tom broke Jake's concentration when he landed next to him. Jake was so startled that he nearly fell over the edge. A quick grab of Tom's hand stopped him, and Tom patted his back when he knew he was safe once more.

"Beautiful, isn't it?" Tom said.

"It sure is," Jake said in reply, still looking all over. Then he stopped. "Uh, Tom?"

"Yeah, Jake?"

"I think we have a problem."

"What?"

Jake's finger was pointing at the answer. Not far from where they had exited the dome, a dozen or so people were congregating. Some had their hands flat up against the dome's inner surface, staring out. Others were pointing directly at the two of them. Most were chatting with one another, though their voices couldn't be heard at this distance. He wondered if once outside the dome, any noise from within could reach them, even if he were standing just a few meters away. The growing crowd seemed very agitated and excited about something.

"I think our secret is out," Jake said.

Tom was now eyeing the scene as well. "One thing is for certain, it doesn't look like they can get out."

Does that mean we can't get back in? Jake wondered.

Almost instinctually, both men leapt back down behind the outcropping. Once they had landed, Jake rubbed the back of his head, nervously. He knew what was coming. Soon, all of Magella would be at that spot, everyone trying to catch a glimpse of the two men who had somehow miraculously made it to the outside world. More than likely, they had been close enough to those people to be recognized, too. Jake was fairly certain that one of them had been his neighbor, Chuck.

If I know that's Chuck, then Chuck knows it's me. Jake thought.

What would happen to them now if they returned? Would they be hailed as heroes or worshipped as gods? Those were nice thoughts, but they probably weren't accurate. Most likely, they would be taken against their will. The Magellan government would investigate, of course. They would send their best scientists to capture Jake and Tom and have them studied. The device would be confiscated and studied in its own right, too. The ending of this entire escapade would not be pleasant. Jake saw one of two possible outcomes: they would be locked up and studied for the remainder of their lives, or they would be killed, either out of fear or over-testing.

"Tom?" Jake asked. He noticed his friend deep in thought as well. Perhaps he was contemplating the same implications as Jake.

"Yeah?" Tom replied, now turning to face Jake.

"What do we do now?"

"Well, let me ask you something. Are you sure that your conversation with the Overseer was all in your head?"

"Given everything that has happened now, I'd say most likely no."

Jake hated to admit it, but it was true. Whether he was comfortable with it or not, all of this *was* happening. It wasn't a dream. It wasn't fake. This was real.

Be careful what you wish for, Jake.

"Well, I guess then it is simple," Tom said. "You either take the Overseer up on his request or you head back inside the barrier and do your best to explain to all of those people exactly what just happened."

That's no choice and you know it! Jake thought, angrily.

He looked out into the vast wilderness laid out before him and contemplated the strange task the Overseer had placed in his lap. Was there really some new promised land out there for him to find? If so, how could he possibly survive long enough to find it? Their packs had a few days' worth of supplies in them, tops. Here outside of the dome there was no water, no vegetation, no animals to speak of… How could this even be possible?

"Do you believe in yourself, Jake?" Tom asked.

"Oh what are you, one of *them* now?" Jake replied sarcastically.

"Look," Tom said, "*I* believe in you, Jake."

"What?"

"I have been around you long enough to feel as though I understand you, Jake. I trust you… probably more than I've ever trusted anyone in my entire life, if you can believe that."

I don't, actually, Jake thought.

"What I'm trying to say," Tom continued, "is that if you want to take this on, this *quest* or whatever it is, I am with you. And if you want to head back and deal with whatever is waiting for us back in Magella, well, I am with you there, too. We are both in the same fix here and I figure we might as well handle it together, as a team… as friends."

Jake looked back at Tom. No other person in *his* life had ever been such a devoted friend and companion. For Founders' sake, Tom hadn't even known him more than a few weeks! A small part of him wondered if Tom was just playing him, trying to gain his trust somehow, but why? There was no real reason for it, was there? No, Jake had to admit that Tom was genuinely being honest with him and had his back, for better or worse.

"Thank you, Tom," Jake said. "That means a lot."

"So, what should we do?" Tom asked.

"You're always asking *me* these things!" Jake said. "What do *you* think?"

"Me? Ah, I don't know. I guess the unknown is better than what waits for us back home. But that's me. I'm used to bouncing around from place to place, not really caring where I end up. For you, this is a much bigger deal. You will be leaving the only home you've ever known."

"You may have lived in a lot of different places," Jake said, "but I don't think any of them were quite like this out here."

"True enough," Tom said. "Still, this isn't as big of a deal for me as it is for you I wouldn't think."

"No, I suppose it isn't," Jake agreed.

"Look, you can take your time thinking about it. We have enough foo-"

"I'll go," Jake said abruptly.

"What?"

"I'll do it. I'll go. Just promise me that whatever happens out there, we'll never leave or give up on one another."

Tom smiled. "It's a deal. I'm in."

CHAPTER 7

"Passion and adventure are for those with short life spans."

-The Book of the Founders

I wish we had been smart enough to grab a couple of horses, Jake thought to himself.

It was too late now. They had already walked for over five hours and any thought of turning around and heading back to Magella seemed a foolhardy task. Even if they could somehow sneak back in just long enough to steal what they needed and not be noticed, it all seemed incomprehensible to Jake at this point. No, they were on their way now, come what may. The Overseer had told Jake that if he were resourceful enough, he would survive. In another day or so, those words would most likely be put to the test.

They had made fairly good time, given the fact that they were on foot. Jake had to remind himself that walking (and even some running here and there) was much easier now that they were outside of Magella. They could cover distances once thought to be marathon-like treks with very little effort whatsoever. As they had progressed further and further away from the dome, the crowd of people had continued to grow. By the time Jake could clearly make out the entire structure, end to end, with one look, he saw what was probably thousands of people lining the inside edge of the dome. Word had spread quickly.

The road was not too difficult to traverse, just rocky and dusty, but mostly flat. As they traveled, Magella still dominated the landscape, hanging there like some all-powerful behemoth. Jake couldn't help feeling a little bit guilty. It was as if the round orb was a hand, constantly reaching out to him, telling him, *Stop! Wait! Come back! Don't leave me!* But, he knew in his heart that he could not listen to those pleas, despite their pull at him being stronger than he had anticipated. He did his best not to look in the direction of Magella and stay focused on the path in front of him. From time to time, he did falter and sneak a peak, though.

By the time they had reached a stopping point for the day, the two men were still in fairly good shape as well as spirits. It was, however, getting dark and both figured they could do for a night's rest. The sun was setting in the west, throwing streaks of deep red and purple across the barren landscape. Jake also noticed something that he had never seen before. How could he? It was the sun's reflection on the surface of Magella's great barrier behind them. It hung there, distorted and bent at a slightly odd angle as if someone had splattered red paint all over that particular section of the dome's surface.

As the sun continued its slow descent out of the sky, the interior of the dome began to light up with all of the resident's candles and lamps for the evening. It was still by far the largest and most significant piece of the landscape. It loomed as a constant reminder of what they had left behind: safety and security. It was ever keeping watch on those who had abandoned it.

Tom and Jake found a comfortable spot on the ground on which to sit. By this time, the sun was completely gone and the Founders began to twinkle themselves into existence. One by one, they began to slowly glow into view, decorating the blackness with their tiny points of light. Jake wondered, as he often did, where in that vast tapestry might his parents be. Could they see him now? If so, what were they thinking of their son, given the past day's events? Were they proud of his bravery or were they ashamed of him for disobeying the commands of the Founders? Jake hoped for the first but feared the second.

Only one of the twins was out in the sky at this particular moment, Dor. The larger and faster twin, Phor, would be racing his way up from the west soon. The legend of the twins told of two brothers born very different from one another. Phor had been born first, Dor second. Phor had been born a strong, capable young man. Dor, on the other hand, had been born weak. So weak, in fact, that his growth had been stunted. He was forever a tiny, child-like creature that could barely take care of himself. His brother Phor, who had grown into a massive, healthy mountain of a man, took pity on his brother. Phor would spend nearly all of his time training, running laps across the sky, but each time he passed his frail brother, he would pause to hold him in a warm embrace. Although Phor could do nothing to help Dor's condition, he would forever be there to show his brother just how much he was loved.

Normally, in a situation like this, Tom or Jake would have made a fire. They had the flint and steel with them, but unfortunately, there wasn't much kindling or wood lying around for them to burn. They had plenty of dirt and rocks, which of course did them no good. The strange thing was that neither of them felt particularly cold. There didn't seem to be a need for a fire, even if they could make one.

"Does this make sense to you?" Tom finally asked Jake.

"Good, I was beginning to think I was the only one," Jake said. "Why aren't we freezing?"

"Not a clue," Tom said, peering out across the nighttime sky.

"Thanks for giving me the creeps," Jake muttered.

Tom laughed heartily. It was cut short, however.

BEEEEEEEEEEP!!!!

Tom and Jake both looked at one another. Jake found his pack and produced the tiny metallic disc. As expected, it was once again glowing blue. Jake couldn't believe that he had forgotten all about the blasted thing. It was the reason for this entire journey, after all. Perhaps the Overseer might make another appearance. At least it would be proof to Tom that he wasn't crazy. Of course, the fact that they were already outside of Magella had probably already made a believer out of Tom.

"That's never a good sign," Tom said, pursing his lips.

"Maybe, maybe not," Jake said.

Jake turned the device over in his hands, studying it. The blue glow was already beginning to fade, but it had been replaced by something new. The flat side of the device was no longer just silver in color. Two sets of red glowing numbers now appeared. They stuck out like a predator's watchful eyes in the darkened night. One of the numbers was unchanged, displaying "4,467.38". The other, however, was moving. In fact, it was ticking down, one number smaller every second.

9,999,999...

9,999,998...

9,999,997...

Even more puzzling was a small blue light that had appeared along the thin edge of the disc. It was no bigger than an ant, but it glowed so bright that it was impossible to miss. Jake tried to turn the disc so that he could get a closer look, but as he did so, the light moved. As the device turned in his hands, the little light flew along the sharp edge so that it was always facing away from him.

"Ok, so this is new," Jake said, brow furrowed.

"Didn't your Overseer friend tell you about this?" Tom asked.

"Sorry, no." Jake replied. "All he did say about this thing was that it was a compass."

"A compass, hmmm? Ok, I suppose that kind of makes sense."

"What do you mean?"

"Well, that little blue dot along the side there, it keeps pointing the same way."

"Yeah, I guess it is northwest, maybe? Why?"

"Well, I would assume that whatever we are looking for would most likely be in that direction, wouldn't you think?"

That seemed to make sense to Jake. The Overseer had told him to "follow the path". Was this that path? He assumed it must be. Good thing they had traveled mostly north on their journey that day. It was fairly close to the direction they apparently needed to go. It would have been awful if they had had to backtrack all that way and start over again.

"Ok, one mystery solved," Jake said, "but what about those numbers?"

"Yeah, those are definitely less obvious," Tom said.

"It looks like one of them is counting down to something," Jake surmised.

"True." Tom replied.

They looked again at the moving digits:

9,999,934…
9,999,933…
9,999,932…

"What happens when they reach zero?" Jake asked.

Neither answered. They just stared at each other for a few seconds, both with looks of slight worry on their faces. Tom ended up breaking the silence, not letting their imaginations run wild for too long.

"I think that as long as we reach our destination before this thing gets to zero, we should be alright," Tom said, "right?"

"So we are on the clock, then," Jake agreed.

"Let's do some quick calculations, here," Tom said. "These numbers appear to be changing every second. There are 60 seconds in a minute, and 60 minutes in an hour, which is a total of 3,600 seconds in an hour. Each day has 25 hours. So, there are 90,000 seconds in a day. If we divide 9,999,900 by 90,000 we get... Hang on..."

How are you doing all of this in your head? Jake thought, but then remembered both how little he really knew about Tom and how bad Jake himself had always been with arithmetic. As long as he could write it down he was fine, but in his head? No. It always seemed as though the numbers would fly away from his thoughts, like butterflies avoiding the nets.

"It's about 111 days," Tom concluded at last.

"111 days! That's close to four months!" Jake said.

"It must be a long ways," Tom said, shrugging his shoulders.

"If we really make it stretch, we have one, *maybe* two days' worth of food in our packs! How in the Founders' names are we supposed to make it nearly *four months* in this wasteland on only that?"

Tom didn't answer. He just stared.

"We didn't think this through, Tom," Jake said, shaking his head side to side. "We've got to go back... resupply somehow... do something!"

"We can try," Tom said, "but I wouldn't recommend it. Half of Magella is probably on the lookout for our return now. I doubt there is an inch of that dome that isn't guarded by centurions from Apex, just waiting to capture us."

"So we just starve out here, is that it?"

"Didn't the Overseer say that as long as we have the compass with us we would be taken care of?"

He said the *Overseer, not* your *Overseer for the first time,* Jake noted.

"Look," Tom continued, "this compass is already protecting us from the cold! Maybe it will help us find food and water somehow, too. Maybe the terrain gets better further down the road?"

It was true. The Overseer had told Jake that as long as he had the compass with him, he'd be safe. He had also talked about being *resourceful,* too, though. What did that mean, exactly? Was he supposed to be resourceful while on his way or before he ever left? The Overseer had also spoken of dangers, out here in the unknown, dangers even the Overseer himself was unaware of.

"I guess we will just have to plug on and hope for the best," Jake said. "No one could possibly carry four months' worth of food on their own. The Overseer must have known that! Somehow, some way, we have to believe that we will be taken care of."

Jake had said the words, but deep inside, he wondered whether or not he truly believed them.

Tom seemed convinced, though, "okay, that just leaves the other number."

Jake looked down at it again. As expected, it had not changed, reading only "4,467.38".

"It's getting late," Jake said. "Two out of three mysteries solved is enough for one day. Let's get some rest."

"Agreed." Tom said.

That night Tom slept like the dead. Jake wasn't quite so lucky. He could have blamed it on the less than desirable conditions, but that wasn't it. In his heart, he worried that he was indeed on a fool's errand. What if they ran out of food? Would his ultimate fate be to die of starvation out in this desolate land, having just left a perfectly good home with all of the comforts and resources he could possibly ever need? That would be quite the turn, wouldn't it? Adventure-seeking moron gets just what he deserves.

As sunrise grew near, he did manage to get a few hours of rest, but they were fitful at best.

The following morning, the two had a small (*very* small) bite to eat and were soon on their way once more. This time, however, they had their compass to guide them. Jake held it flat in his hands and turned to the northwest. Sure enough, the little blue dot on the edge of the compass faced directly ahead.

Jake didn't have the compass out all of the time, but he did remove it from his pack frequently to make sure they hadn't strayed too much from the proper direction. On the third such instance, he discovered something. He was fairly convinced he had solved their third mystery.

"They've changed," Jake said, still trudging along behind Tom.

Tom stopped, causing Jake to nearly run into his back. He then turned around. "What's changed?"

"The other set of numbers. Look!"

Jake held out the flat side of the device in front of him so that Tom could see it. The "clock" was still counting down, of course:

9,996,876...
9,996,875...
9,996,874...

Sure enough, though, the number below it had also changed. It was not actively moving as the number above was, however. It was static, though it was now a different number than before. It read:

4,465.13

"It's smaller than before," Tom said, but only by about two."

"How far would you say we have traveled so far today?" Jake asked.

'Oh, I don't know, probably a little over two kilometers," Tom replied.

Jake just smiled. Tom got it, Jake could see it in his friend's face.

"Well, only four thousand, four hundred and sixty-five more kilometers to go!" Tom said.

No wonder we needed nearly four months, Jake thought to himself.

"That is an average of about forty kilometers a day," Tom said. "Very manageable, especially out here with the lower gravity, as long as we don't get sidetracked."

As long as we don't get sidetracked, Jake repeated to himself.

Jake figured that they could even take a few days off here and there, to rest or gather supplies. Ugh, supplies. Jake was leery on their prospects in that area. The landscape had still given them both no indication that it had any plans on changing. It was as barren as ever. The Overseer had told him that they would be taken care of. Jake wished he could say that he believed him, but deep down he didn't. In moments like these, his brain often trumped his heart.

The two continued along their journey, with not a lot changing, either in their pace or the look of the world around them. Jake continued to scan the horizon, hoping desperately to see some speck of green. Over and over he was let down as more dust and rocks would appear. Jake almost felt as if the Overseer was mocking him, laughing over the fact that sweet, gullible Jake actually thought there would be anything worth finding out there.

Behind them, the world of Magella was steadily growing smaller. Jake and Tom could still see the curvature of its top, but the area where the dome had met the ground was now gone, blocked by the horizon of the red surface the two had been traversing. So much of the lower portion of the dome's surface was gone, in fact, that they could no longer see even the tallest trees or structures inside of Magella. It was all just sky now. Jake knew that as they continued, the dome would not only get smaller in their view, but it would eventually be obscured completely by their current landscape.

After traveling about twenty kilometers (according to the compass), the two figured they had traveled enough for their second day. They had done a fairly good job rationing their food, but Jake's stomach was continually grumbling at him, as if asking, "is this it? Is this all I get today?" Jake did his best to keep his pleading stomach out of his thoughts. A different plea, however, he could not ignore.

"I've got to pee," Jake said, throwing his pack on the ground near Tom. "I'll be right back."

Tom probably wouldn't have cared if Jake had unzipped and let the urine flow right there in front of him, but old habits did die hard. They were as far away from civilization as Jake had ever been and yet he still felt the desire to hide somewhere to do his business. They had passed a small cave a few minutes before stopping and Jake figured that would be as good a place as any. They had yet to find a single scrap of evidence of indigenous life living outside of Magella, at least yet. Jake figured that the chances of him peeing into someone's home were pretty slim.

As Jake trotted back the direction in which they had just come, he was amazed at just how little of Magella he could see. The upper portion of the dome was still clearly visible, but only a small amount. It bulged up into the sky like a distant, giant eyeball, searching for those it had lost. Jake shuddered.

And then he shuddered again, this time chills running up his spine.

This isn't that cursed dome, Jake thought, *this is something else.*

The feeling grew stronger. He was getting colder. It wasn't long before Jake could actually see his breath exhale from his mouth in a plume of smoke. Soon thereafter, Jake felt as if thousands of tiny needles had begun sticking their tips deep into his skin. They dug deeper and deeper, until finally all he could feel was pain, rippling up and down every last centimeter of his body. They relentlessly pulsated with pain, growing stronger every second. His ears began to ring. It started like some distant church bell, but soon it was as if his entire head was inside the bell itself. It drowned out all other possible sounds, making the soundtrack of his world in that moment one loud, long, unrelenting tone. Jake covered his ears with his arms. It made no difference. He shook his head side to side as if the sound could have been expelled from his head like water out his ears. No luck.

He looked down at his arms. The veins inside had begun to bulge. His skin was turning a strange purple color, speckled with splotches of deep magenta and even black in some places. His fingers were also expanding, ballooning out to the size of small hotdogs. Stars began to appear in Jake's vision, which was strange considering the fact that the sun had not yet set for the day. These tiny speckles of light danced around Jake's field of vision and began to multiply exponentially.

It was only when he tried to inhale that he realized he was probably going to die. Something had gone wrong with his lungs. For some reason, they refused to bring in more air for him to breathe. He continued to try to suck in something, *anything*, but they stubbornly refused. The twinkling stars soon gave way to darkness. It wasn't the darkness of the night sky in the middle of the night, but an all-consuming, complete and total black. The last thing Jake saw before everything melted away was the world turning completely on its side. It all ended with an abrupt bang.

Chapter 8

"The faithful will survive while the faithless will surely die."

-*The Book of the Founders*

"Jake! Jake!"

The world was a dark grey haze. Two indistinguishable forms floated through Jake's field of vision, but that was all. Slowly, those forms began to take on more defined shapes. One was clearly a human face and the other... well he still wasn't quite sure what the other was. It floated just above the man's (yes, he *was* a man, Jake could see that now) right ear.

"Jake, are you alright?"

It was Tom's voice. It had to be. What had happened? Things were coming back in small pieces now, like waking up after a strange dream. He had been dying. That had been it, right? The world around him had slowly dissolved right in front of his eyes, but he wasn't dead. Had he survived somehow? What had caused all of that pain, the stars, the blackness? He still had more questions than answers but his brain was too fatigued to ponder anything for too long.

"T-tom?" Jake managed, weakly.

"Jake!" Tom shouted again, perhaps a bit too loudly, right into Jake's face. Jake's eye flashed open wide for a moment. "There you are!"

Jake's vision continued to pull in sharper delineations. He could clearly make out Tom's face now and he looked visibly shaken up, eyes darting this way and that. The strange little object to Tom's right turned out to be the mighty twin Phor, burning brightly in the night-time sky. More memories were returning to Jake's mind. He must have passed out for some reason. He remembered he had been on his way to take a piss and...

Jake's hand shot down to his pants. They were wet.

"Yeah, well, there wasn't much I could do about *that*," Tom said sheepishly.

Jake felt sufficiently confident that he could pull himself up to a sitting position. When he was up, he was able to get a better grip on his surroundings. It looked as though he was sitting right where he had originally passed out. The cave wasn't even all that far away. He looked back at Tom.

"What happened to me?" Jake asked.

"I'm not entirely sure," Tom said, "but I sure am glad to see you aren't dead. You had me worried there."

"How long was I out?"

"Not long, maybe half a minute or so. I happened to see you topple over and I came running. At first you weren't breathing. I figured that was it, end of the line for you."

"End of the what?"

"Nevermind. The important thing is that you started breathing again, fairly quickly after I got here. It took you a couple of minutes to completely come back."

In that moment, Jake noticed something hanging from Tom's back. It was one of their packs. *Jake's* pack. What was Tom doing with that? Tom seemed to notice that Jake was now staring at it.

"Oh yeah, I grabbed that before I came over here."

"Why?"

"I don't know! We have each packed emergency med kits, I figured I might need to use something."

"But why mine? Yours has a med kit in it as well, right?"

"Yours happened to be closer, alright?! Sheesh, you try to help a guy out..."

There are dangers beyond your borders, Jake, the likes of which you will not fully understand. Keep this device, this compass of sorts, with you at all times and you will be protected.

For some unknown reason, the Overseer's words came to the forefront of Jake's thoughts in that moment. Tom had grabbed Jake's pack, not his own... and it had contained...

"Tom, is the compass still in there?" Jake asked.

"Yeah, I think so..." Tom said as he pulled the pack off of his back and tried a few of the side pockets. Finally he retrieved what Jake was looking for. "Here it is!"

Jake plucked the compass out of Tom's hand. That must have been what saved him. It wasn't anything Tom had done, it just had been the presence of the compass.

It keeps us safe, but only if we keep it close enough to us, Jake thought. Perhaps that was why all of those people back in Magella couldn't follow them out of the dome. Jake, Tom and their compass had been too far away.

"I think this saved me," Jake said, holding the device up in front of Tom's face. "It must be some kind of a proximity issue."

"You mean if we get too far away, it stops working?" Tom said.

Jake nodded, "Exactly. Whatever it does, it must make it so we can breathe outside of the great barrier."

"What, you mean we aren't able to breathe the air out here?" Tom asked.

"I'm not even sure if there *is* air out here," Jake replied.

The following morning, Jake felt well enough that they could continue on their way, following the direction the compass had laid out for them. Jake still kept the compass in his pack and Tom seemed to be more diligent about not wandering too far away at any time. The going got tougher as the road began to rise slightly in elevation, but it still seemed nearly effortless, at least compared to what walking had been like back in Magella. The view was still much the same: a lot of rocky formations and red dust covering nearly everything. As the two climbed higher, the wind gusts began to pick up. There were a few times that Jake nearly toppled over, but Tom was always there to extend a hand and help him stay upright.

By midday the ground seemed to level off. Behind them, the tiny spec they had glimpsed of Magella that morning was now gone. Only the pinkish sky and the brown and red dust-covered land remained. It was now that Jake truly felt their isolation. Before, it had been a strange and yes, scary situation. But now, with Magella completely out of sight, Jake felt like a stranger in a strange land more than ever.

When they stopped for another miniscule bite of food, Tom had gobbled his up in seconds and then was up, scanning the land that was laid out in front of them. Jake had the sense that something was bothering Tom, but he wasn't completely sure. Once he was done with his few bites of cracker and a couple of beans, Jake joined Tom.

"What do you see?" Jake asked.

"Trouble," Tom said.

"What is it?"

"Take a look," Tom said, pointing straight ahead.

Jake looked in the direction they had been walking all morning: almost directly northwest. At first he wasn't sure what Tom was getting at. It looked the same as everything else, whether he looked north, south, east or west, but after a few moments he caught it. When looking northwest (as well as north, mostly) it looked as if the horizon line was not as far away as it should have been. They had gone up in elevation slightly, but that wasn't it. It was as if the whole world just stopped, ended.

"I had noticed it a little before we stopped." Tom said. "At some point we are going to reach the edge of this."

"The edge of what?" Jake asked.

Tom just shrugged his shoulders, "I don't know, I guess we'll find out when we get there."

The two trudged on, now unsure of what the compass had in store for them. As they continued forward, the horizon grew in size, never revealing any further land beyond it. Nothing but pinkish sky could be seen beyond. Not in his wildest dreams could Jake have imagined what they saw when they reached the end of the road.

When they arrived, Jake shuffled forward, one tiny centimeter at a time. It was impossible, but there it was: the world *had* indeed completely ended.

Looking down over the edge, the wall of rock seemed to fall down forever. There was no bottom, as far as Jake could tell. It was as if the entire world had rotated on some unknown axis and there was now a new horizon line, except that it was straight down. He had to close his eyes and take a few deep breaths to keep from toppling over. That was *not* something he was prepared to do, given his current location. Eventually Jake backed away from the edge. One could only look for so long.

Looking out to where the real horizon should have been, there was only sky. A hazy collection of clouds hung about, demarking what was clearly the end of anything solid on which to stand. Looking left and right, the cliff stretched out as far as the eye could see both to the east and the west. Perhaps some of the old stories had been true. Some of the more senile (or at least *supposedly* senile) members of the New Salem community had said that out in the great wilderness there was a point where the world just ended. The land would stop and the sky would continue on forever, marking the edge of the perceivable world. Like most everyone else, Jake had dismissed them, figuring that it was easy to make up stories about a place that no person could ever visit.

But now here he was, looking out into the exact same picture that had been painted for him all those cycles ago. Perhaps he was the fool after all. Perhaps those he had lovingly referred to as "the old crazies" were actually the smart ones. The world had come to an end and there was nowhere to go. The device still persistently pointed forward, out into the void. He had followed his directions up until this point, but he was not about to jump out from the ledge. That kind of leap of faith he was not prepared to make just yet.

Jake supposed that one possible solution would be to climb down the cliff face and hope that at some point they would reach the bottom, but they hadn't exactly planned on this kind of travel. Both Jake and Tom had some climbing experience working down in the mines, but nothing that came anywhere close to this. Besides, neither of them had packed any climbing gear with them. One slip and they would fall down for... well, perhaps forever?

Is *this* what the Overseer's compass had been taking them to? They still had months of time left! They still had over four thousand kilometers in which to travel! The only way they might be able to continue forward was if they had some kind of airship that could fly them out into the clouds. Such things were pure fantasy, or course. Although, so was leaving the dome only a few days ago. Still, Jake figured that if they were meant to fly out into the clouds, the means by which to do that would have been provided to them. Nothing felt right about any of this.

What a waste all this was... There was nothing but rocks and dirt out here to begin with and now even that is gone!

Jake was still contemplating the implications of what lay before him when he felt a tug at his left jacket sleeve.

"Look!" Tom said. "There *is* a bottom. I knew it!"

"There is?" Jake said and attempted once more to take a precarious peek over the edge.

"You have to look out away from the rock wall," Tom said. "You see? There's a break in the fog just out there..."

After a few moments Jake found it. It was sticking out amongst the waves of swirling orange. It was clearly the same rocky surface on which they had spent the last couple of days walking. Jake's eyes returned to the cliff face and attempted to look straight down once more. He tried to imagine where it might possibly hit the floor. It had to be an even longer distance than they had traveled all day. It didn't matter if they had proven the kooky old men back in New Salem wrong. This was impossible. Reaching the floor of that canyon was a fool's errand that would most certainly end in death for both of them.

"What do we do now?" Jake asked. "We can't possibly get down there."

"I agree," Tom said.

"So what's our next move?"

"We go that way," Tom said, pointing to their left, along the edge of the gorge.

"But that's not the right direction," Jake said.

"Think of it this way," Tom said. "What would you do if you found a giant boulder right in the middle of your path?"

"Go around it."

"Exactly! You'd just go around it. We have to do the same thing here. The cliff face of this thing runs almost exactly east to west. So, we head west and hope that eventually we can work our way north again. Let's just pray that this canyon isn't as wide as it is long."

Seven hours later, Jake and Tom knew their answer. With still absolutely no end in sight to the cliff riding along in front of them, Jake began to wonder if the damned thing would just continue on forever. Only one thing gave them hope: they could now see the far side of the mighty canyon. It was hard to make out at times, but it was there: another rock wall that climbed back up on the far side. It was so far away that Jake could stick out two fingers horizontally and cover it up completely.

Finally, exhausted and without much hope of seeing an end to their current path, Jake and Tom decided to stop for the day. The sun was on its way out of the sky anyway. It would be dark soon and the last thing either of them needed was to have one of them fall over the edge because they couldn't see where they were stepping. The two found a spot far enough away from the edge of the canyon so that any possibility of falling down or, Founders forbid, rolling into the huge hole in the ground would be out of the question.

As the sun made its way down, Jake could now clearly see the outline of the great pit along side of them. As he looked west, the canyon continued to slice through the ground to his right like an enormous crack in the biggest piece of glass in existence. The horizon line to the west was cut into a jagged shape that looked much like a square with its top edge missing. It was in that moment that Jake saw it, almost by accident. The deep reds of the setting sun were splayed all over the landscape before them. All, it seemed, except for one tiny point directly in front of them. In that small area, the red was distorted slightly, making it a darker shade, almost black. Jake looked closer. There was a slight sparkle of light bouncing off of...

...it couldn't be.

Could it?

It was.

Jake was looking at the faint outline in the distance of another dome.

Chapter 9

"Challenge the Founders at your own peril."

-The Book of the Founders

"**C**ome on! Come on! Let's go!" Jake was shouting, pack already strapped to his back.

"I've been walking all day!" Tom moaned, "I'm tired! I need sleep! It can wait until tomorrow!"

Jake was walking himself in circles now, clearly not even talking to Tom anymore. "I knew it! I knew it!" he said, pumping his tight fists. "We aren't the only ones! Ha ha! I *knew* it!"

"No!" Tom said, in a more forceful tone now. "Give it a rest, will ya?"

"Come on, Tom, we gotta go, we gotta go!" Jake said, now breaking his circular path, grabbing Tom's jacket by the collar with one hand and pointing into the night with the other. "It's an entirely new world, and it's right over there! How can we possibly just sit here and, and... *go to sleep* of all things! Do you honestly think I could possibly sleep at a time like this?"

"I could!" Tom shouted, brushing Jake's hand off of his collar.

"Come on, Tom! Isn't this why we are out here in the first place? To find a new home? This could be it!"

"Jake, we aren't even heading in the right direction anymore! This can't be what the Overseer had in mind."

"Maybe, maybe not. But still, at the very least we could replenish our supplies. The Overseer did say we would be able to survive if we were resourceful out here. He was right! Here's our chance to get some more food. We won't have to starve to death!"

"I think I can make it through the night without starving to death."

"Fine, you stay there. Do whatever you want. I'm going."

"You can't, Jake!"

"Why not?"

"Because you'll kill me, genius!"

"Oh, right, the compass… well, I guess you'll just have to come with me, then!"

With that, Jake took off at a run. Tom had to scramble to close up his pack, throw it over one shoulder and hurry off in pursuit.

"Sonofabitch…" Tom muttered.

It didn't take too long for Jake's run to slow to a light jog and then eventually turn into plain old walking again. Back in Magella, he wasn't exactly well known for doing a lot of cardio. Tom caught up within seconds. The two walked in silence for most of the journey, Tom apparently resigned to the fact that no matter what else he might say, Jake was bound and determined to continue until they reached this new wonder. Unfortunately, Jake's body ended up having the final say.

They had traveled so long that the sun was once again rising into the sky, shooting rays of bright light onto their backs. Ironically, Tom was doing alright, but Jake was finding it difficult to take many steps without shuffling from side to side. Quite often he was dangerously close to falling over completely. Finally, when Jake seemed as though he was going to make a rugged impact with the ground, Tom held him by the shoulders and eased him down to a sitting position.

"We rest now," Tom said in the kindest voice he could muster. Jake answered by falling over to his side and passing out instantly. Later, when Jake finally awoke, he noticed that Tom was already up and about.

How long was I out? Jake wondered to himself.

"Finally, you're awake," Tom said, approaching Jake.

"What time is it?" Jake asked, groggily.

"It is hour fifteen," Tom said.

Hour fifteen? Yikes, I've already slept most of the day away! Jake thought, *I suppose Tom was right last night. Better to have slept during the night than through most of the day. Besides, if that thing is as big as Magella, we still have quite a ways to go...*

Jake peered out at the new dome. It was already much bigger than he had last recalled... probably because he was half-dazed through most of the walking the night before. As was the case when they had left Magella, only the top portion of the dome could be seen. As they got closer, Jake knew they would see more of the outer shell and eventually, what lay on the ground underneath it.

However, something was already different about this particular dome. Even though they could see the top portion of it, the color seemed off. Instead of viewing in to see a bluish sky and white clouds, all Jake could make out was a flat brownish-red color that was caked all over the dome's surface. It looked to be opaque, in that light was still making its way through, but it was definitely not clear, as Magella's dome had been.

That wasn't even the weirdest part. Jake wasn't completely sure at this distance yet, but it appeared as if the very top of the dome was missing. The outline that he could see wasn't one long, complete arc. Exactly halfway across, at its highest point, the arc abruptly stopped and was replaced by a shallow, jagged-looking "U" shape. The dome looked like an egg of which an enormous baby bird had broken its way out.

Tom gave Jake a look that seemed to say, "yeah, I know."

Neither said a word to one another. There was no need. They were both thinking the same thing. Jake grabbed a few bites of food. They were getting dangerously low now. There was probably only enough for anther day's worth of rationing. He had already gotten used to the feel (and sound) of his stomach constantly rumbling. Within a few minutes of completing his measly excuse for a meal, he packed up his things and continued on his way towards the new dome. What other choice did they have? It was right along their current path anyway. Might as well venture a look-see.

A day later, Jake and Tom were officially out of food. After gulping the last morsel down, Jake looked to the dome before them, appearing more and more now like a pointless endeavor, praying to the Founders that there was something inside that would help them. The structure now dominated the landscape, sitting there like a gigantic discarded relic. Not just the top portion, but the entire surface of the dome was brownish-red in color. Jake could now clearly see that there was indeed a hole in the top of it, too. The kilometers-long opening had a jagged edge that cut across what was once a smooth, solid surface. Cracks shot down from the opening towards the ground like veins.

What's happened here? Jake thought to himself.

Later that day they passed what Jake had to surmise were large chunks of dome, imbedded in the ground like giant daggers. Some were the size of a house. Others were bigger. Others were much, *much* bigger. Enormous mounds of sand and dirt spread out from the insertion point of each piece in all directions. Like the rest of the dome these pieces were brownish-red in color. On closer inspection, it became clear that much of the dirt and dust that the wind had kicked up outside had become stuck to them.

They had traveled close enough to one piece in particular that Jake could touch its surface. It felt smooth, but cold. He had wiped the dirt from its surface to see that underneath it was indeed clear, like glass. It looked as though each piece was nearly as thick as Jake was tall. The entire encounter added to the growing sense of dread in Jake's heart. He doubted that they would find anything different when they reached the rest of the dome.

When Jake and Tom had made it to the base of the dome itself, Jake's palm made contact with its surface. His fears were confirmed. It held firm, just like he was touching a solid wall of rock. He knocked on it with his fist next. It made a kind of a *PING, PING, PING* sound. It felt and sounded less like something thick and solid, but more lightweight or even hollow. The thought gave Jake an idea. He reached inside his pack until he found it: a small chiseling tool from Morzellano's mine.

"You brought that with you?" Tom said.

"I figured I might need it," Jake said.

"Do you really think that little thing is going to make any kind of difference?"

Jake just shrugged his shoulders as if to say, "who knows?"

Holding on tight and mustering all the strength that his starving body could manage, Jake swung the tiny chisel towards the dirty dome surface. Unfortunately, it had exactly the result Tom figured it would.

"I thought perhaps at least it would leave a mark or something!" Jake said.

Tom just shook his head.

"If this dome is like this all the way around, there is no way to get in," Jake commented.

"Too bad the hole is on the top," Tom said.

Jake nodded. He wiped a bit of the dust from the dome's surface with his hand in an effort to see what was inside, but when he peered through, all he could see was more brown. The inside surface of the clear barrier must be caked with the stuff as well. Damn.

As expected, this was a fruitless venture. Jake had been excited when they had first discovered this second dome. It had meant that Magella was not alone. Other worlds also existed! Other beings besides their own people were out there, too! It had been a revelation. But now, looking at this old, decrepit dome, Jake wasn't so sure anymore. Perhaps those that had constantly argued that the people of Magella were the only living beings in the universe were right. Perhaps long ago, other domed worlds, other whole societies, had existed, but no more. Maybe now, Magella was the only one left.

This is the wrath of the Founders, Jake thought to himself, trying to avoid a shiver. *These are the people that had turned away from them and had destroyed themselves.*

A single tear rolled down Jake's face as he realized that in all likelihood, he was looking upon the remains of his ancestors, who, blinded by their own greed and thirst for technological advancement, had damned all of humanity. It was here that the human race was nearly crushed out of existence. They thought themselves superior to the Founders and they had paid the price. Now, all that was left was a dead world, a monument to the kind of destruction of which only human beings were capable. It made him miss the safety and security of his own home all the more.

For the remainder of the day, Tom and Jake trekked counter-clockwise around the outside of the dome. As they walked, they began to creep closer once again to the giant gorge that cut through the ground like the leftover path of an unbelievably huge snake. Their only choice now was to continue to try and circumnavigate it somehow. The device kept pointing northwest even though they were now heading mostly just west. And, as always, the little counter on the device continued to click away.

9,549,789...
9,549,788...
9,549,787...

A few more chunks of the domed surface littered the landscape as they walked. When they got to the northernmost part of the circular base of the dome, where the dome was at its closest to the canyon, they even saw a piece of crystalline dome, taller than a city block, hanging precariously out over the ledge of the canyon. It had landed edge-first into the ground and then gravity must have taken over, pulling it partway into the chasm. And there it stayed, sitting like some cock-eyed sideways wall, forever on the brink of tumbling over but never quite making it.

For some morbid reason, Tom found this to be a great place to stop for the night. They never got close enough to touch the teetering wall; it was still too far away for that. The dome itself was a good five to ten kilometers away from the pit and the two did their best to stay more or less within arm's reach of the dome's surface. The following day, however, they would leave that path and continue to use the canyon as their guide, leaving the failed dome behind them.

As the twinkling, tiny lights of the Founders began to fill the sky, Jake was unnerved by how many of them he *couldn't* see. The dirt-covered dome beside them had blotted out nearly half of the sky now. It made Jake feel even more alone than he had before. He was used to having the gods of his knowledge and understanding keep a watch over him each night. Sure, when he had been inside of his tiny cube of a home back in Magella he was unable to see them, but if he was ever feeling lonely, all he needed to do was step outside. Now both Magella and half of the Founders were gone from his sight.

He felt the most alone he had ever felt in his entire life. Even having Tom with him didn't seem to help. He was abandoned, spit out into this wasteland to suffer and die. He was starving to death and his only hope for finding food sat right beside him, its impenetrable barrier refusing to let them in. It might take them days or even weeks to find another dome, if one even existed like Magella, which seemed a long shot at best to Jake. After that amount of time, both Tom and Jake would be long dead. Jake had to come to grips with reality. He was going to die.

He thought of his parents. They had always been so confident and faithful. How did they do it? Even back when they were alive, there had been struggles. They always seemed to find a way to rise above it. How would they react if they had seen the things Jake had now seen? Faced the same desperation?

"Where are you, dad?" Jake said softly to himself.

It was in that moment that Jake's eyes found the small, bright blue star along the dark horizon... his father's star.

That is our special star. Whenever I'm away, you can look at this star and know that I am with you.

Strangely, the star lined up almost perfectly with the far right edge of the dome. That was the weird thing... there *should* have been an edge there, but there wasn't. The dirt-smeared dome should have made it impossible for him to see his father's star, but there it was, shining its faint blue glow. It reminded Jake of the compass's odd propensity to shine nearly the same shade when something strange was about to happen. It looked as if his father's star had punctured its way through the dome while the rest of the stars hadn't. If that were true then that would mean...

Jake was up and on his feet immediately.

"Come on, grab your gear," he said to Tom.

"Not this again! Go to sleep!" Tom cried.

"Come on, Tom! This is important!"

"What's going on?"

"I think I've found a way in," Jake said with a grin.

Chapter 10

"Excess is the downfall of man."

-The Book of the Founders

It was early the next morning before Tom understood what Jake had been talking about the night before. The morning sun was peaking up over the far horizon, spilling bright oranges and yellows across the ground and up onto the side of the dirt-covered dome. They had been traveling around the side of the dome most of the night and hadn't noticed the change in one particular section of the dome's surface. It had been right there in front of their faces the entire time. The sun now made it abundantly clear: there was a hole cut into the side of the dome.

This hole, however, was much different than the gigantic one they had seen at the top of the massive spherical shield. Instead of being random and jagged, this opening was a perfect rectangle, probably about a hundred meters tall and fifty meters wide. The piece that had been cut out lay flat on the ground. It had fallen forward, inside the dome, and had completely flattened anything unlucky enough to have been sitting in its path. As expected, it was covered in red dust.

Tom approached Jake, who was already standing in the middle of the wide opening. For the first time, they could finally see what was inside this new habitat, although, the word "habitat" would have to be used loosely. It looked as though no being had made this place home for years. It was hard to see very much from where they were standing, but it was not encouraging. Debris was spread everywhere. Gigantic pieces of stone littered the ground. Either they had stumbled upon a part of this dome that was a garbage dump or they would be hard-pressed to find anything of value here whatsoever. For the moment, the two of them tried to put that out of their heads. At least there was a way in now. At least there was a chance to find something they might need, or so they hoped.

"How did you even see this last night?" Tom asked.

"I had a little help from my dad," Jake said.

Tom cocked an eyebrow at his friend.

"Ok, let me explain," Jake said. "When I saw this opening last night, it was from the side. A profile view, if you will. I saw a star that should not have been visible if this opening hadn't been there. It was ever so slight, but I could tell that a small part of the edge of the dome was missing."

"It doesn't look so small now," Tom commented.

"No, no it doesn't," Jake agreed.

"How did this get here?" Tom asked. "Who did this? Look at the edges! This is precision work."

The two men took a long, hard look at the opening cut into the side of the dome. The edges were not only perfectly straight, but smooth as well. Jake ran one of his hands up and down along it. He couldn't have cut his hand even if he had wanted to. There wasn't a single sharp edge to speak of. It was all nicely rounded off, as if he was feeling along the side of an extremely wide pipe.

"Nobody back home has ever been able to find a way to break through the dome." Jake said. "What kind of technology could have done this?"

"Well, one thing to remember is that this dome is, ah, broken, right?" Tom said. "Maybe it's a lot easier to break through when the dome is, uh, you know, turned off."

"Perhaps," Jake said, staring up to the top edge of the giant, invisible doorway. "My chiseling tool didn't even dent it. I am guessing whatever cut this hole had to be absolutely *enormous.*"

"And there is another thing to consider," Tom commented. "This appears to have been cut from the *outside,* as if someone was trying to get *in,* not *out.*"

There was a brief moment when neither of them said anything.

"Well, we better see what's in there," Jake said at last. "We came all this way, didn't we?"

With that, Jake climbed up onto the rectangular piece of the dome's outer shell that was in their path. As he walked forward, he cocked his head up slightly in an attempt to get a better view of their surroundings. A few steps later, his left foot slipped on the dust-covered surface of the cut-out door. Tom saw it and made a bit of a hissing sound as he inhaled quickly. Jake was able to steady himself with no harm done.

"Tread lightly," Tom said as Jake continued to walk, albeit a bit more cautiously now. "We still know next to nothing of what we are dealing with, here."

Jake nodded as Tom climbed up onto the massive hunk of door behind him. Just past the door was a large pile of rock. Jake gingerly made his way up with Tom close behind. Once he was up and on his feet, he was able to get a much better view of the world before them.

His heart sank. It was a complete wasteland. The chunks of rock and garbage they had seen from the doorway continued on for kilometers upon kilometers. All of the structures (or what had at one point been structures) around them were either crumbling to pieces or had long since fallen completely apart. The few that were still intact reached to dizzying heights. There was hardly a structure that wasn't at least fifty meters tall and many shot up to heights easily ten times that. Some had toppled over and crashed into each other, creating gigantic piles of rocks and debris.

There were so many pieces in places that Jake and Tom had to do quite a lot of climbing just to get anywhere. Everything was covered completely with red and brown dust, just like outside. Jake wasn't sure if anything in here had been a different color. If anything had, the harsh winds of the outside world had long since driven it away, along with any signs of life. Bones of every kind were scattered all over the ground. They were mostly human (well, Jake assumed they must have been- they didn't look any different than the human bones he had seen before), but there were also a few small animal skeletons from time to time. They seemed to be mostly feline or canine.

"This place is just one big tomb," Tom said. "Who in their right mind would want to break their way *into* here?"

"Us," Jake said. His stomach rumbled, as if on cue.

"Oh, right."

After hours of climbing around what Jake could only describe as a decimated city, they were able to see out much farther into the interior of the dome. The "city" they were in was atop a cliff of sorts and much of the rest of the dome was filled with a low-laying valley. From their vantage point, the reality of the dome's fate became heartbreakingly real. Many more buildings covered the landscape. There had to be at least ten other cities that they could see and probably dozens more that they couldn't. They were just as decimated as the one they had seen up close. Even this far away, one could see toppled structures and gigantic heaps of trash.

It also became clear that the city they had entered was actually one of the smaller ones. Compared to some of the other places, it could be argued that what they had just traversed may not have even been considered a city at all- perhaps just a small village. The others had were expansive with more structures, some reaching nearly twice as high as the tallest building in their original metropolis.

But even those were dwarfed by the most massive structure Jake had ever seen (except for the dome itself, of course). Its base was wide- probably the same size as the city they had just explored. From there, it just got ridiculous. It rose up for what had to be at least a dozen kilometers. Along the way, all kinds of tubes and pipes raced across its surface, interconnecting with one another at least a hundred times. Jake had no idea what they were all there for, but it had to have something to do with the top of the structure. The top of it grew into a fairly small point, but at this distance, it could probably still be the size of a city block- Jake couldn't tell. The crazy patchwork of tubes all seemed to coalesce at this point. The tip pointed directly into the cracked opening at the top of the dome.

"Those crazy bastards," Tom said. "They actually did it."

"Did what?" Jake asked.

"They found a way to break through the dome," Tom said. "Look, that… well whatever *that* is… it has to be some sort of giant weapon of some kind… designed specifically to penetrate the dome."

"I never in a million years would have thought that would be possible."

"Hell lot of good it did them. That is certainly what killed them all."

"Why did they want to leave so bad?"

"Why did you?" came Tom's reply.

That had stung a bit. Tom was right. Before their little adventure, Jake had spent years dreaming of life beyond that giant clear wall. The world that everyone else seemed to think was a safe and secure home had seemed more like a prison to him. But would Jake have gone to these lengths if the technology were available to him at the time? Would he have risked everything just to know if it was possible? He didn't know. That was the scary part. He really didn't know.

"I would say let's go explore it," Tom said, "but we have more important matters to attend to, like finding food."

"Yeah, you are probably right," Jake replied. He wasn't sure that he wanted to anyways. It was all a little bit too creepy for him.

"The best plan is to probably go back to the city and look for anything that is salvageable." Tom said.

Jake snorted. "Fat chance, but okay."

The two men spent the next two hours back in the city pouring through what could only be described as useless junk. Everything had rotted, and not just the food. There weren't even any decent tools or clothing to be found. Jake's heart sank even further. It had all been a waste. Even finding the entryway had ended up meaning nothing. They were not going to be able to find anything here of help and certainly not any food, which was their most desperate need of all.

Even though he knew that logic stated that he should pack it in right then and there, Jake kept his mouth closed and kept looking. Fairly early on in their search, Tom and Jake decided to split up. They both knew that they couldn't stray too far away from one another. Both agreed that if they started to feel funny at all, they would immediately head back in the other direction and call for help. The only sound other than themselves that Jake and Tom could hear was the whipping of the wind here and there so they assumed that being able to hear one another would not be too hard of a task.

Jake stepped over what he assumed used to be the base of a wall. Inside was a small staircase leading down under the ground. He peered down, but couldn't see much, just the floor in the corner of some kind of room covered with (what else?) reddish-brown dust. He carefully made his way down. There was no railing, but thankfully it ran along the side of a wall, so he used that to steady himself. The stairs creaked and cracked as he walked. About halfway down, one of the stairs broke beneath his foot, pieces falling to the ground, dust flying everywhere. He considered turning around at that moment, but his curiosity and his need to find something they could use were far too great.

We absolutely CANNOT leave here empty-handed, Jake said to himself. If they didn't find something to eat, they were as good as dead-both Tom and Jake knew that.

At the end of the stairs was a room that was in fairly good shape. Once Jake got out from the end of the stairs and stepped further into the space, he noticed that it hadn't taken the same kind of beating that much of the surface had. Light from the outside still poured in from the opening at the top of the staircase. Some articles of furniture were nearly completely intact. There was a couch, a couple of chairs and a table in the center of the room. It looked different from most tables he had seen, however, with buttons and knobs on its side. What they were supposed to do was lost on Jake. Their original purpose had more than likely long since died with their operators. On the wall hung like a picture, was a large piece of flat glass. This was the most puzzling to Jake. It wasn't reflective glass, so it couldn't have been used as a mirror. There were no knobs or buttons this time. More mysteries.

On the far side of the room there was a door. He walked over and peered in. It was hard to make out most of what was inside. The light from up on the surface was having a hard time making it this far in. The room was significantly smaller than the one he had just been in. There was an object in the corner that came up to Jake's knees and looked as long and wide as Jake was tall. It had to be some kind of bed, with an long object lying on top of it. He crept inside and let his hands do most of the looking for him. It felt cold, smooth... almost round... then, a hole, then another... then a slightly smaller hole...

he snapped his hand back. It was a skull. As his eyes adjusted to the darkness, he looked closer. Sure enough, it was a human skeleton. Not only that, but it was cradling a much smaller human skeleton. The two must have died lying in bed together. Jake had seen enough. He turned to go.

But what he saw when he turned around made him fall to the ground. A figure was standing right in the doorway, but it was obvious that it wasn't Tom. It was wearing black athletic gear with all sorts of pouches and gizmos strapped to it. It fit snugly to a very chiseled male body. The man had to have been in the best shape of his life. His face was obscured. He wore a leather cap that covered every inch of his face except for his eyes- and those were covered with a sleek, black visor that stretched nearly all of the way around his head. On the right shoulder of his outfit was an unfamiliar white symbol. It looked sort of like an upside-down "U" to Jake. The stranger had something in his hand. Jake's only assumption was that it was a weapon of some kind, because it was pointed right at his head.

Still sitting on the floor from the shock, Jake shook himself back to reality. He had to act fast. He had no idea what this new visitor had in mind for him, but he wasn't about to sit around and find out. His hand reached up onto the bed next to him, searching for something he could use to defend himself. The first thing he touched was a bone belonging to one of the long-since deceased occupants. It was long and thick.

Good enough, he thought.

He quickly swung it up and out in a long arc. The bone connected with something and soon Jake had his answer when he heard a clattering on the floor. This was it. This was his opportunity. He was instantly on his feet, barreling straight through the doorway and through his assailant. The stranger went down hard with a grunt, obviously not expecting Jake's quick reaction. Jake allowed his legs to keep himself moving forward. He looked back to see the strange new man already picking himself back up off the floor. Before he could look straight ahead again, Jake's gut ran into the weird table in the middle of the room, knocking the wind out of him.

No time to worry about breathing, Jake thought sarcastically as he pushed around the table and kept going.

Once back on the surface, Jake could see Tom was still searching through rubble and finding nothing. Tom picked up a can that had lost its contents long ago, brought it up close to his face, then wrinkled his nose a bit and tossed the can to the ground. It took a few small hops and then settled under some slightly burned paper. Tom turned as he heard Jake's frenzied footsteps approaching him.

"Jake, I know you are curious and all, but don't you think that is a little bit disrespectful towards the dead?" Tom said. "Plus, it's kinda gross, buddy."

Jake took a quick look at the bone still in his hand. He hadn't even realized that he had carried it all this way. Without a second thought he threw it to the ground and proceeded to grab Tom by his collar and shake him wildly.

"You... me... over... down... go... gotta go!" Jake managed to spit out amongst a plethora of wheezes, coughs and labored breaths.

"Wha?" Tom asked. "Slow down, there. Take your time, Jake. What's up?"

Jake did as he was told and took a few seconds to compose himself, hands placed on his knees as he tried desperately to take a number of deep breaths. All he really needed was four words anyways...

"We are not alone," he said.

Chapter 11

"You are my chosen ones, regaled and blessed above all others.
You, I have kept safe, while all others have perished."

-*The Book of the Founders*

Jake was now bent over, heaving heavily. Running for extended periods of time always seemed to set his lungs on fire. The gut-check by the table down in the room where he had been attacked hadn't helped, either. The air was coming back to him now, but slowly. He wasn't too comfortable waiting this long to begin with. Tom didn't seem to be grasping the fact that they had to move, and fast.

"Not alone?" Tom said. "You mean there are people here who survived this? Or maybe people like us? Visitors from out of town?"

"Look, can we discuss this later?" Jake said. "We have more pressing matters at the moment."

With that, Jake grabbed Tom by the shoulders, turned him in the direction of the entryway they had come in and pushed. Tom seemed to get the hint and started moving his legs. Within seconds of them getting on the move, a long spear of blue light sailed through Jake's peripheral vision. It struck the side of the building next to them, blasting a hole in it the size of his head. Dozens of tiny rocks rained down upon them. Jake looked behind them. Sure enough, there was the mysterious man in black, now accompanied by three other men, dressed in identical outfits. In their hands each of them was holding the same strange object that had been pointed at Jake's head just moments earlier.

Another one fired. This time, the beam of blue light missed Tom's head by mere centimeters, hit the ground and blew rocks, dust and debris all over the two runners. Jake struggled and nearly fell, but Tom was quick to grab him from under the arm, pull him up and steady him, all while still pressing forward. The dust obscured their vision for a moment, but soon they were through it, leaping over rock piles and aged remains that were scattered all over the ground.

More shots were fired, exploding the old, tattered structures all around them. They were running out of road to run across. Tom motioned to his right and shouted, "this way!" They both quickly ran around a corner and stopped for a moment.

"This is crazy!" Jake said. "With those weapons or whatever they are that they have, we are as good as dead. It is still at least another five or six hundred meters to where we came in."

"Well, I guess we'd better take matters into our own hands," Tom said.

With that, Tom pulled his bow from its carrier and ran inside the nearest building that was more or less intact. Jake followed. Once he had made it through the doorway, Jake noticed a set of stairs. Tom had already scrambled up them and was pulling an arrow from his quiver. Jake craned his neck to look up. There was a small window up there, facing the direction of their pursuers. Tom pulled the arrow back and released. The look of hopeful expectation on his face soon changed to a look of disgust... then fear.

"Move!" Tom shouted as he scrambled down the stairs as quickly as his legs would allow. Jake took the hint and bolted from the building just as Tom was exiting it himself. As they made their way outside, the entire upper story of the structure exploded, sending man-sized boulders flying in all directions. They quickly found another doorway in which to hide from the falling projectiles.

"I take it you missed," Jake said once they were safely out of the way.

"No, I didn't miss," Tom said. "I hit the guy right in the chest."

"Then what happened?"

"That's just the problem. Nothing."

"Those suits they are wearing must be strong enough to deflect arrows."

"Whatever the case, we are seriously outmatched here."

"Our best bet is to lose them, if we can."

"Not too likely, but we've got no other choice. Come on."

Jake and Tom sprinted back out of the building just as their pursuers rounded the corner and spotted them. More blue light, more explosions, more chaos. Somehow they managed to stay together and keep going. The chase continued throughout the mess of the old, decomposing city. More often than not, the ground was not flat, but rather covered with all kinds of obstacles that needed to be avoided. About every few meters, one of them would trip, stumble or completely fall over. The escape attempt was not exactly going to plan.

The pursuers in black were closing the gap between themselves and Jake and Tom. Before long, it was all over. Jake and Tom had run themselves right into an alley with no apparent exit other than the way they had come. The group of black-clad strangers quickly blocked off any possible escape routes. Jake was the first to put his hands up.

"Please," Jake said, "don't kill us. We are strangers here. We had no idea anyone was still alive. Please, just let us go in peace."

All four still had their weapons raised on Tom and Jake, but did not fire. The one out in front (probably the leader, Jake surmised) tilted his head slightly in an inquisitive manner. He then used his non-weapon hand to turn a small dial that was attached to the side of his leg, by the knee. What came out at first sounded more like some massive creature clearing its throat, but soon words formed…

"Stop running," the man said.

Although to Jake it sounded more like "stoop rooning".

"Well, as you can see, we have… no real choice there," Tom pointed out.

"No real choice," the man in black repeated.

"Noo raal cheweece"

At that moment, Jake noticed something moving, back behind their four new guests. He wasn't sure, but he thought that he saw another figure peering around from the side of one of the buildings. Before he knew what he was looking at, it was gone.

"What do you want from us?" Tom asked.

There was a slight pause and then only, "death."

"Great," Tom smirked, "and here I was all worried."

"First," the leader said, "give us the compass."

"Compass? What compass?" Jake asked.

"The compass! It is the disc that gave you freedom. Give it to us. NOW."

As before, Jake saw someone peak out from one of the buildings. Jake could see them clearer now. In one of its arms, it held a weapon, not unlike the ones used by their pursuers. At least Jake thought it was. It was still difficult to make out too many details at this distance. He wasn't sure what he was looking at, but figured he might as well take a chance. It wasn't as if their current situation could get much worse. He had to go with his gut on this one.

"Tom?" Jake said. "Do as I say and don't ask questions."

"What?" Tom asked.

"I said don't ask questions!" Jake shouted.

"GIVE IT TO US…" the leader screamed. "NOW!!!!"

"DROP!" Jake shouted.

Both men hit the deck. From far away, a blast of blue light came screaming in and hit the leader square in the back between his shoulder blades. He didn't explode like many of the buildings had earlier, but it seemed to have done the job. He fell to the ground like a sack of potatoes and didn't move a muscle. The other three immediately began looking around them in all directions, weapons raised and roaming for the source of the shot.

"Who the hell did THAT?" Tom asked.

"Who cares, MOVE!" Jake yelled.

Tom and Jake got up and ran as fast as they could out from the alley. The other three men were so distracted that they let Tom and Jake run right by without any resistance whatsoever. Streaks of blue light flew in all directions now. Jake had no idea who had fired what where or when, he just did his best to stay out of the way. In the chaos, he lost track of Tom. Dust was everywhere. It was nearly impossible to see anything through all of the particles floating in the air. After a good deal of scrambling around and hoping that he wouldn't get shot, he found a small crevice between two structures. He did his best to wiggle into it and then stayed there, hoping he was far enough out of the way not to be noticed.

After several minutes, the sounds of screaming, explosions and running feet dissipated. Either everything was over or those still involved had moved far enough away not to be heard anymore. Jake waited a minute or two more, just to be sure. Then, very carefully, he ventured a look out from his hiding place. He saw one body, dressed in black, lying on the ground. Everyone else had gone. He figured it was as safe as it was ever going to be and stepped out.

He figured wrong.

The end of one of the strange new weapons dug deep into the small of Jake's back. One of the black clad men had been just outside of his hiding place, waiting for him. Jake turned and looked. The man's visor and head cover had been stripped. He was just as human as Jake or anyone else underneath. Jake didn't know what he should have expected, but at least something more, well, *different*. The man's body was covered in dust and had a couple scratches. One particularly deep gouge in his right check was bleeding a decent amount.

"Get on your knees!" the man spat.

"Wha-" Jake managed before being shoved to the ground. Streams of pain ran up both of his legs. He couldn't see his assailant anymore, but he knew the man was there. The end of his weapon poked painfully in the back of Jake's head. It then pushed harder, causing his head to tilt forward.

"GIVE ME THE DISC!!"

"I don't know what you are talking about!" Jake pleaded.

"GIVE ME THE-" *CRACK!*

The pressure of the weapon on his neck immediately disappeared and he heard a loud THUMP from behind him. He turned around and was amazed at what he saw...

It was a woman.

And she was handing Jake the now dead man's weapon.

"Tha-thank you," Jake managed as he took the weapon from her. She seemed almost disinterested in him, scanning the area around them for more assailants. As soon as Jake had grabbed hold of the weapon, he studied it. It was in the shape of an "L" with one end that flattened slightly as it approached the tip. That was the end that been pointed at them constantly. The other end of the "L" must be the grip, then. How did it fire, though? He had no clue how one might create the blue fireworks that were shot at them earlier.

For the first time, Jake was now able to get a good look at his rescuer. Her clothes were well worn and looked as if they had been through hell and back. She wore a grey jumpsuit that fit tight to her thin, yet surprisingly muscular body. This seemed a reasonable clothing choice, considering how she had moved about so seamlessly just a few moments earlier. There were dark marks streaked all over it and even a few small holes here and there. Sheathed in a holster that hung slightly below her hip was another mysterious weapon, just like the one she had just handed him. It looked as if she had a number of other hand-to-hand type weapons attached to her body as well, but it was impossible for him to be able to tell exactly what they all were. Most hung from a black belt about her waist while a larger one was attached to her back, it's handle sticking up just above her shoulders. Her hair was dark brown and tied up in a tight bun in the back of her head. Her face was smeared with dirt. Underneath it all, there was a thin face chiseled with grim determination.

"Wh- where's the rest of them?" Jake asked.

"Dead," she said.

It sounded to Jake like she had said "Daad." This was yet another peculiar accent.

"I just hope there aren't more," she continued. "Come on, let's go find your friend."

"Wait," Jake said, "I, I don't even know your name."

"It's Meela," she said.

Jake extended his hand. "Nice to meet you, Meela. I'm Jake."

She had a look of confusion as to what to do at first, but eventually grasped Jake's hand with her own, "Jake… interesting name…"

Before setting off to find Tom, Jake walked over to the two dead soldiers. They had to be military of some kind, he supposed, by the way they were dressed and armed. Bit by bit, he began to grab what he could of their belongings and stuffed them in his pack. It was obvious they wouldn't be needing them any time soon. When he came across their canteens, his heart skipped a beat. He quickly gulped down a sizeable amount from one but soon had the cap back on. Who knew how long they may need to ration it. When Meela saw what he was doing, she offered him a suggestion.

"Take his clothes, too," she said.

"Good idea," Jake said, remembering how they had deflected Tom's arrow. "They might come in handy some day."

He pulled at the material of the uniform, examining it more closely. It felt somewhat smooth and porous, but tough enough to deter projectiles. Whatever it was made out of, he had never seen it before. He removed the man's gloves and turned over one of his hands. In the man's palm was either a tattoo or a very old burn mark, Jake wasn't sure. The marking appeared to be another upside-down "U", just like the one on the right shoulder of the uniform. Jake looked confused. Meela looked bored.

He got the hint and didn't ask. He finished stuffing the clothing in his bag, and was surprised just how small it would pack down when folded. Before he finished getting it all in, Meela approached one of the bodies and with considerably less strain than Jake might have guessed, she turned it over onto its chest. The overturned body revealed a small pouch, lying on the ground. Jake couldn't believe that he had missed it earlier when stripping him.

Meela snapped the pouch open and pulled out a small silver object. No, it couldn't be. Jake looked closer. Sure enough, it was. There in Meela's hand was another compass, identical to the one he had in his pocket at that very moment. Well, perhaps not *exactly* identical. There was something different about this one, and it took a second for it to register for him. It didn't have any numbers or tiny blue light on it. No light to guide the way, no numbers counting down, no numbers tracking distance. Just plain silver all over its surface. So, it wasn't exactly fair to call it a compass like theirs, then, was it? Maybe it just hadn't been activated yet or something.

"Want to keep that one?" Jake asked.

"No thanks," Meela said, tossing it to him, "I already got one."

When Jake got just about all that he could fit into his pack, which included a new silver disc, he stood up and scanned the area. Meela gave him a slight smile and took off at quite a quick pace. Jake did his best to catch up. They didn't have to go far. After only having traveled one city block (or what remained of one) Meela had spotted Tom. That was a blessing. Jake knew all too well that the range of these devices didn't extend very far at all.

Tom was inside a crumbling building that was missing all of one wall and part of another, sitting in a chair at a rickety old table that was somehow still standing, even though half of its legs were gone. It was as if the guy had been having his afternoon tea in the midst of all of the chaos. He was decidedly cheerful when he saw Jake and their savior, Meela. He smiled as only Tom could and extended a hand.

"Nice to meet you, my dear," Tom said, shaking Meela's hand. "I take it all of our pursuers are gone?"

"Yes, they are gone," Jake answered for her.

"And do we have *you* to thank for that?" Tom asked, nodding at Meela after they had completed their handshake.

"I've encountered them before," Meela said. "I was able to track them and thankfully get the drop on them this time. My name is Meela, by the way."

"So, Meela," Tom said, "who are you, exactly? This may or may not shock you, but you are the first other living person we've encountered out here… whatever *here* is."

"Well, besides those four dead guys," Jake chimed in.

Meela grunted and grinned slightly. "They call themselves the Omega Order."

Someone's changing the subject, Jake thought to himself. He kept his mouth shut on the issue, though.

"I started encountering them a little more than one cycle ago," Meela continued, "but I've never seen them venture this far to the east before. They usually stay west of the great canyon."

"So it *does* end!" Jake said.

Tom elbowed Jake in the side and then gestured for Meela continue.

"Yes," Meela said, "it ends, but far to the west of here. When I've encountered the Omega Order in the past, they have stuck mostly to the northern side of the canyon. They have been expanding their search."

"Search for what?" Jake asked.

"These," Meela said, holding up a disc of her own. Like the first one they had found, it didn't have any numbers on it. It seemed to Jake as though these devices must be somewhat common, although at this point, he figured that his had to be unique with its directional light, countdown clock and distance counter. He wondered if he shouldn't keep that tidbit of information to himself, at least for the time being.

"These are what make it possible to survive outside of the domes," Jake said.

"Yes," Meela replied. "Plus they make it possible to enter and exit them at will."

"Well, at least those that are functional," Tom said, looking out the window at the devastated world all around them.

"Each dome has only one," Meela said. "At least, I *think* each dome has only one. Either they were looking for the disc located in this particular dome or they knew you were coming and had planned that little ambush of theirs."

Jake figured it was probably the latter. It wasn't as if he and Tom were trying to hide from anyone while they had been traveling. Hell, they hadn't even been sure if there was anyone else outside of Magella other than just the two of them. Now they knew better. It had been Jake and Tom's first encounter with other human beings outside of Magella and those humans had tried to kill them. At least this new one didn't seem to be ready to destroy them... yet.

"So, it seems logical why they want these devices," Tom said. "Since they have the power to leave and enter new worlds, those who possess most or all of them also possess all or most of the power."

"Exactly!" Meela said. "But, from what I've learned through my, um, encounters with them, they are not just looking to build their collection."

"Oh?" Jake asked.

"Apparently, there is a special one that they are quite excited about," Meela said.

"Special how?" Tom asked. Jake gave him a quick look. Tom looked back for just a second and then his eyes were once again locked on Meela's.

"I don't know really," Meela said. "They call it 'the compass'. It is supposed to lead them somewhere, I think."

Don't tell her! Don't tell her! Jake thought to himself.

Tom didn't tell her. "Where does the Omega Order come from?" he asked.

"A dome, just like all of us originally," Meela said. "It is far from here, near the great mountains. It seems to reason that they found their dome's disc and now they are on the search for others. They have been working their way out from their home, systematically looking for as many of those discs as they can find."

And now they are here, Jake thought. *It won't be long now before they find Magella. What will happen when they do? What will happen when they find no device? Will they destroy everything in their fruitless, desperate search?*

"How many of those discs do you think they have found?" Jake asked.

"It's hard to tell," Meela said. "Maybe a dozen? Maybe more."

Jake couldn't help his curiosity now. "How many domes are there?"

Meela laughed at that. "Think I've explored the entire world, have I? Jake, I don't have any idea. Since I've been out here, I've seen a total of fifteen different domed worlds, not including this one."

Jake's entire worldview just exploded with that one simple sentence. *At least fifteen different domed worlds.*

"And they are alive?" Jake asked.

"As in they don't just have a bunch of skeletons laying about, yeah," Meela said, still laughing.

Jake couldn't believe it. The world just became a whole lot bigger and more complex than he had ever imagined. Being a citizen of Magella had always made him feel special. They were the chosen ones, after all. Now, he was discovering that there were *other* chosen ones, perhaps dozens, maybe even hundreds! This wasn't right. This flew in the face of everything the Founders had taught them.

"So, what's your story?" Meela asked casually. "I take it you are from somewhere east of here, otherwise I suspect we would have run into each other before now."

Tom took it upon himself to describe their journey thus far. Jake noted with a sigh of relief that Tom had been careful to leave out certain details. There was no mention of the Overseer or numbers that had appeared on the device's surface. No path to follow, no countdown clock. As far as Meela was concerned, these were two guys who had stumbled across their dome's device and were now exploring the outside world. He was quick to mention at the end that they hadn't eaten in nearly two days because they had run out of food.

"Seriously?!" Meela shouted, like a mother scolding her poorly behaved children. She removed a handful of what looked like twigs from her pouch and threw them across the table at Tom and Jake. Both men grabbed at them greedily and began munching instantly. The sticks were kind of bitter, but otherwise they had a slight cinnamon-like taste to them. Both men devoured them in seconds. Soon, Meela had tossed out half a dozen more. "That's all I have," she said finally.

"Thank you!" Jake said, through a mouthful of food.

"Yes, thank you for the food," Tom said. "And thank you for your patience with us. As you know, we are still new to all of this and it has been a bit jarring for both of us."

"Of course," Meela said, with a look on her face that seemed to say "what else was I supposed to do?"

"That only leaves one more question," Jake said. "Who are *you?*"

"That answer is… complicated." Meela replied.

CHAPTER 12

"Do not fear. All is provided."

-The Book of the Founders

Jake, Meela and Tom were now standing back at the entrance to what Tom had lovingly christened "the dead dome". Jake looked up once more at the opening cut into the dome's surface. Had it been the Omega Order that had created this or had it been someone else, years earlier? For that matter, just how long ago had the society inside killed themselves in an attempt to escape? The irony was that the means for their escape had been sitting somewhere inside with them the entire time. Perhaps it was still sitting in there somewhere?

On their way back out to the seemingly artificial entrance to the dome, the three had stopped at the bodies of the other two dead Omega soldiers. They had taken as much as could be carried between Jake's pack, Tom's pack and Meela's satchel. No more devices were found, however. That was probably for the best. The Omega Order would not be happy to discover that not only had four of their troops been killed, but one of their prized discs was now gone as well. Jake wondered to himself if they shouldn't just leave the disc they had found behind. Maybe the Omega Order would think the men had died in an accident and then leave them alone? But, that wasn't very likely. Besides, Jake and Tom had had targets on their backs before ever entering that dome, even though they had had no clue at the time.

A deep, rumbling growl broke Jake from his thoughts.

"What the hell was that?" Tom asked.

Soon, they had their answer.

A great blur of black swept across Jake's field of vision, from left to right. His head quickly followed it and found an unbelievable sight: a giant panther had Tom pinned to the ground. Its mouth was opened, bearing a pair of the biggest fangs Jake had ever seen. Its ebony cheeks were pulled back, whiskers stuck straight out in a posture of aggression. It roared directly into Tom's face. Jake assumed Tom had only seconds before that lovely face of his was no longer so lovely.

"TOM!!" Jake shouted.

The panther turned its head to Jake and bellowed even loader.

Nice move, Jake thought to himself.

"DAISY!!" Meela said forcefully, stomping over beside the giant feline.

Daisy? That gruesome creature's name is Daisy?

Almost immediately, the cat pulled back from atop Tom and walked over to look up at Meela's face. Tom instantly scrambled backwards like a crab until he had banged up against the dirt-smeared outer casing of the dome. There he sat, breathing heavy, never taking his eyes off of his attacker. Meela regarded the great beast for a moment or two and then flicked its nose with her finger. It shook its head from side to side a few times and then reared back its face and used its large tongue to lick the spot where it had been hit. Finally, it sat down and lazily looked about, as if nothing was the matter at all.

"What in the Founder's names just happened?" Jake asked.

"Sorry about that," Meela said. "I forgot all about her."

"So, what? This monster is your *pet?*" Tom said.

"More like companion," Meela said. "And she was just being protective of me. She doesn't particularly like strangers."

"You don't say..." Tom mumbled.

"She just needs to get to know you," Meela said. "Tom, hold out your hand."

"Are you joking?" Tom said.

"She won't hurt you. Come on!" Meela said.

Tom reluctantly did as he was told. It was all he could do to keep his hand from shaking profusely, though. As the giant cat stood up and approached, his body stiffened, sitting just a little bit more upright. The cat stopped only a few steps away from Tom and extended her head forward. Her nose was almost bigger than Tom's entire hand. Her nostrils flared and then they finally made contact with Tom's fingertips as she turned her head and rubbed the side of her mouth along Tom's hand, leaving a good amount of saliva along the way.

"I think she likes you!" Meela said.

"Charmed," came Tom's reply as he attempted to wipe the wet onto his clothes.

Meela then led Daisy over to Jake to give him a smell as well. As she did so, Tom made his way back up to his feet, palming the dome's gritty surface for help along the way. Daisy seemed just as content with Jake as she had with Tom, though he didn't get quite as much slobber. All the while, Meela was petting the creature's head, occasionally giving a few scratches behind its large, triangle-shaped ears.

"I left her outside," Meela said. "The terrain in there didn't look too stable."

"She must have been standing away from the door, behind the dirt-covered dome surface," Tom said. "That's why she didn't see us until now."

"But, how did she survive that far away from you?" Jake asked.

With that, Meela simply took hold of a thick, leather collar around the cat's neck that Jake had only noticed just then. She pulled it around until Jake saw a white, circular container attached to it. He knew exactly what must be inside of it. So, their total number was actually four devices: one for each human and one for the gigantic, terrible beast Meela kept as a pet. Jake wondered if Meela was ever afraid that the Omega Order would kill Daisy and take the thing, but he laughed to himself at the thought. After what he had just seen with Tom, he knew Daisy could defend herself just fine.

"We usually stick close together," Meela explained, "but for the times that we are apart, I like to know that she is safe."

"Why don't you just get a horse instead?" Tom asked. "Wouldn't that be safer?"

"And easier to ride?" Jake chimed in.

"Horses don't work out here," Meela said. "It has something to do with the gravity, I think. They can't make the adjustment. They always just topple over. Most of the time they end up breaking an ankle and need to be put down. I went through about five horses before I figured that one out. Megacats, on the other hand, are much more sure-footed."

"How did you get her?" Jake asked.

"I found her when she was just a cub," Meela said. "She was starving and I nursed her back to health. We used to domesticate these animals back home, so I took it upon myself to raise her. It was nice to have a friend after so much time out here on my own. Daisy and I are now just about inseparable."

"Daisy," Tom said. "Cute name."

"How long were you out here?" Jake asked.

"Almost five cycles," Meela said. "Until those Omegas started showing up, I thought I was the only one."

"You mean you don't actually live inside any particular dome, then?" Tom asked.

"No, I gave that up a long time ago," Meela said. "I guess you could say I always had a hard time fitting in. Eventually, I just decided to live out here."

"Nice," Tom said, eyeing the landscape.

"But how did you survive?" Jake asked. "There's nothing out here!"

Meela just smiled. "I got good at stealing. It was easy enough to sneak into a dome nearby and sneak back out again without being noticed. As far as I can tell, I don't think I've ever been spotted. And if I ever *was* spotted... well, let's just say people are really good at seeing what they want to see. Most, I assume, would probably dismiss me as their eyes playing tricks on them or some figment of their imagination."

"Do you have a set home or do you just roam around like a nomad?" Jake asked. "Do you live near here?"

"You know, I really should get going," Meela said, adjusting her satchel.

"Wait, what are we doing?" Jake asked, looking back and forth between Tom and Meela.

"Do whatever you want," Meela said matter-of-factly. "I'm leaving."

"Leaving as in we can come with you?" Jake asked.

"Leaving as in stay the hell away from me," Meela said as she leapt up on Daisy's back. The giant cat didn't seem all that fazed.

"Come on," Jake protested walking beside Daisy and peering up at Meela like a small child begging for food. "We need your help! You know things we don't, you..."

"YOU," Meela interrupted, turning around so that both her and Daisy's faces were staring Jake down, "both have most likely been targeted by the Omega Order. I haven't made it this far by being stupid. I feel for you, I really do, but I'm not willing to risk my own safety on either of you. Do yourselves a favor and head back to wherever you came from and keep a low profile. You don't want to be out here. Life inside the domes is safe. Life out here is dangerous. You two have already proven to me that you have no business spending any more time outside of your home. I'm leaving now and if I catch either of you following me, I'll shoot you myself."

With that, Daisy and Meela took off out into the dusty evening. The sun hung low in the sky, casting long shadows behind the two as they departed. As Jake watched the pair go, he felt as though their best chance at surviving out in the wilderness was leaving as well. Before long, the mysterious woman and her beast had completely disappeared from sight. Red dust began to fill the space they had occupied only seconds earlier.

The winds were beginning to whip up again. They did that from time to time outside. One had to be prepared when they did or the low gravity would sweep you up into the air. Jake remembered all too well his experiences with the gusts of the outside world when he had first exited Magella. He wondered how Meela handled those kinds of situations when they happened. He realized he'd never know now. She had abandoned them.

Both Tom and Jake knew their primary goal: food. It was a matter of finding another dome, this time hopefully populated by living things, and stealing what they needed, much like Meela had become so accustomed to doing. Once again, Jake wished that Meela hadn't ditched them. She was a bonafide expert at this kind of thing and they really could have used her help. But she was gone. Tom and Jake would just have to be careful and figure things out for themselves along the way.

Jake and Tom continued their way along the ridge of the canyon, pulling away little by little from the dome that had proven life existed outside of Magella, but had done little in the way of meeting their basic needs. Days passed. The two saw nothing but sand and rocks. Jake had to remind himself how long they had been outside of Magella before they had come across the first dome. The elements were not the worst of it. Again, for reasons unknown to Jake or Tom, the device kept them temperature-controlled right around a comfortable 25 degrees Celsius.

The worst of it was the lack of food. Long ago, when Jake was little, he had complained before a meal that he was "staving". His father had taken him by the arm and looked at him hard in the face. "You don't know what starving feels like, son... not REAL staving," he had said. Jake thought that he was now beginning to understand just what his father had meant all those years ago. His hunger for food was more than just some kind of rumbling physical desire in his belly. It was *painful*. It *hurt*.

The best they could do was continue moving forward and continue to hope. Jake's lips were beginning to crack from dehydration. They forced themselves to only take a few swigs of water every few hours in an effort to conserve it. The lack of food was troubling, but the lack of more water was a true emergency. As the days progressed, though, it became clear that Tom was far worse for the wear than Jake. Jake spent much of his time just trying to keep Tom upright and still walking. Both he and Tom knew that even though they both desired to stop and rest, it would be to their detriment. Any additional time spent not moving forward was that much more time for them to starve to death.

The two tried to keep hopes high that they would find another dome soon. Jake often wondered why Meela couldn't have at least pointed them in the direction of the closest one. She must have known she was condemning them to death with her departure. Many times a day, Jake would peer at the road ahead of them (if one could call it a road) as well as the landscape to either side of them, desperate to find a little clear bubble, popping up out of the ground.

And then, Jake found it. It was off to the south of their current path, a fair distance away from the gigantic chasm, which frustratingly, still looked as though it would go on forever. At first glance, Jake figured that it was just the sun's rays or perhaps his own eyes playing tricks on him. But, as they turned and began to head southwest, there it stayed, right in front of them. Even with this new hope on the horizon, Jake knew they still had at least a day or two's travel, especially at their labored pace. The new dome's presence was a miracle, but Jake was worried it might not be close enough for them to reach before he collapsed on the ground for good. He looked over at Tom, stumbling beside him, eyes half open, mouth caked with blisters and cuts.

Three hours after the sun had set, Tom had collapsed. Jake stumbled over to him in an effort to help, but as soon as he loosed his legs to kneel beside his friend, they had given out completely. He fell right on top of Tom, who didn't even flinch. The two lay like that for the next six hours.

The following day, once the two of them had gained enough strength to stand once more, Jake was able to make out structures inside the dome. They were shaped kind of like bubbles or mushrooms. It was unlike anything he had seen before. Everything seemed to be round or spherical in shape. From here it was difficult to tell, but he was fairly certain that this dome was still intact. The last one had allowed the awesomely powerful wind of the outdoors to sweep in and cake the sides of everything with a reddish-brown paste. So far, it didn't appear as if that was the case here. They would have to get closer to know for sure.

Another unique feature for this particular dome was that it was embedded into the side of a large mountain. Was this one of the great mountains that Meela had spoke of? Most likely not, considering that this seemed to be the only sizable mountain anywhere nearby. Plus, if the Omega Order had spent over an entire cycle exploring the outside world, visiting possibly dozens of domes, then logic would dictate that they had to be quite a bit further out than this.

Only about three quarters of the dome's outer surface was visible, while the rest was imbedded into the side of the mountain. Jake figured that this could work to their advantage. With Tom's condition worsening, he would be less than useless in any kind of food-finding mission. Jake would need to find a cave near the base of the mountain where Tom could rest while he looked for something for them to consume. So, the two changed directions, now heading for the foot of the mountain instead of the dome itself.

Sure enough, there were plenty of caves to choose from once they arrived at the foot of the mountain. With the mountain now between them and the dome, Jake was certain that nobody inside the dome had seen them approach. Sure, if someone had an incredibly high-powered viewing device, they could have spotted them a day ago, but Jake had to put those thoughts out of his mind. He gingerly helped Tom to the floor of one of the caves, almost toppling over himself in the process. Tom's eyes closed almost immediately as he made contact with the ground, his body on the cusp of total shutdown.

At this distance, Jake could work his way around the rocks and within half a day he would be by the edge of the dome. Jake emptied both of their packs onto the floor of the cave, hopeful that he would soon return with each of them filled with food and water. He also put on one of the suits worn by their previous attackers at the dead dome. At the last moment, he threw Tom's bow and his quiver of arrows over his back.

Why not? He thought to himself.

Lastly, he grabbed their "new" device and placed it inside of Tom's pocket. It was time to test just how reliable it was. Jake kept their original device, the compass, in his own pocket. However unlikely it was that someone would stumble upon Tom in the cave, he was not prepared to risk losing both his friend and the savior of all of humanity (well, at least according to the Overseer).

When he was all suited up and ready to go, he looked back at Tom, who hadn't moved a muscle, save for the brief risings and fallings of his chest as he continued to breathe. He was fairly certain that Tom had already allowed the long, deep tendrils of sleep to burrow in and drift him off to more pleasant circumstances.

"Sorry about this, Tom," he said, rubbing the neck of his friend. "I'm sorry that bitch Meela allowed this to happen to us. I'll do what I can. Just hang on."

CHAPTER 13

"Attempting to take on life's challenges all by yourself
almost never turns out the way you would like it to."

-*The Book of the Founders*

A s soon as the sun had begun to set, Jake was out of the cave and on
his way. He just hoped that Tom would be alright. It pained him
to no end leaving his friend like that, but he had no choice. Tom was
not in any shape to do, well, *anything.* Jake let the low rays of the sun
guide his footsteps as he made his way through the uneven path of
rocks, down and around the side of the jagged mountain.

As expected, it took Jake many hours to traverse the distance to
the new dome's edge. Because so much of his journey had been behind rocks that obscured his view, Jake didn't really get a good look
at what was inside the dome until he was nearly there. Even when he
got so close that the dome nearly enveloped everything around him,
the reflection of the sun's deep red rays still made it difficult to make
out much of anything inside. All he really saw for most of his journey
were shapes and impressions, mostly of the rounded variety.

By the time he reached the edge of the dome, he was covered
completely in darkness, as he had expected. He knew that he needed
to find an entry point where he would not call attention to himself.

He also knew that the device, as well as he himself, would glow blue as he entered. He took a quick look around the general area just inside the dome and was relieved it appeared deserted. The closest structure that he could detect was at least a kilometer away. He really wasn't able to decipher all that much in the dark and he gathered most people were either asleep or didn't use any kind of illumination at this hour. *All the better,* he thought as he slid through the clear structure.

It was difficult for Jake to navigate through the area of brush just inside the dome's surface once the blue glow that hailed his arrival had dissipated. He just needed to be very careful as he walked, as the ground inside the dome wasn't any smoother than it had been outside. Any misstep could mean a twisted or broken ankle. He couldn't afford for that to happen. Tom was counting on him.

When Jake finally got close enough to touch one of the bulbous, rounded buildings, he took a moment to sit and rest. He crouched down to where it met the ground. It was the first time he was able to get a really good look at the strange architecture. The width of it was around thirty meters, almost like a mini dome, except for the fact that it wasn't clear. He let his hands move about its surface. It was incredibly smooth. He wondered just what it was made out of, and could easily spend weeks here, exploring the area. He had to tell himself "no" once again. Tonight he was a thief, not an anthropologist.

Just as he was getting up to move again, he heard a laugh from inside. He froze, rethinking his plan. He was already halfway up from his crouched position. Before long, his legs began to ache. In excruciatingly slow motion, he lowered his body back down, careful not to make any additional noise. He kept his ears attuned to any other sounds. For a few seconds, nothing happened. Then he heard two female voices. They were either arguing or joking with one another. Jake guessed that it must have been joking, since it had been laughter that had tipped him off in the first place.

The voices inside grew in volume. Either the joking was intensifying or they were getting closer to him. Before Jake had a chance to react, two figures flew out of a door he hadn't noticed before, less than a meter away from where he was sitting. He immediately shot up and ran around the edge of the house (he assumed it was a house) and out of their range of sight. He only hoped that they were so into whatever it was they were doing that they hadn't noticed him. It was still fairly dark out which hopefully would continue to keep him camouflaged. More giggles and laughter came out of the two girls, now just out of view around the side of the building. He couldn't make out any real words at all.

Trying to still stay crouched, Jake continued his way around the circular building, away from the two figures. If they were outside, then chances were good that nobody was inside. When he stopped moving, he noticed a window just above his head. When he stood up fully erect, his eyes could just peek over its bottom edge and he could see a chair, a bed and a few other pieces of furniture inside. As expected, no one was there. The room was small, which meant there could be a risk of someone entering from another room. He had to be cautious. He continued around the house until he came to another window. He chanced another peek inside. It was some kind of gathering space or living room this time. As before, there was no sign of anyone. He kept going.

Soon, there was another window, giving him the sense they were all evenly spaced around the building. He peered in again. As luck would have it, this room was some sort of kitchen. Bits and pieces of food lay about, including apples, cheese, blueberries, crackers and a glass pitcher of water. There was even what looked to be a gigantic fresh loaf of bread sitting on a table. Jake's stomach growled in agony at the sight. The window had no glass, so the various aromas of the kitchen's contents reached his nostrils. That was all it took. Within seconds, he had leapt up off of the ground and was wiggling his body through the open window.

As soon as his feet hit the floor, Jake knew that his decision had been pretty stupid. The seductive smell of the food had drawn him carelessly into the room, and now inside, he had no idea if the girls would return or if anyone else lived here, for that matter. It was too late now. He had to grab what he could and hope no one showed up. He unzipped one of the packs as quickly and quietly as he could and began to stuff anything edible that he could find into it. The bread was first. It took up a lot of space, but he knew that it would fill them up the best and could last them a good long while.

Jake continued to grab various items from the counter and the cabinets. Some things he recognized, others he didn't. He didn't discriminate. If it looked edible, into the pack it went. Once plenty of food was in both packs, he needed to figure out just how to get the water. The pitcher didn't look like it was very transportable. As silently as he could, he began opening cabinet doors, searching for whatever he could that he might be able to use to carry the water back to Tom. As he searched, he gobbled up this and that, and drank liberally from the pitcher of water on the counter.

Food in my belly will leave more room for food in the packs, Jake thought, obviously trying to justify his eating while his friend lay far away in some cave, starving to death.

He found many strange devices that he could only assume were used to help prepare food. He also found plates, bowls, cups, a few utensils, but nothing to carry the water. If he had to, he supposed he could just carry the jug out of there and be very, very careful, but just as he was running out of hope, he found a spherical container with a rubber stopper the size of a baby's fist plugging up a hole in its side. It didn't look too practical to him. There was no way to really set it on the counter. It took some balancing, but after some careful holding and pouring, Jake filled the sphere all of the way up to the hole. Only a few drops had hit the floor.

As he was turning to set the pitcher back on the counter, he heard a door slam. He was so startled that the pitcher slipped from his grasp and smashed into a multitude of tiny pieces, all over the floor. He also nearly lost the sphere, now filled with water. A bit of the liquid dribbled down its side, out of the hole at the top. Jake cursed under his breath. Quickly, he grabbed the rubber stopper and plugged up the sphere so he wouldn't lose any more of its contents. He slammed it into one of the packs, squashing some of the food as he did so.

No longer caring about being completely silent, Jake zipped up the pack as fast as he could and looked for a place to hide. The best he could do was a cabinet that wasn't facing the entryway to the room. It was fairly empty, thank goodness, but it was small enough that he once he had wiggled inside it, he began to feel a bit claustrophobic. He felt like a fool. There was no way he would be able to stay hidden for long. Soon, he could hear voices, the same voices that he had heard outside, he was certain. They were coming his way.

"...how should I know?"

"Well, maybe we should get someone."

"Come on, it was probably just Buster or something."

"Your pet rat? I highly doubt it."

"Well, I don't care. I'm checking it out. You can go hide under a chair if you wish."

"May the Founders protect you, I'm out of here!"

"Fine."

Wait... *what?*

Had that woman just said "the Founders"?

Jake heard two pairs of footsteps, one coming, the other going. The pair of steps heading in his direction were measurably softer and slower than the pair that were leaving. Then, he heard an exasperated sigh, followed by a gasp. The woman had discovered that not only the water pitcher had shattered, but most of her food was missing as well. It was only a matter of time before he would be found. He thought about making a break for it out the window, but soon dismissed that as being too difficult. The window was fairly high up, plus there were too many objects in the room between here and there to trip him up.

"Breeka! Breeka!"

The other pair of footsteps came stomping back. It seemed as though her friend had not gone too far, after all.

"What is it? Are you alright?"

"I think we've been robbed!"

"Robbed? Why in the world..."

Abruptly the two stopped talking. Jake wasn't quite sure why. For a long time, nothing seemed to be happening. Just silence. He wondered what had happened. He decided it was time to go for broke. He had hoped to avoid any direct contact with anyone here, but circumstances (*or my own stupidity,* he thought) had forced his hand. Carefully, he pulled the bow from his back. He had to keep it awfully close to his body as he brought it around, ever conscious that even a little knock against the side of the cabinet would spell his doom. Getting an arrow from the quiver proved to be even more difficult. He pulled it up, out and over his head slowly and carefully. The tip of the arrow scratched the top of the cabinet for a second, creating a brief grinding sound. Jake prayed the two women had not heard.

Finally Jake had the arrow set perpendicularly along the edge of the bow. He tried to slow his breathing and relax. He would just scare them with it and then take off out the front door. No problem. He counted down slowly in his head.

Five... four... three... two...

Suddenly, before he could finish, the door to the cabinet flew open. There was Meela, of all people, standing there, hands on her hips, head tilted slightly to the side. She looked like an annoyed teacher, glaring at Jake, the disruptive student. He looked down and saw the two women he had been listening to, both sprawled across the floor, clearly unconscious.

"Just what the hell do you think you are doing?" Meela said.

"I, uh…" Jake tried.

"That's Tom's, isn't it?" Meela said, pointing to the bow in Jake's hands. "Do you even know how to use one of those?"

Jake had no answer this time. Not even a grunt. He just lowered his head, as well as the bow, in defeat and stepped out from the cabinet. Meela snatched the bow and arrow from his grasp before he realized what had happened. She had been right, he was totally unprepared for any of this. He would surely have been discovered if she hadn't intervened and…

"What did you do to them?" Jake asked, looking down at the two bodies on the floor.

"Just put them to sleep," Meela said, holding up her laser weapon. "There is a setting on these that works much like a mild sedative. Don't worry, they never even saw me coming. They will wake up about an hour or so from now, feeling just fine, figuring that some burglar had knocked them out or something. You didn't even know these weapons had that particular setting, did you?"

Jake shook his head.

"Let me ask you something," Meela continued. "Have you even attempted to fire one of these yet?"

"Well, not exactly…" Jake said, realizing that he hadn't even brought one along. The one that Meela had handed him in the dead dome was currently sitting up in the cave with Tom.

"I knew it!" Meela said. "I told you two that you had no business being out here! I told you to go home! Why didn't you listen to me?"

Meela turned in frustration and made for the door to exit the kitchen. Jake quickly grabbed the two packs and followed. Entering the next room, he realized the unique design of the place. This new room had to be the center of the entire building, which was itself a large circle. Above him hung some kind of light fixture or piece of artwork made out of glass that looked like a giant finger pointing down at him. It seemed to say, *what are you doing here? Intruder! Intruder!* All of the other rooms were shaped like pieces of pie that jutted out from this middle space. All around him there were doors, all lining the circular wall. Each, he supposed, led to the different rooms in the home.

They passed through the only open doorway, and that led down a long hallway decorated with bluish-green shapes painted on the walls. There were no straight lines. Everything seemed to weave in and out of another, creating what looked like almost moving, *living* images. Their feet marched down the hard floors, and Jake halted behind Meela as she stopped in front of a giant, circular door. She lifted the latch, swung the door open and hopped out. As Jake stepped through, he felt a hand grab his collar. He was thrown around to the side and slammed against the smooth outer surface of the house.

"From here on out, you do exactly as I tell you, alright?" Meela said, her face twisted in anger.

Jake nodded his head vigorously.

It was now that Jake noticed Daisy, Meela's megacat, who had been waiting patiently for them outside. Her dark fur made it nearly impossible to see her in the darkness. She looked more like a pair of glowing eyeballs, floating a meter above the ground. Jake figured this worked to Meela's advantage as she snuck her way in and out of domes, undetected.

Meela nabbed one of Jake's packs and strapped it to her back. Jake did the same with the other pack, but it ran into Tom's quiver of arrows, which was also strapped to his back. He kept reaching for the other strap with his free arm, but he was unable to find it around the quiver. He even leaned over to try and find a better angle, but all that accomplished was the quiver spilling all of its arrows onto the ground. Meela sighed and helped him pick them up.

Jake felt like a clumsy idiot, standing there in front of Meela, fumbling with his supplies. How stupid he had been taking that bow with him! He had no business taking along a weapon he couldn't handle. Hell, he had no business doing any of this! Once again, his thoughts turned to the Overseer. What in the Founders' names did the Overseer see in Jake? The only thing he seemed to be good at was screwing everything up for everyone else.

Once his pack was more or less secure on his back, Jake looked up to see Meela already on Daisy's back. She extended her hand. He took it and she yanked with such force that he thought he must surely have dislocated his shoulder, but in a blur he was perched on the black cat's back, arm sore but still functional. As he adjusted his pack, he started to slide to the side and had to grab onto Meela's waist to keep from falling.

You are completely and utterly dependent on her, Jake thought to himself. As fed up with himself as he felt, he also felt strangely content sitting there with his arms wrapped around Meela's warm midsection, his head so close to her back that he could hear and feel her soft inhales and exhales. For a brief instant, things in this strange, weird world outside of Magella no longer felt scary or dangerous. He felt safe and secure… at home even.

Within seconds the three were silently speeding across the strange, alien countryside, heading once more for the desolate world outside.

Chapter 14

"A hunter hunts, a teacher teaches, a farmer farms, and a sailor sails, each according to his gifts and experience."

-*The Book of the Founders*

"**Y**OU?!?" Tom yelled in shock and surprise. "What the hell are *you* doing here?"

"Saving you from your own stupidity," Meela said bluntly.

Meela stepped forward and dropped one of their packs to the ground, food spilling out. Just like that, Tom was done asking questions. He greedily snatched as many items as he could and began stuffing them into his mouth. Soon he also found the circular water jug and drank his fill from that, too. Jake found a few morsels in the other pack and began to chew on them as well, his stomach now ready for round two. Meela abstained from eating. She looked far from starving to Jake.

It took most of the day for the two men to fully regain their strength. Meela had to stop them from eating too much from time to time. She had explained that they needed to be slow and incremental about it, otherwise the food would just be wasted. She spoke with the confidence of someone who had gone through this very thing herself once or twice. By that evening, both men felt much stronger, but still far from completely recovered.

Mcela was standing watch by the mouth of the cave, looking out into the starry night sky. She had been that way for hours, not saying a word. She was like a doctor just after surgery. The hard work was done. Now it was just a matter of waiting while the patients healed themselves. Looking up at her from his seated position on the floor of the cave, Jake once again felt like a child that needed to be held by the hand. Meela probably had much more important things to do than to look after the two of them, but here she was, biding her time until he and Tom were well once again. And when that happened, then what? Probably the same as before: she's ditch them all over again, happy to be rid of the annoyance.

"I'm sorry, Tom. I screwed up," Jake said.

"What happened?" Tom asked.

"Do you really want to know?" Jake asked back.

Tom thought for a second and then said, "no, I suppose not. I bet I can guess and get fairly close, though."

Jake just chuckled and handed Tom one of the two packs, still filled with all kinds of strange foodstuffs. Many didn't even look edible, but in times like these, neither of them was particularly picky. Tom grabbed a handful of little orange balls and crammed them into his mouth. Jake did the same. The taste of sweetness attacked his taste buds to such an extent that he nearly coughed them back out. Meela looked at them for a second and then turned back around again, continuing to keep watch. For what, Jake wasn't sure. Perhaps Omega troops that may have seen his shenanigans the night before, as Meela had. Daisy lay between the two half-starved men and Meela, taking another of her many cat naps that day.

"Do you trust her?" Tom asked.

"Meela? I don't know," Jake said. "The woman has saved my life twice now, though."

"She doesn't seem happy to be here."

"I think she feels like we are somehow her responsibility now."

"What do you mean?"

"Like we are too dumb to take care of ourselves."

Tom snorted.

"You know I can hear you, right?" Meela said, still looking in the other direction.

"Well, are we right?" Tom asked, figuring he might as well push the issue now.

"As you said yourselves, that's now two times I've saved your asses," Meela said, turning around.

"And it's two times we are grateful," Tom replied.

"Thank you, Meela," Jake chimed in.

Jake and Tom took the opportunity to stand up, albeit shakily.

"I don't need your thanks," Meela said, approaching them. "I need you to stop making dumb decisions."

"Now wait just a damn minute!" Tom said, jabbing a finger directly into Meela's collarbone.

If Tom had been attempting to intimidate her, he had failed miserably. She grabbed his hand mid-poke, pulled it up and twisted his entire body around so that now she was holding his right arm behind his back. Jake saw her weapon come out of its holster on her hip and lodge itself into the small of Tom's back. She leaned in close so that her nose nearly touched the back of Tom's neck.

"Don't you ever touch me," Meela growled.

"Fine, fine!" Tom said. "Will you let go of me now?"

Meela did as she was asked and reholstered the laser weapon.

"I just want to make one thing clear," Tom said, now his turn to lean in close to her. "Although we are grateful for all that you have done for us, you have to agree that when you left us outside of that destroyed dome, you were basically leaving us to die. You knew full well that we were nearly starving when you met us. A few cinnamon sticks thrown across a table weren't going to change that. You knew that by the time we would make it to another dome, *if* we would make it to another dome, we'd already be as good as dead."

"I know," Meela said, backing away a little, "and that is why I came back. But YOU need to understand reality, mister. You made the poor choice of not leaving home with enough food. That is not MY fault. You also didn't take my advice and go home. That was good advice, fellas. Life out here isn't some game. I thought I made that clear to you. But no, on you trudged, throwing good sense to the wind! When you left that destroyed dome, I watched you, hoping that you would head back the way you had come, to the southeast, but you didn't. At first I thought I could just let you deal with the natural consequences of that decision. Turns out I couldn't."

"So now what?" Jake asked, looking back and forth between Meela and Tom.

"I'm convinced that if the two of you are bound and determined to stay out here and are going to have any hope of surviving, you are going to need my help," Meela said.

"What does that mean?" Jake asked.

"It means," Meela said, "that I am taking you home with me."

"To what end?" Tom asked.

"You want to live out here?" Meela said. "Fine. But first, you need to learn how to survive in this world. I can train you. I can show you how to hunt, how to steal, how to defend yourself properly."

Jake thought about his clumsiness with Tom's bow and knew she had a point.

"Do you truly want to live out here or not?" Meela continued. "If the answer is yes, then you need my help. If the answer is no, you need to turn back now and head home."

Jake wanted desperately to explain to her their mission, to tell her all about the numbers and the little blue dot, to tell her about the message he had received from the Overseer, to tell her that their true goal wasn't to live out in this wilderness, but only to move through it, to some unknown destination. Neither he nor Tom had said a word to her about it, though. Both knew that it was likely too far-fetched to be believed. Hell, Jake still wasn't completely convinced that Tom believed his story about his conversation with the Overseer.

And yet, all of that didn't matter. It all boiled down to one simple fact: neither Tom nor Jake could trust Meela. In this particular case, however, they knew that if they were to have any hope of completing their task, they needed help. As much as Jake hated to admit it, Meela was correct in her estimation of the two of them. They were laughably unprepared for the dangers and challenges of this strange new world. Their only hope of completing the task laid out to them by the Overseer was to take her up on her offer.

Jake and Tom looked at one another. Jake could tell without a word spoken that he and Tom were on the same page in their conclusions. The resigned expression on Tom's face was all that he needed to see.

"Ok, Meela," Jake said. "We'll go with you."

Meela smiled. Well, maybe just a little. "Finally," she said, "you have made a smart decision. Now, let's start packing up our gear. We leave in ten minutes."

Without another word of protest (even though they both felt incredibly weak), Jake and Tom got right to it.

An hour later, Jake, Meela and Tom were at the foot of the mountain. All three then climbed onto Daisy's back, one at a time. The large feline had protested somewhat when Tom, the last of the three, had climbed aboard, letting out a deep moan and arching her back, but that was it. For an animal used to only transporting one person around, the addition of two more seemed to actually go remarkably well.

As they sped across the dusty plain, Jake marveled at the quickness with which they now moved. If this was Daisy's speed with three passengers aboard, he wondered just how quickly she could move when it was just Meela. Smashed in the middle of the three riders, Jake found that he once again had his arms about Meela's waist. He could also once again feel the warmth of her body pressed against his. Those familiar feelings began to bubble up. He thought to himself that if he could just stay attached to this woman, perhaps everything would be alright in the end. Part of him wondered if that was all he felt, though.

A few hours later, they were now far enough away from both the mountain and its spherical companion that the two once again appeared to be blending into the landscape. Being careful to hang on to Meela seated in front of him, Jake reached around to the side of his pack and pulled out the compass. Given where the sun was hanging in the sky, he suspected that they might very well be heading back the way they were supposed to go. He gave the disc a quick look. Sure enough, they were back on track, heading nearly the same direction as the little blue light on its edge told them to go. They were heading more west than northwest, but it was close enough in Jake's mind. At least they weren't backtracking any more.

After a few seconds of studying it, Jake noticed Meela snap her head around to look in Jake's direction.

"What are you doing?" she asked.

"What?" Jake answered.

As quickly and carefully as he could, he placed the device back inside his pack. Had she seen the numbers or the little blue dot? He hoped that he had been quick enough for them not to be noticed, although Meela had already proven that she was generally one step ahead of Jake and Tom on most matters.

"You are going to want to keep that thing secured," Meela said. "The last thing we want to do right now is stop because you dropped something."

"Uh, right," Jake said.

Meela turned back around and said no more. Jake sighed.

Later that day, they decided to stop sooner than expected, mainly for Daisy's sake. She didn't look it, but Jake had to assume that the megacat's back was in a lot of pain from all of the hauling. She was strong, but she wasn't exactly intended to be a pack mule, either. They had traveled so far that the dome they had left was no longer even visible. Jake's groin ached somewhat, but it was nothing compared to how all of that walking the past few days had made his feet feel. He thought to himself that if it was ever possible for him find and train up his own megacat, he was going to do so as soon as the opportunity presented itself.

Shortly before settling down for sleep, Jake took a seat on a small, flat rock next to Tom, who was sitting on a rock of his own. Meela was off tending to Daisy, which was probably for the best. Jake wasn't stupid. He knew that Meela saw them more as a charity case than as a couple of new friends. He wasn't all that shocked when she hadn't stuck around to chum it up with him and Tom. Instead of one tight group of four, their party was more like two tight groups of two.

"Hey Tom, I've been meaning to tell you something," Jake said.

"Yeah? What's that?" Tom asked.

"It's about yesterday when I left you in that cave."

"I know, I know, you're sorry."

"No, it's not that. It's something else. When I was inside, I happened to hear one of the locals say something... something about the Founders."

"*Your* Founders?"

Jake hated it when Tom said things like that.

No, not MY Founders, Tom. OUR Founders.

"Yeah! They know about them, too!" Jake said, gesturing back the way they had come. "I heard someone actually use the word 'Founders' when I was in there."

"Why are you so surprised?" Tom said. "If you do indeed believe that the Founders created everything, then wouldn't it make sense that they had created those people as well?"

"I suppose you are right. It just seems so strange to hear the Founders' names mentioned all the way out here. It kind of makes me a little homesick."

"You and me both, even though I think the idea of the stars coming down from the heavens and making all of this out of nothing is a bit far-fetched."

"Then how do you explain what I heard in there? If the Founders were just made up by the people of Magella to explain the unexplainable, then no one outside of Magella should know anything about them, right?"

"Then perhaps their ancestors and your ancestors knew each other before any of these domes were built," Tom said. "Or, maybe you were just hearing things."

"That's a bit of a stretch."

"You hearing things? I don't know, Jake, you were pretty out of it, even before you left to go in there."

"No, you idiot, a stretch that our ancestors all knew each other!"

"You sure? I think a stretch is believing that magical fairies from the sky twinkled everything into existence."

Jake just shook his head. "Goodnight, Tom."

The journey went on the following day without major incident. A few times the wind picked up and nearly blew Jake or Tom off of Daisy, but the instances were few and not anything too dangerous. Meela's position on the feline's back never faltered. She had already told Tom and Jake stories of wind storms that had been over ten times as big and over twenty times as powerful as the ones they were experiencing that day. Storms that were so severe that anything not solidly part of the landscape was blown away forever, storms that would rage on for months at a time. Jake wasn't sure how Meela had survived these encounters in order to tell these stories, but he didn't push it. She had proven to be quite the survivor already.

As the days passed along the course of their journey, Jake happened to notice a number of domes, far away in the distance from time to time. He counted at least four that he could be certain of. His heart ached to go explore these unique new worlds, but the reality of their mission (and Meela's) kept him from ever saying anything about it. He could only imagine what there might be to discover inside those distant globes. So far, he hadn't seen much: a destroyed world and a home inside a small village, which was obscured mostly by the dark of night.

It was late in the afternoon one day when the group was just coming up on the western cliff of the great canyon. Jake knew that Meela had told him the canyon did indeed have an end, but it was nice to actually see that end for himself. They had seen the edge of the canyon for the majority of the day and would be at its precipice at any moment. Jake couldn't wait.

It was here that Meela had spotted them: a group of Omega soldiers, off to their north. Without saying a word, Meela dismounted Daisy and was soon pulling a startled and confused Jake and Tom down off of the cat, too.

"Hey, what's the big idea?" Tom protested.

"We have company!" Meela responded. "Just stay low! We are in a fairly rocky area. If we keep to the ground, and are lucky, we might avoid detection."

"The Omega Order?" Jake said, falling down to his chest. "What are they doing here?"

Now all four of them, including Daisy, were as flat to the ground as their bodies would allow. Jake looked around. Meela had been right. The ground all around them was anything but flat, rising and falling like waves. Perhaps if they just stayed put for a few hours the Omegas would pass them by and they could continue on their way. If anything did happen, Jake felt much more prepared than he had since stepping foot outside of Magella. They had Meela with them, after all.

"We can't stay here!" Meela said.

Ok, well forget that, Jake thought.

"Why not?" Tom asked.

"Because they are heading right in this direction!" Meela barked. "If we stay here, they will be upon us in a matter of minutes."

"Minutes?" Jake said. "I thought you just spotted them?"

"I did!" Meela said. "This group is not on foot."

"More megacats?" Tom suggested.

"Not exactly." Meela said. "You'll see. For now, we need to get out of sight. Head for the edge of the canyon. We're only a few kilometers away now. You see that hill over there?"

Tom and Jake both looked to their right. It was hard to tell from their current angle, but Jake thought he could see a mound of rock, atop of which appeared to be a large boulder. It sat up there rather precariously, like it would tumble down at any moment. Jake figured that that must be what Meela was talking about. Even if it wasn't, it was as good a place as any to hide for the time being.

"Ready?" Meela asked.

"Ready!" Tom and Jake said in unison.

"Ok, NOW! RUN!!"

All three humans took off at a sprint. Daisy got the idea quickly enough and soon was following them. Within seconds, she had caught up and was running along side of the group. Now that he was upright, Jake could see the hill with the big rock on top even better. The boulder wasn't exactly a boulder at all. It was all one complete structure, although at its skinniest, it couldn't have been any wider than Jake himself. Its base, however, was wide enough so that perhaps even a dozen people could hide behind it if they wanted to. Unfortunately, it was still more than a kilometer away. Jake just kept churning his legs, hoping beyond hope that they hadn't been spotted.

The shot of blue energy that blew a hole into the ground just to his right gave Jake his answer.

Chapter 15

"Offering your bed to a stranger who claims to be in need is a blessing indeed for that stranger. It will remain to be seen, however, whether or not it is a blessing for you."

-The Book of the Founders

"**D**ammit all!" Meela cursed between clenched teeth.

"I think they've found us," Tom said, still running.

"You think?" Meela shouted back. "You two keep going and don't stop until you get to some cover."

"What about you?" Jake asked.

"I'll see if I can slow down our friends," Meela said.

Meela stopped in her tracks and turned around, weapon already drawn. She fired a few shots back toward their attackers and then took off at a sprint to the north, away from Jake and Tom. A dozen or so steps later she launched herself up into the air. It looked to Jake like a bird taking flight. As much time as he had already spent outside of Magella, he was still awed whenever he saw the affects of the lower gravity. Meela continued to sail through the air (or lack thereof, if Jake's assertion was to be believed) and eventually landed far up on top of a rocky hill of her own. She fired off a few more shots.

It was working. The bolts of dangerous blue energy were no longer flying in the direction of Jake and Tom, but were now being fired only at Meela, perched high above them all. She was doing well enough for herself, dodging this way and that, firing back multiple shots. Jake had no idea if any of them had hit their marks at all. He realized then that he hadn't actually seen any of the Omega troops yet, just the frightening affects of their energy weapons.

When Jake and Tom reached their destination, Tom immediately ran around the far side of it and crouched down, chest in the dirt. Jake, however, ran only until he had just rounded the outer edge of the hill and then halted. He allowed himself a moment to peek back toward the direction that they had come, curious how Meela was doing. He couldn't see her or their pursuers. In fact, he didn't even see Daisy. Where had she gone? Was she helping Meela somehow? It seemed logical enough. That cat was as loyal as they come.

"Jake!" Tom shouted. "What are you doing? Get over here!"

Ignoring Tom and still looking, Jake then noticed a large shape, coming at them quickly. The closer and closer it came, the clearer and clearer view he was able to get. It was a strange contraption resembling a bike he had ridden back home, back before all of this had happened, time that seemed like ages ago now. This bike was different, though. It seemed thicker, bulkier and it didn't have any wheels. Its chrome-colored surface was caked with dirt and grime. It just seemed to float over the ground, effortlessly. It would be upon them in mere seconds. Its driver fired off a handful of shots in Jake's general direction. One landed dangerously close to Jake's left foot.

Jake pulled back behind the hill and joined Tom, cursing himself for being so damn curious. He gave Tom a look that seemed to say, "yup, buddy, I screwed up." Tom just sighed and pulled his bow from behind his back and loaded an arrow. The weapon had done no good the last time he had used it, but he had no other choice right now.

Both men looked up when they heard a loud roaring sound. Seconds later, the strange floating bike sprang into view, careening around the side of the hill.

Tom raised his bow and cocked an arrow. It was a useless gesture. The black-clad man on the bike already had his laser weapon raised and pointed directly at them. Tom shot the arrow anyways. The rider on the bike shot his weapon and before Tom's arrow had even traversed half of its intended distance, it had been reduced to ash, falling harmlessly to the ground like someone peppering their steak.

"Damn," Tom cursed.

It was then that Daisy appeared. With a mighty bellow she leapt from behind another rocky outcropping towards the bike. The Omega soldier had no time to react. He had barely turned when all four of Daisy's paws made contact with his chest, knocking him from his bike and digging their claws deep inside him. The man hit the ground with an "Ooof!!"

Arrow-proof? Yes. Daisy-proof? No.

The megacat had the man completely pinned down. He tried to wiggle to get free, but that only made the cat's claws dig deeper into his torso. His helmet flew off in the struggle. He screamed in pain and surprise. Daisy roared back in response, her gigantic incisors nearly touching his face as she did so. The man's eyes grew wide with terror and he fell silent. Then, either in an attempt to put the man out of his misery or just out of pure blood-lust, Daisy bit down on the man's neck. Blood spewed out in all directions. A few gurgling sounds escaped from his throat, and then nothing.

Daisy raised her head and looked at Jake and Tom. Her eyes were wide and her bloody fangs were still barred. This was not some pet. This was a wild, crazed creature. For a moment, Jake was certain they were next on the menu. Meela had proven she could control the beast, but she was nowhere to be seen. Hell, she might even be dead now, for all that Jake knew. Daisy growled again, jowls curling even farther up her ferocious face, blood dripping down into the red sand.

"Easy, there," Jake said, extending his arm out and facing his palm up towards the gigantic feline. "Easy, girl."

Another growl, this time softer. The megacat took a few steps toward Jake and Tom.

"Easy!" Jake said again, doing his best to sound like he was in control of the situation, knowing deep down inside that he was failing miserably.

Daisy growled once again, even softer this time and it would be her last. She stopped and tilted her head slightly to the right, as if slowly coming back to reality from her murderous psychotic episode. Moments later she was seated on the ground, licking spilled blood from her paws, hardly noticing Jake or Tom. Both men let out simultaneous sighs of relief.

"How many more of them are there?" Jake asked, looking down at the blood-soaked corpse on the ground.

"I don't know," Tom replied. "Meela was the one that saw them first, remember?"

"Meela..." Jake said. "We should go find her."

"No," Tom said. "She told us to wait here!"

"You can stand around and get ambushed again, if you'd like. I for one am going to see if I can help."

"Help how? Sheesh, Jake! Isn't that why we joined her in the first place, because we can't defend ourselves? Hell, she even took your newfound laser weapon away because it was too dangerous for you! These are trained killers! What are you going to do, throw rocks at them and hope for the best?"

"I have to do something," Jake said. "I can't just let her die out there."

For a second or two, Jake considered stealing the Omega soldier's bike, but then thought better of it. If he wasn't able to use their weapons properly, then the chances of him getting into an accident on *that* thing were probably pretty high. No, he would do things on foot. Tom had been right, though. He didn't have anything with which to defend himself. He thought for a moment and then tore open his pack and pulled out the small chiseling tool he had taken with them from the mine back home.

Better than nothing, Jake thought to himself.

"Jake, don't," Tom pleaded one last time, slowly shaking his head.

Jake didn't reply. He simply ran back in the direction from which they had come, hoping that he would see Meela, either already victorious, or at the very least close to it. He wanted to help in any way that he could, but his heart pleaded that he wouldn't have to be put in harm's way. As he ran, he saw no sign of Meela or any member of the Omega Order. There were a couple of smoldering remains of laser shots, but that was about it. He kept running.

Soon, he heard laser blasts. They sounded like loud, sharp shrieks, like the kind hawks make when they are about to attack their prey. The sounds were coming from the edge of the canyon. He altered his path and headed straight for it. When he was close enough to see the drop-off, he could also see Meela, darting from one rocky growth to another, exchanging fire with a single Omega soldier. The soldier was facing away from Jake, still focusing on his target. Jake picked up speed. When he felt he was close enough, he pushed off of the ground hard.

It dawned on him mid-air that he had no real plan.

Without enough time to think of something else to do, his feet made contact with the Omega troop's shoulders and the impact sent the two men flying. They bounced across the rocky landscape as one: a single mass of flailing arms and legs. Both of their weapons flew from their grips, but it would be to Jake's advantage. A little chiseling hammer versus a deadly laser blast wasn't the best of odds. When the two of them finally came to halt, Jake noticed that both of their heads had not landed on the ground, but rather were hanging out over the edge of the great canyon, looking down to the rocky floor that seemed it would take a lifetime to hit if either of them were to fall towards it.

Jake gasped in his shock and then was quickly snapped back to reality when a fist made contact with his right check. His head exploded in pain. Nerve endings he didn't even know existed felt as if they were on fire, all over his face. He tried to return the favor, but all he got for his effort was a fist that now had exploded in pain as well. The Omega soldier didn't seem fazed in the least. He kept coming. Another blow to Jake's face. Another. And another. If Jake didn't do something quickly, he would be reduced to a bloody pulp... a bloody pulp that would probably be falling over the edge of the cliff and into the abyss below.

Jake tried to move his head out of the way and was marginally successful. The fists of the man on top of him impacted dirt instead of flesh a couple of times in a row. In between jabs, Jake spotted his little chiseling tool laying just to his right, handle sticking out away from him. He reached for it, but was only able to get clumps of red sand in his hand. Meanwhile, the punches from his attacker continued. Jake fought through the pain and reached out even further. He was just able to grab ahold of the little hammer by its head.

As soon as it was in his grasp, Jake wheeled the hammer down on his attacker's neck. Since it was only the handle that made contact, all it really did was distract the Omega soldier for a brief second. Jake threw his weight towards the Omega soldier and wrapped his right arm around the man's neck. He tightened it as hard as he could, desperately hoping that his attacker would run out of air soon. It didn't seem to be working. The man suddenly wrenched his upper body to the side. The surprising maneuver caused Jake to lose his grip. He then felt a full-body blow to the chest. Then he was falling.

He looked around. He had been hit *up,* but now he was coming back down again. His chest almost felt as bad as his head, but that wasn't the worst part. The worst part was when he had opened his eyes. He could see that he was now hovering over the great canyon, falling down towards certain death. He could see the ground along the canyon's rim beside him. If he reached out enough, perhaps he could grasp on to something…

No luck. The edge of the gorge flew up past his head. He reached out in an attempt to grab anything that might at least slow down his descent. No luck there, either. He was subjected to rocks flying up with the rest of the canyon wall, pummeling his poor hand. He kept grasping. More rocks slammed into it. It soon felt as if he was going to lose all feeling in his hand completely. He could only imagine what it must look like now, all battered and bruised.

It was then that Jake remembered the hammer that was in his other hand. He repositioned it so he held the handle properly, and then swung the claw of the head into the rock face as hard as he could. Miraculously, it stayed put. Jake's body snapped back from its fall and he nearly lost his grip, but he was able to hold on. He took hold of another piece of the rock wall with his other hand while his feet found purchase on a few larger rocks below. After a couple of careful steps, he was able to put all of his weight on his feet. He was still desperately hanging on to keep from falling, but at least his initial descent had stopped.

He looked back up to the top of the rock wall. It had to be at least forty, maybe fifty, meters back up to the top. Had he really fallen that far? There was no other choice but to climb back up. With his damaged left hand, he was having his doubts if he could even make half that distance, even if he could find the right rocks to grab ahold of.

In that moment, his left foot slipped out under some small pebbles. He was forced to use his bad hand to keep from falling.

This is going to take a miracle, he thought.

Just as he was deciding which rock to reach for first, he saw a man, clad all in black, go shooting over the edge (and Jake's head) and fall screaming down into the great chasm. Jake quickly turned to look down behind him, but the man had already disappeared into the haze. The screaming continued until the man was so far away that it was impossible to hear it anymore. Jake assumed that it would still be quite awhile yet before the poor bastard would reach his final destination. He took a deep breath. He had to focus. If he didn't, he would end up just like the man plummeting to his doom.

He looked up in an attempt to figure out just what had happened and was rewarded with a fat piece of rope flying out from the edge above and flopping against his back. The mere surprise of it all nearly caused him to lose his grip. He quickly grabbed ahold of the rope and put his chiseling tool back in his pocket. His left hand screamed at him in pain as it wrapped around the rope. Jake tried his best to ignore its pleas. He gave the rope a couple of quick tugs. It didn't move. He then looked back up and saw two smiling faces looking down at him: it was Meela and Tom.

"Hold on tight!" Tom said. "We'll help you up!"

Jake did as he was told, desperately hoping that the other end was securely attached to something else up top and not just being held by Tom or Meela. It took some doing (especially when he tried to grip the rope with his left hand), but he was able to slowly make his way up the canyon wall and to solid ground once more. When he finally made it to the top, he rolled over onto his back, catching his breath. Both Meela and Tom were staring at him.

"The prodigal son returns!" Tom bellowed, arms wide.

"Th-the... who?" Jake struggled to get out.

"Nevermind," Tom said.

"That's three, now," Meela said happily, clearly enjoying herself.

"Sorry, buddy," Tom said, now leaning over and patting his friend on the chest. "Meela says there is one more out there. We've got to move!"

"Ugh," was all Jake could manage at the moment.

"Don't blame me," Tom replied, "I tried to stop you from being stupid again, didn't I?"

With the help of Meela and Tom, Jake gingerly got to his feet. He took a quick scan of the area. No Omegas in sight. Good, maybe they were lost. He did happen to see Daisy, though, standing up on all fours. He also saw one of the Omega Order's hovering bikes floating next to Meela, her hand on what appeared to be its controls. Either she had captured one from another attacker or perhaps Tom had brought it over from their earlier encounter. Whatever. It didn't matter in that moment. They had to get going.

"I'm taking this," Meela said, regarding the bike. "You and Tom can ride Daisy. Try not to fall off, ok?"

Jake nodded and then pulled himself up on Daisy's back. She let out a bit of a groan and craned her neck in his direction. There was still plenty of dried blood on her face. Jake shivered and tried to remind himself that they were all friends here. Tom climbed aboard behind him. Neither of them were armed, at least not in any manner that mattered. Tom had his useless bow and arrows over his shoulders and Jake's little hammer was still tucked away in his pocket. Both men knew the score: they were to simply stay alive. Meela would do all of the fighting for them.

"Daisy, GO!!" Meela said as she hopped aboard the bike.

As soon as Daisy took off, Jake nearly broke the only command Meela had given him. A handful of fur later and he was able to steady himself. Daisy didn't seem to mind. Jake wondered if the megacat had any idea where she was going. With no Meela in front to guide them, they could be headed anywhere. Wherever they were going, they were going there *fast*. Daisy's paws whipped across the landscape in a black blur. Jake looked behind him to see that Tom wasn't faring too much better himself. The poor guy was seated right above Daisy's hips, so with every footfall, his body was being bounced up into the air a few centimeters. Only by hanging on tightly to Jake's waist was he able to keep from being bounced off completely.

Looking behind Tom, Jake also saw Meela on her hovering bike. She was about thirty meters behind them, constantly moving her head side to side to look behind her. Jake dared to hope that perhaps they had escaped quickly enough not to be noticed. But then he saw it: another hover bike far off in the distance, heading their way. Jake watched the tiny vehicle as they continued to fly across the landscape. It was getting bigger. Not by very much, but over time it would catch up to them. Unless, of course, Daisy could run faster, but he was fairly convinced that this had to be her top speed.

A few minutes later the firing started. Most of the shots missed them by wide margins, but one landed dangerously close to one of Daisy's paws as it padded across the ground. Meela fired back in retaliation, but none of her shots hit their marks. Soon, Jake could see that Meela was pulling away from him and Tom, slowing down. When the other bike got closer to her, she pulled her ride to the left, into an area more densely populated with uneven, rocky structures.

I hope you are a good pilot, Jake thought.

A minute or two later, Jake saw Meela's bike blast out of the rocky area, the Omega soldier still hot on her tail. Many shots were still fired. One hit the Omega's bike and Jake thought that perhaps Meela had disabled him somehow, but he kept coming. If anything, he was actually speeding up. Meela shot again. This time, there was a large explosion just behind where the Omega soldier was seated.

Trails of thick, black smoke were left in the bike's wake, and the bike began to slow. Meela turned forward once more and grinned. She rotated her fists forward, propelling her bike closer to Jake and Tom. It wasn't long before Meela was once again along side Daisy and her two riders.

"Just a little farther. I think we might actually lose him!" Meela shouted as she sped ahead of them.

Ten minutes later, Meela stopped her bike and leapt off. Jake, Tom and Daisy likewise stopped. Jake had a hard time figuring out just where they were. There were a handful of strange tower-like rock formations maybe a kilometer away in either direction, and they could still see a small portion of the great canyon to their southwest. Other than that, it was no different than anywhere else outside of the domes, just more red dust and sand everywhere! Was this some other strange double-cross? He had a bad feeling in the pit of his stomach, a larger version of that feeling he sometimes got when he had left something important at home and was already at the mines for work.

Jake and Tom dismounted Daisy, who still seemed agitated, looking around, especially in the direction from which they had just come.

"Nice place you got here," Tom said, taking a few steps around and holding his arms out wide. "Personally, I would have picked a different spot, but to each their own."

Meela ignored him. She was bent over and frantically looking around down at the ground. Jake leaned to the side for a better look. He hadn't noticed it before, but there was some kind of small, metallic rod sticking out of the ground. It had a couple of circular holes going through it, up and down the side. There was a considerable amount of rust on it as well, especially at the top. It couldn't have been more than a few centimeters tall, easily missed if you weren't looking for it.

Meela finally found what she had been looking for, and she pulled up forcefully. Jake saw an old looking metallic ring come up out of the sand and heard a CLICK sound. A small piece of the ground gave way. It took a second for it register: she had just opened a trap door, buried in the sand. Jake looked back at Tom who himself seemed mildly impressed.

It was Daisy who noticed the man first. She let out a frightening roar and all three of her human companions turned to look at her. It was then that they saw it too: their Omega pursuer wasn't finished yet. His hover bike, still coughing out black smoke, sped directly towards them. A few shots were fired in Daisy's direction, chasing her away. Meela tried to call for her to come back, but it was useless. The cat was sprinting over the dusty red terrain. She then tried to reach for her weapon, which was now holstered, but didn't have the time. While still in motion, the man on the bike jumped from it and landed on Tom.

The force of the impact knocked Tom backwards and into Meela. She then fell backwards herself into the hole in which she had just opened. Jake could hear a few bangs and grunts as she went down. Working purely on instinct, Jake charged Tom's attacker. Before Jake was able to take more than three of four steps, however, the black-suited soldier turned from Tom and fired his weapon in Jake's direction. The shot hit Jake in the lower right leg, which exploded in pain. He fell to the ground, screaming.

"Give it to me!" the man yelled, turning back to face Tom. His hands clasped themselves around Tom's neck.

Jake could only lie there and watch the scene play out, unable to do anything about it.

"Give it to me!" the man said again. "Now! We know you have it!"

"Have whhhat?" Tom managed through some gasping.

"The disc we have been looking for! Not just any disc, is it? I am sure you know that by now! No, yours is special. It is the compass we have been seeking! Give it to me now and I will make your deaths painless. A quick shot to the chest will be all it will take. You will hardly feel anything. If you resist, I guarantee you that your passing will be beyond painful. The Chancellor will see to that!"

Tom answered by trying to wiggle free, but it was useless. Jake could see his friend's eyes slowly closing.

"Seven of our men are now dead because of you!" the man shouted. "I no longer have the patience for this! Where is it? Does the boy over there have it? Should I shoot him again, some place more vital, perhaps?"

"Ghnnooo!" Tom said.

"Then tell me where the compass is!"

"Ghnnever!"

"Fine, then pain it is!"

"Exactly!" A voice said.

A shot of blue energy hit the Omega soldier directly in the chest, knocking him backwards onto the ground. Tom grasped at his neck, now free from his attacker's hands, taking a number of labored breaths. Both Jake and Tom looked to find the source of the voice and found Meela, her head sticking back up from the hole in the ground she had fell into just moments before. The weapon in her had still had a small trail of smoke rising from its muzzle.

CHAPTER 16

"The Founders are connected to all living things and all places. Their influence is spread throughout the entire world."

-The Book of the Founders

"**D**on't just stand there, help me!" Meela said.

She was already completely out of the hole in the ground and had her hands on the controls of the smoking hover bike. She hadn't jumped aboard it, but rather was guiding it along the ground while walking beside it. Tom approached her as instructed.

"No, not this one, *that* one!" Meela said, nodding her head in the direction of the other bike, the one that didn't look like it was about ready to explode.

Jake still lay on the ground, now in the fetal position, watching everything take place around him. "Don't worry, I'm fine!" he said sarcastically.

"Oh, quit complaining," Meela said as she continued to push the bike forward as it floated over the ground. "Haven't you even been shot in the leg before?"

"What do you think?" Jake said.

"You'll be fine. Just hang on. We have to take care of these first."

"What *are* we doing with these?" Tom asked, now walking his own bike along side of Meela's.

"Just ahead there, do you see it? Looks like a small cave in the rocks?"

Jake couldn't see what Meela was talking about from his position on the ground but the lack of a reply from Tom told him that his friend must have found what she was talking about. About five minutes later, Jake felt something like wet sandpaper wipe across the back of his neck. He turned over and saw a gigantic pink tongue, now sliding up over his nose and forehead.

"Hi, Daisy," he said.

A few minutes later, he heard Tom and Meela's voices, growing closer.

"...sure we should just leave them in there? I would think they would be fairly easy to find."

"They are turned off now. The junked one will stop smoking soon enough. Stop worrying so much. Those bikes were a great find! If I can repair the junked one..."

"Oh, hey, cat."

Jake could now see Tom, standing almost directly over him. Daisy looked up in Meela's direction as she approached. Instantly, Meela gave the megacat a flick to the nose.

"What was that, huh? Running off like that?" Meela said.

Daisy lowered her head in shame.

"Ugh, good-for-nothing cat." Meela continued, looking away.

"Ok, so do we stash the corpse in the cave as well?" Tom asked, pointing to the body of the Omega soldier laying on the ground a few meters away from them.

"Corpse? What corpse?" Meela said.

"What?" Jake said.

"I only stunned him," Meela said, matter-of-factly. "You two seem to be prime targets on the Omega Order's hit list and we need more answers."

"Are you crazy?" Tom said. "Do you have any idea how risky this is?"

"It couldn't possibly be as risky as taking on you two," Meela replied. "Now, come on and help me get Jake inside. We'll come back for *him* in a bit."

Tom carefully helped Meela lift Jake up off the ground, trying hard not to bump his injured leg into anything. Jake found that he could hop fairly well on one leg, as long as he had Tom and Meela holding him up on either side. Once at the opening in the ground, he was able to lower himself in without too much difficulty. The hole itself was a perfect square, roughly a meter wide in each direction. The trapdoor, which was made of wood as far Jake could tell, was hanging to one side. A very rickety looking vertical ladder led straight down into a sea of black. It reminded Jake of the entryway into the room where he had met the first of the soldiers from the Omega Order, back in the dead dome. Images of the parent and child laying dead down there together popped back into his head. He couldn't help but shiver a little. He shook it off.

Jake gingerly stepped in with his good foot and found a rung on the ladder. As he made his way down, he had to be careful not to slip from the rungs, whether it be his hands or his foot. There was also his mangled left hand to consider.

What a piece of work I am, Jake thought to himself.

Reddish sand was falling everywhere, like some bloody waterfall, making it difficult to get a decent grip or even a decent look around. Jake gently hopped from rung to rung, further down into the darkness below.

A good fifty rungs later, he had made it to the bottom. Meela and Tom had gone back for the stunned Omega soldier and had awkwardly transported him down the tunnel, lit only by the remaining rays of light that streamed down from outside. The soldier's head may have smacked into the rungs of the ladder a few times. Tom didn't seem to mind all that much.

Once everyone was in, Meela lit a few candles. It was hard to see very much, but the room they were in appeared to be a makeshift kitchen. There wasn't a lot there, just a few cupboards, a counter, a saltbox, and what looked like a washbasin. A few scraps of food littered the countertops. The light from the candles didn't extend much farther beyond that, but Jake could see that the walls weren't walls at all, just jagged rock. He could barely make out what had to be a man-made doorway, cut out of the rocky wall.

"You know, your cat is still up there," Tom said, pointing back up the ladder with one hand and wiping dust off of his pants with the other.

"She's fine," Meela replied.

"You mean she just stays up there?" Jake asked.

"She has her own cave a kilometer or so north of here," Meela said. "Don't worry. I keep it well stocked with food for her. Since she and I are about the only living things out here, I'm not too worried about some other creature stopping by and stealing it."

"Nothing buys loyalty like a full stomach," Tom commented.

Meela just snorted as she walked past everyone and back to the bottom of the entry tunnel. She contorted her body around the bottom of the ladder and felt for something back in the darkness. Another pull (on what sounded to Jake like another metal ring) and another CLICK came from the top of the ladder. This time, there were also sounds of something like rotors or gears that accompanied the whole production. What little light had been streaming in from the surface up above had now disappeared. Another avalanche of sand poured down from the surface, creating little mounds on the floor. Jake assumed that back up top, the wooden door, now closed, would only be visible for a matter of seconds. The strong wind would surely kick up another thick layer of sand, hiding it from view once again.

"Did you build that yourself?" Jake asked.

Meela smiled. Then she said, "everything you see down here was either built or brought in by yours truly. This used to be just a simple cave, underground. I've expanded some of it, but the natural geography is more or less as I found it."

Tom nodded. "So, what do we do with our guest?"

"I have some more rope in the back that should secure him fine," Meela said. "I wasted my good rope pulling your butt out of that canyon, Jake. Hang on."

Jake hopped on his foot a few more times, watching as Meela left the room and was enveloped in darkness. "The leg's fine, no worries!" he said, once again trying to soak his comments with as much sarcasm as he could muster.

When Meela returned with a length of thick, white rope in her hands, the unconscious man on the floor began to move, albeit only slightly. Meela noticed this right away and set the rope down on the table. She pulled her laser weapon from its holster and pointed it at the man on the floor, who was now groaning a little bit, and fired. He was still once more.

"There," she said. "That should put him out for at least a good six hours. Plenty of time to figure out what to do with him."

"Are you sure that's safe?" Tom said, pointing at Meela's weapon.

Meela just shrugged her shoulders and placed the weapon on the table.

An hour later, their uninvited houseguest was fully secured to a kitchen chair. The thick rope made several revolutions around his torso and legs. His arms were wrapped behind the back of the chair

AWAKENING

and secured to the same piece of rope holding his feet together. Jake was no professional, but it looked like a top-notch job to him. Tom had removed the man's visored helmet and set it on the floor next to him. The face of the man underneath was older than Jake had expected. He had salt and pepper hair and a face filled with unkempt stubble. There were numerous scabbed over scratches on his forehead and cheeks. The man's head hung there limp in complete defeat.

Once the member of the Omega Order had been taken care of, Jake's leg had *finally* been attended to. Meela had applied some kind of balm to it that took the pain away almost instantly. It was just like washing dirt away from one's skin. One second the pain was there, the next it was just gone. The really strange thing was that there didn't appear to be a wound in his leg at all. Jake had felt the pain (boy, had he ever), but his injured left leg looked no different than his right. Meela wrapped the wounded area in a light bandage and told Jake to try putting some weight on the leg. To his amazement, Jake found that he could. It still hurt somewhat, but he found that he could walk around without too much effort. Next, she went to work on his hand, following the same protocol.

Tom yawned and stretched. "Well, do you want to give us the tour?"

"Knock yourself out," Meela said, getting up. "I'm going to bed. I'm sorry I can't offer you two something nicer than the floor to sleep on. I never figured that I would have visitors."

"We'll be fine," Jake said.

"At least we're not tied to a chair," Tom said, smiling.

"Thank you for giving us a chance, Meela." Jake said.

"Just don't let me regret it," came her reply.

Once Meela had left, Jake decided that he would go ahead and take a look around, while Tom elected to scope out a nice piece of floor and get some sleep. There hadn't been much to the place, from what Jake could tell. He supposed that if you were never expecting visitors, you had no need to make it look presentable. Meela indeed had just stuck to the bare essentials. Besdies, anything that Meela owned had to have been carried around fifty to one hundred kilometers from wherever it had been stolen. That would indeed help someone decide just how important each item really was. Anything not an absolute necessity wouldn't make the cut.

Some areas within the cave folded in, creating makeshift rooms. The closest they came to being completely separate spaces was an opening that was still about a meter wide, or more in some cases. The main artery was more or less designated in different ways as you made your way through it. First came the kitchen and then the bathroom, complete with a lovely hole in floor. Jake didn't need Meela to explain to him what that was for. He just hoped that the hole was deep. Really deep. No door for privacy there. Well, they'd all be super-chummy soon enough, wouldn't they?

At the end of the central room was where some of the smaller caves split off. One was for Meela's bedroom. Jake couldn't help but peek. There was no door, after all. The view he got was more than he bargained for. Meela, standing in the middle of the room, just getting into her nightclothes. He turned away in surprise. He had to catch his breath for a moment. He was used to seeing a different kind of Meela: a dirt-caked, rough and tumble warrior. The Meela he had just seen in that bedroom was a different one all together. In his mind's eye he could still see her soft, shapely body. Founders, she was gorgeous! He quickly returned to the central room to continue his self-guided tour. He just hoped she hadn't seen him.

One of the other smaller caves was completely abandoned with nothing was in it. He supposed that it wasn't a requirement that ALL areas be used. The third and final offshoot, which was smaller than the rest, was a work area. Either by natural phenomena or by painstakingly hard work, a shelf of rock longer than Jake was tall jutted out from the wall. On it was all kinds of tools and gadgets, most of which Jake hadn't the first clue how to operate. He wondered how many different cultures this pile of hardware before him represented. Jake eventually returned to where he had started, only to find Tom, already fast asleep.

The next morning (or at least he thought it was morning, it was hard to tell without being able to see the sky), Jake got up from his spot on the floor next to Tom and stretched. His friend was snoring away happily, so he tried to move as quietly as possible, as not to wake him. After tiptoeing around Tom, Jake saw a single candle lit in the kitchen, where he found Meela sitting at the table, staring at a mug filled with a dark liquid. Stream was rising out of it. Their Omega friend was seated at the table with her as well, still tied up and slumped in the same position they had left him the night before. It all looked like some absurd tea party.

"What's that?" Jake asked, pointing at her mug.

Meela jumped a bit, "Oh! Jake! I didn't even know you were there."

"Sorry," he said.

"This is called 'coughing', I think," she said, lifting up the mug in her hand.

"You mean like when you are sick?" Jake asked.

"I guess. It has a bit of an acquired taste, but I love the stuff. Want to try some?"

"Sure."

Meela held out her mug to him, and he put it to his lips. He took a very hesitant sip. Well, it had the right name. He had to turn away from Meela as he worked to control all of the hacking. "Eeck! It's so bitter! How can you drink that?"

"I told you, it's an acquired taste. I hated it at first, too, but now I have some every day that I'm home."

"You are welcome to it," Jake said, handing the mug back to Meela.

"Ok, thanks," she said with a smile.

"So, how did you get the water to make this?" Jake asked. "I couldn't help but wonder how you deal with that particular issue. If you have to steal everything you use or consume, I would think you would be spending an awful lot of your time just hauling water from the domes to here. I know it would be less safe, but wouldn't it just be easier to stay inside a dome where water is available?"

Meela smiled. "Oh, there's no need. There is plenty of water outside of the domes."

Jake thought back to when he and Tom had nearly died of dehydration. "*What?*"

"Well, perhaps not in the way you think. It is deep down below the ground in aquifers. You had aquifers back in Magella, right?"

"Well sure, but those were inside the dome. Only the dome provides those kinds of things."

"Well, in this case the outside world does as well. See that over there?" Meela pointed to a small sink in the corner, complete with a long, curved faucet. Jake had never noticed it until now.

"You made that?" Jake asked.

Meela chuckled a little at that. "No, not the sink itself. I stole it and the pipes I needed, but I did do all of the plumbing myself. The aquifer out here is not as far down as you might think, especially given the fact that we are already a decent ways below the surface."

"You know how to do that?"

"Necessity is the mother of invention."

"Indeed." Jake looked over in the direction of where he knew Tom to still be sleeping. "You don't think I woke him, do you?"

"I doubt it," she said. "He didn't wake when I walked by or when I made this drink we are now both enjoying so much… nor you for that matter."

"Hey Meela, can I ask you something?"

"I suppose."

"What happened to you? Really? Why are you down here, out away from all other living things? I mean, you had to have come from one of those domes out there somewhere. Why did you leave?"

"Why did YOU? I don't believe for a second that you two were stupid enough to actually *choose* to leave the safety and security of your home. What were you thinking?"

"Well, we, we were..." Jake started.

"There's nothing for us back there anymore," Tom cut in, grabbing a chair at the table, pulling it back, and taking Jake completely by surprise. Where the hell did he come from? Meela didn't seem fazed in the least.

This is nice, Jake thought. *Now we are a happy little group of four at our creepy tea party.*

"No?" Meela said, nonchalantly continuing the conversation, as if nothing had happened.

"Not really," Tom said. "Whatever is in our future is out here now."

"You mean death," Meela said, "because that is all you are going to find out here. You two little bunnies should have stayed home. I wish I had a choice. I was forced out."

"How?" Jake asked.

Meela sighed, eyeing the two men at the table with suspicion.

"Well, I guess since I invited you both into my home, I might as well tell you the story," Meela said. "In order to really understand what happened to me, you first need to understand where I came from. My home was probably quite different from yours. It was one of deep religious fervor."

"Actually," Tom interjected, "you're not that far off."

"Oh, really?" Meela said.

Jake gave Tom's chest a small smack with his hand. "He exaggerates."

Tom winked. "Not much."

"Let me ask you something," Jake said. "Have you ever heard of beings called... the Founders?"

Meela sat there for a few moments and then said, "hang on a second, I'll be right back."

Soon after she left from the table, it was Tom's turn to hit Jake.

"What are you doing?" Tom asked.

"Come on!" Jake said. "You remember what I told you about that woman I overheard in that other dome!"

"Jake, we need this woman to trust us! She is going to help us survive out here! The last thing we need to do is scare her off with your wild stories of magical beings!"

"Look, I just-"

Jake's sentence was cut off by the loud *THUMP* of something massive hitting the tabletop. The impact was so severe that the little candle even jumped up into the air. Its tiny flame still stayed lit, though, somehow.

A huge tome was lying before them, bound in red leather. It looked as if it must be decades, if not centuries, old. It seemed strange to Jake that a woman like Meela had *any* books laying around her place, let alone one this large or old. There were three words written on the cover in an elegant script, indented into the leather and colored gold. Jake turned the book around on the table so that he could read it right side up. He caught himself for a moment when he saw what was written on the cover.

It read: "The Book of the Founders."

"Where did you get that?" Jake asked.

"Where else?" Meela said. "From home."

CHAPTER 17

"Beware the demons of this world, for they
may take on many shapes and forms."

-The Book of the Founders

"**G**rowing up back home, absolutely everything in life had a god, a Founder," Meela said. "A Founder for the sky, a Founder for the ground, a Founder for the sun, a Founder for the sea, a Founder for day, a Founder for night..."

"No, no," Jake said. "That's not right. There's..."

"Who's telling this story, me or you?" Meela barked.

Jake just scowled.

"He's sorry," Tom said. "Please continue."

"Thank you," Meela said. "Each Founder had its own temple where we would worship them. Each had its own season of the sun's cycle that was designated for their worship. Also, each area under our particular dome was assigned a different Founder. The home I grew up in was on the edge of a great lake. It was so large, it took up nearly a tenth of the total area under our dome. It even ran up against the edge of our dome in places. So, as you can imagine, our area's Founder was the god of water.

"At a very young age, I had built myself a small raft that I would paddle out away from shore and lay on for hours in the afternoon sun. It was my way of getting away from others. I wasn't exactly a social child. It seemed as though the longer I spent around other people, the more annoyed I became with them, especially my family. My two older sisters were the worst. They so often would make up rules about how I was to act around them or what possessions were theirs and not mine. They saw fit to run my life any way they pleased and my mother and father did little to nothing to stop it.

"So, whenever possible, I got away. My raft was my sanctuary. While I was upon it, nobody could tell me what to do. Nobody could run my life but me. Many times, I would paddle all of the way out to the dome's edge and stare out into the vast landscape of red. It was quite the strange sensation, I have to tell you: the waterline was a good four or five meters above the ground outside of that invisible barrier. It felt as if I was floating in the air.

"When I got older, I designed a device that allowed me to dive below the surface of the water for minutes at a time. I used some old clothing fabric and created a half-spherical cover to a round wooden frame. It was then only a matter of attaching a few weights to the sides of it. When it submerged, a bubble of breathable air remained under the half-sphere. I would dip my head in and out of that air bubble to watch the different sea life that called the lake home.

"After a few cycles of doing this, I grew even more curious. For all of the times I had explored under water, I had never found the bottom. I often wondered how far down it really was. I was determined on one particular trip that I would find out. So, I paddled out to the middle of the lake again, jumped in with my little diving device and made my way down, not to return until I had felt the touch of the ground beneath me. It was a lot farther down than even I had expected it to be, but I did find it. I was a bit worried about the trip back up. I really wasn't sure that I had enough breathable air left. I began to panic. And then…

"My foot touched something… something altogether strange. The rest of the ground was muddy. My feet had i sunk in to my ankles and I had to kick hard just to get them to come loose… but this… *this* was rock solid… and *smooth* to the touch. I had come this far. I had to find out what it was. I took a deep breath and dove down so that I could search around with my hands for it. It was deep in the muck, so it took some digging to get it out, but eventually I dislodged it. As soon as I had it in my grasp, I looked up for my bubble so that I could catch my breath. It was gone.

"To this day, I really have no idea what happened to it. It may have floated away with the current, but that would have been extremely unlikely. The current there can be strong at times, but not so strong that it would move something that far that fast. It wasn't as if I could see that far under the water, though. It usually looks like pea soup down there. Plus, I had just kicked up a decent amount of dirt into the swirling water. Later, I had thought that perhaps one of the larger sea creatures had done something to it. Some of them can be quite violent, but most of the time they leave you alone if you leave them alone.

"Whatever the case, my supply of oxygen, however limited it was, was now completely gone. I had to make my way back to the surface on my own. I was quite an accomplished swimmer, but even I doubted my ability to make this ascent. There was no other choice, though. I had to try. So, I kicked my legs as hard as I could and pulled my arms with all of my might. As I made my way up, I felt such pain as I'm sure I'll never experience again in my lifetime. My lungs felt as if they were going to explode from the inside. My heart felt as if it were on fire. I started seeing bright shining stars appearing in my vision. Everything began to blur, and then, miraculously, I was somehow at the surface.

"The immediate intake of oxygen was wondrous, delicious and even a bit painful itself. After several minutes of hyperventilating while floating on my back on the surface of the water, I was able to regain full consciousness again. With my back arched, I could easily keep myself afloat with hardly any effort, and could concentrate on getting my breathing back to normal.

"Once I had my wits about me, I scanned the area for my raft. I had to swim for about an hour before I found it, all the while still clutching onto that strange new object I had found. Once I did find the raft, I collapsed upon it and blacked out for most of the rest of the day. When I awoke, the sun had set and the stars were out. After taking time to get my bearings based on the stars' orientation in the sky, I began the slow trip back home.

"When I got there, my entire family was asleep. I was shocked to discover that no one had even been the least bit worried about me. They were all snug in their beds, comfortably snoozing away without a care in the world. I guess they were all so used to me running away from any kind of human contact that they assumed I was just gone again and would return when I saw fit. Still, it hurt to think that even though I had been gone for nearly an entire day, no one had felt compelled to investigate.

"I never did get to sleep that night. I used what remained of the early morning hours studying what I had found. It was a little wider than my open hand, silver and shaped like a squashed ball. I was frustrated to find that there was nothing special about it. It was just a strangely-shaped piece of metal. All the same, I was so mad at my family (and everyone else for that matter) that I decided I would never tell them about it. I kept it on me almost everywhere I went and when I didn't, I had a safe hiding place for it underneath one of the floorboards in my room.

"Then came the day that changed my life forever. I was back out on my raft, the strange object tucked safely away in a pouch beneath my clothes. Once again, I decided to float out to the dome's edge and gaze out at the landscape beyond. Now, if the device had been where I could have seen it, I suppose I would have noticed it glowing blue, but I didn't. As I got closer to the edge, I extended my hands out to rest them on the dome's edge as I often did when looking out. Except this time they didn't rest on anything. They fell *through* the dome, as if it didn't even exist! The rest of my body followed. That landing hurt. Not as much as my near-death experience swimming back up to the surface a few months earlier, but it was still painful enough for me to double over. The shock of my new environment didn't help, either. One moment, I was floating on water, the next, I was face down in red dirt.

"I got up onto my feet as soon as the pain dissipated and looked back at where I had come from. A wall of water was in front of me and my little raft was floating about three meters above my head. It was like looking into a fish tank. A few small fish did swim by and give me uninterested looks as I stared back at them. My first instinct, of course, was to place my hands back on the surface of the dome to try and make some sense of what had just happened. And of course, upon doing that, I fell back *into* the water, through the dome once more."

"So, wait a second," Tom said. "You mean to say that everything else just stayed inside? I would have thought that all kinds of water and fish and stuff would have come out with you. You probably know by now the range of these things."

"Don't ask me how it works," Meela said. "I didn't build the damned things. Anyway, I fell into the water and eventually floated back up the surface. By the time I got back up on my raft, I was so scared that I grabbed my paddle and made for home like there was no tomorrow. When I arrived, I ran for my room and hid under the covers of my bed, not wanting to come out for anyone or anything. Now, if I wasn't already prone to locking myself in my room on a regular basis, perhaps someone might have thought something was wrong, but they didn't. I heard one knock a little later in the day letting me know that the evening meal was ready if I wanted any. I didn't move.

"The following morning, I gathered up enough inner strength to exit my little cocoon and re-join the rest of my family. It had been a trying experience for me the day before and for the first time in a long time, I actually looked forward to being around other people. What I saw after leaving my room that morning was not at all what I was expecting. Two men were at the door. One look at their clothing and I knew precisely who they were: Priests of the Second Order. Now, I won't go too deep into the hierarchy of the Holy Priesthood, but suffice it to say that these two men were in the highest rank of priests allowed to speak to such simple people as my family. These priests were hardly ever seen outside of the temple, so for them to make a special trip like this one was saying something. I didn't hear everything that was said, but I knew they were talking about me. Their eyes grew wide when they first noticed me and from that point forward, they kept looking back at me as they spoke to my parents.

"A few minutes later, the two men at the door entered our home and grabbed me. I was kicking and screaming telling them to stop as they dragged me outside. I still remember looking back at the open doorway to my home as the priests continued to carry me away. There stood both of my parents. I will never forget the looks on their faces. They weren't looks of confusion, anger or even sadness. They looked calm, perfectly at peace, as if nothing was the matter. Their little girl was being carted away to Founders' knew where and they just stood there, not doing or saying a damned thing to stop it.

"The priests locked me in the back of a horse-drawn cart and I was brought to the water god temple. Deep down below on its lowest level were a series of cells. There were only half a dozen or so. I was left there for over two days without one person ever visiting me to give me food or water. No one even came to tell me why I had been taken there in the first place. Finally, one of the priests made an appearance. It was explained to me that the priesthood had declared me as a 'Demockadle'.

"What is that?" Tom asked. "I've never heard of that before."

"The best way to describe it would be an 'unwanted', 'undesirable', 'other' or... 'demon.'" Meela said.

"Demon?" Jake asked. "You mean a creature of evil or something?"

"Yeah, something like that," Meela said. "They were convinced that I had now become, or always had been, some sort of evil non-human entity. Needless to say, I was shocked, sickened and saddened all at the same time. Here were my parents, the very people who had supposedly loved and cared for me my whole life... the people whose responsibility it was to keep me safe... throwing me out like trash and dismissing me completely because some stupid, pious priest had told them to."

"You mean they never did anything to fight this?" Tom asked.

"Nothing," Meela replied.

"How sad," Jake said.

"Story of my life," Meela said. "If there is one constant in this world it is this: you can't trust anybody."

"Someone saw you fall through the dome, didn't they?" Tom said.

"Yup. A fisherman, I think. It doesn't really matter."

"Stupid, ignorant, superstitious fools."

"Pretty much."

"So, what was going to happen to you, now that everyone thought you were this Demagrackle or whatever?"

"Demockradle." Meela corrected him.

"Right, that."

"Well, the punishment is death."

"Death?!" Jake exclaimed.

"My people do not tolerate infestations of any kind," Meela explained, "no matter what form they may take. I was to be put to death immediately. "

"How?" Jake asked.

"The Founder god of fire sees to that. Not a fun way to go, but of course, fire cleanses all," Meela said.

"Indeed," Tom agreed.

"The same night I was told declared a demockradle, I was set to be executed," Meela said. "Justice is quick when it is 'the will of the Founders', after all. I was led out of my cell below the water temple and forced to walk barefoot over six kilometers to the temple of fire. There, they led me up to the roof and strapped me to a gigantic spire. The thing was massive. It was as thick as a fully-grown man and as tall as five of them standing on each other's heads. There were still ashes up there, too... of those who had been sacrificed before. I can still feel the sickening crunch beneath my feet. I nearly vomited a few times. Once I was secured, they began to set the kindling. When it was in place, they left me for a few moments so they could light their torches.

"What happened next I fully believe was just blind luck on my part. It was just a happenstance and nothing more. Within a matter of a few minutes, one of the most powerful and destructive storms I've ever seen swept in. The priests couldn't even keep their torches lit in all of the wind. Then, the rain and lightning came. Before I knew what had happened, the wind had grown so intense that it snapped the spire I was attached to. I saw it crumble and fall over the side of the temple. For all I knew, it had fallen on top of some of the people on the street who had gathered up to watch me burn and praise my passing from this world. Whatever the case, it didn't matter. I was free.

"My bonds came loose easily enough. The poor, dumb priests were probably too busy scrambling to save their own lives to even notice me at this point. I made my way around to the back of the temple, away from any prying eyes, carefully watching my steps as I raced across the steep shingled roof. I nearly slipped and fell a couple of times. The drop to the ground would have been farther than my drop out of the dome had been. Most of the crowd had scattered by now, desperate to find some kind of cover. Once I reached the back wall of the temple, I scaled my way down the side, using different pieces of the opulent architecture to help my descent. When I hit the ground, I ran… and ran… and ran…

"Luckily, the priests had been in such a hurry to kill me that they didn't bother changing my clothes. I was barefoot, sure, but the rest of my outfit, along with the pouch where I had hid my strange object from view, was still with me. I hadn't put two and two together about that little disc and its connection with my ability to leave the dome. If I had, I probably would have screamed about it when they were accusing me of being an evil spirit. In any event, my main focus at this point was to get away. I spent the night in an old man's barn, riding out the storm.

"The following morning I awoke to a world gone mad. It was as if all of Coustea had been told of my escape."

"Wait, what's Coustea?" Jake asked.

"It is the name of my home, the cursed place," Meela said as she spat on the floor. "Everyone was convinced that the storm was caused by my 'evil magic'. I did my best not to be seen, but just about every living soul was looking for me. In the end, it became clear that I only had one choice. I made for the edge of the dome. The priests had said that I now possessed the power to do so at will, so I figured I'd give it a shot. It was better than staying in a place that now considered me a monster.

"I stole a few things along the way, but I was just a child and I didn't plan anywhere close to an appropriate amount of food or other supplies. Before long, I was outside of the dome again, this time by land, with a small pack on my back, and the wind whipping me around like a like a leaf. It took me a while to realize that it was that little disc of metal that was making it possible to enter and exit the domes. By the time that happened, I was far away from Coustea.

"I nearly starved out there. I have no idea how I made it, but eventually I came upon another dome. I couldn't believe it. All my life, I had been told that we were the only living things in all creation, and here was a whole other society of people who looked just like me! Well, their eyes were slightly wider and their hair a bit darker in general, but pretty close. I did my best to blend in, not get noticed. It didn't take long before I became an expert thief. I never stayed in one place long, and I never, ever made friends with anyone. After I felt I had overstayed my welcome there, I moved on in search of other places."

"Other domes, you mean," Jake said.

"Precisely." Meela said, "I figured that where there were two, there must be three or four or… well, you get the idea. Over time, no matter how long I stayed anywhere, it never felt like home to me. I couldn't stay. Before too long, I stumbled upon this place. If it were possible, I would stay down in here in this cave and never come out. Unfortunately, as you both know, nothing is sustainable outside of the domes. There always comes a time when I need to go out and brave the world above."

"To steal," Tom said.

"I will tell you," Meela said, "stealing doesn't seem nearly as morally objectionable when you are starving. When you are starving, dying... all bets are off. A switch in your brain seems to turn on that takes out all thoughts other than getting your hands on some food."

Tom and Jake nodded. They both knew all too well.

"Now," Meela said, "since I have come clean and told you my story, I think it is only fair that the two of you do the same."

"What do you mean?" Jake asked, shifting in his seat slightly.

"What, you think I didn't hear what our friend here said to you up top before I knocked him out?" Meela said, jamming her thumb in the direction of the Omega Order soldier. "I heard everything. Where is it? Where is this special disc? This compass of yours?"

CHAPTER 18

"Do as the Founders command you, for they know more than you could possibly imagine."

-The Book of the Founders

"I know full well that you two aren't outside of your dome on some merry little romp just for the fun of it," Meela said. "That special device that the Omega Order has been looking for... you have it, don't you?"

Jake looked to Tom. Tom nodded back slowly to Jake, as if saying, "it's alright."

Jake reached down into his pants pocket and retrieved the compass they had found down in Morzellano's mine, all those weeks ago, and set it on the table. The tiny blue light on its edge pointed right at where Meela was seated at the table. She ran her finger over the small dot a few times and then looked back up to Jake and Tom.

"Is that it?" she asked. "What am I looking at?"

"That light always points in the same direction," Jake said. "We came to the conclusion that it is pointing the way we need to go. Turn it over."

Meela did as she was told and picked up the device. There were the two numbers in red, one reading "3,732.58" and the other, still counting down.

7,998,467...
7,998,466...
7,998,465...

Jake was shocked at how much smaller the numbers on the clock were. He began to think back on how much time they had spent doing things other than following the path the device had set for them. It appeared as though they still had plenty of time, but it was obvious they needed to get back on the move as quickly as circumstances would allow. Jake had no idea how much time would be needed here with Meela in order to be properly trained. He hoped it was the ultra-short course, not the extended version.

"So, I take it this is some kind of clock?" Meela said.

"Well… um, yeah, actually we thought that, too." Tom said.

"The members of the Omega Order called this a compass. If this little blue dot tells you what direction to go, my best guess on the other number is that it is some kind of indicator of distance?" Meela said.

"Wow. Yeah, that's right." Jake said.

"So, this is leading you some place," Meela said. "Where are you going?"

Jake and Tom paused for a moment. Jake was a little unsure what to say next. Do they tell Meela about the Overseer and Jake's quest to save all of humanity? Was Tom thinking the same thing? Jake pictured how the conversation would go, explaining to Meela that a projection of some strange man had told Jake he was to find a new home for everyone. In all instances, he saw the same result: Meela laughing in their faces.

"What's the deal, fellas?" Meela said, breaking the silence, "Still not sure you can trust me?"

"It's not that…" Jake said.

"Alright," Tom said, "if you really must know, this device, this *compass*, is leading us to a new home for humanity."

Jake had been right. Meela did laugh. Only a little bit, though.

"So, what exactly does this new home look like?" Meela asked.

"We don't know." Tom said.

"Then how do you know it's even there?" Meela asked. "Who told you?"

Jake sighed. There was no sense in leaving anything back anymore. He told the entire story to Meela: how they found the device, Jake's conversation with the Overseer, their decision to leave Magella, everything. To her credit, it looked as if she actually believed them. Maybe the whole thing wasn't quite as ridiculous as it sounded in Jake's own mind, after all.

"Wow," Meela said. "So you are on some kind of quest, then, huh?"

"Given to me by the Founders," Jake said.

"Maybe your Founders, but not mine," Meela said.

"You don't believe in them anymore, do you?" Tom said.

"Would you, after what I've been through?" Meela said. "Look, I believe that you were contacted by someone or some*thing* with that device of yours, but if you think I am going to believe that you have been sent on some holy journey by the Founders themselves, then you're crazy."

Meela then pointed at the Book of the Founders, still laying on the tabletop.

"See this book?" she said. "Do you know what this is?"

"What?" Jake asked.

"Control," Meela said in a forceful tone. "A means by which to keep us silly little humans from misbehaving. Or, I suppose, from doing what an elite group of people have deemed misbehaving. I've seen it all the time, Jake. People in power want only one thing: to stay in power. How do you do that? Well, you write big books like this one that shape the world in a way that you like best and then you tell everyone that it is 'holy' and if they don't follow it, they will all die."

"Religion can be a powerful motivator," Tom commented.

"Indeed," Meela agreed. "Jake, don't be some stupid pawn in this selfish game."

"What's a pawn?" Jake asked.

"A blind follower," Meela said, now raising her voice somewhat. "Someone who only does what they are told but doesn't think for themselves. In other words, you."

"I am not just blindly following!" Jake shouted, pounding his fist on the table.

Suddenly a low moan came out of the imprisoned fourth member of their party. All eyes turned in his direction. He shifted his head side to side slowly, moaning a bit more. His eyes were opened, scanning the room and its three other occupants. They blinked in quick succession, either adjusting to the light or trying to figure out just where they were. The man's attention soon turned to the woman who had shot him.

"Good morning!" Meela said, a fake smile plastered on her face.

"What is this place?" the tied-up man asked. "What am I doing here?"

"We need information," Meela said, "and you're going to give us some."

"Am I now?" the man said.

"Yes, you are," Meela said, producing her laser weapon from beneath the table and placing it on top. Its tip was pointing directly at the Omega soldier's chest. "Check it, you'll see that it is set simply to 'pain'. The same setting you used on my friend, here, if I am not mistaken."

Meela then leaned in Jake's general direction and said, "each shot is non-lethal, but is incredibly... well, you can read the setting."

She then turned back to their captive and continued. "I find it interesting that your kind have created weapons with such a setting. What do you think that says about you?"

"You are using that setting as a means to threaten me right now. I don't think you have the right to question our motives," the Omega soldier spat back.

"Perhaps not. In any event, if you do not give me sufficient responses to my questions, we'll have a chance to see just how many shots at this setting a human being can endure."

The man just scowled.

"We know that you have obviously figured out how to exit and enter the domes by means of these devices," Meela said, nodding down towards Jake's device, still set on top the table. The flat section with the numbers was face-down again and the small blue light was facing away from their captive. For all the tied up man knew, it was like any other device the Omega Order had used. "We also know that you have been searching for others. How did you know of their existence?"

The man in front of them stayed silent, still scowling.

"Really?" Meela said. "You want to get started this quickly, huh?" Meela placed her finger on her weapon's firing mechanism.

"Wait! Wait!" the man said.

Meela released her finger.

"The reason we know about the others is because we've always known," the man said.

"Wait, what do you mean, 'always known?'" Jake asked, shuffling in his seat, apparently now ready to join the interrogation.

"My people have always known there were devices created that would allow us to leave the domes," the man said. "We just didn't know what they looked like. It wasn't until the first device was discovered beneath the surface of our home dome that we finally figured it all out."

"But how did you know that you could leave the domes?" Tom asked.

"It is part of our history," the man said, "passed down from one generation to the next. It is common knowledge. We had spent centuries searching and up until a few years ago, we were unsuccessful."

"And knowledge of the other devices as well? That was passed down, too?" Jake asked.

"Yes," the man said.

"But why steal the others?" Tom asked. "To what end?"

"We're greedy," the man said simply.

"You know what?" Meela said, standing up from her chair. She picked up the weapon from the table as she walked towards the Omega soldier. "That sounds a lot like a lie to me. Boy, I hate liars. I'll give you another chance, though. Want to tell us why the Omega Order is *really* hoarding as many of these devices as they can get their hands on?"

Meela raised the weapon. Its tip was now mere centimeters from the man's forehead.

"Ok! Fine! Just put that damned thing down!" the man yelled.

"That's better," Meela said, doing as she was told.

"Alright, it *is* out of greed, in one sense," the man said, "but it is more than that. As I am sure you all have figured out by now, these devices only have a certain range. Only a handful of people can use one at a given time. With more devices in our possession, more of our people can venture outside of our dome and into others. We know through our history that each dome has only one device, hidden somewhere inside. We began by looking in the same place ours had been found: in the rock beneath the surface. As it turned out, nearly all of the others were found in very similar circumstances. We soon became very efficient at our job. The motivation is simple: the more devices we find, the more of our people can leave our dome."

"Very good!" Meela said. "You are almost there! Mind telling us the rest?"

"That *is* the rest!"

"Really? *Really?* Does any of this make sense to anyone else? Your 'order' is fully-funded, organized and driven… and you are after something. Don't waste our time telling us you just want more of your people running around out here! Who cares?!? You didn't think we had forgotten what you had said back on the surface, did you? What was that word again? Oh right, you said *compass*. These devices sure don't look like compasses to me. Sure, they are fun to use, great for getting to new places and meeting new people, I have no doubt. The word compass implies that you are being led in a specific direction or to a specific destination. So, as I said, mind telling us the rest?"

If the man seated in front of them could have scowled even more than he already had been, he would have. Not a word was uttered. This time, Meela didn't hesitate. She shot him in the shoulder.

"AAAAGGGHHHH!!!" The man screamed.

Jake shivered at the sound, knowing all too well what a shot at that setting felt like.

The man tried to look down at his wound, as if expecting to see some great gaping hole there, but it looked no different than it had before. He jostled around in his roped-in prison, but to no avail. Eventually, he gave up and sat there, head lowered. Jake looked at Meela. He had to admit to himself that he never expected her to fire the weapon. He figured that she would do a lot of gesturing and posturing, but that would have been it. He wondered if Tom felt as uneasy at the scene unfolding in front of them as he did.

"YOU TRIED TO KILL US, YOU BASTARD!" Meela said, thrusting her arms out to her sides and jutting out her head in the man's direction. "Do you think this is some kind of game? Tell me what I want to know, or I'll unload every last shot this thing can fire on you!!"

"Yes, I tried to kill you and I swear I'll finish the job if I ever get out of here!" the man growled.

"Maybe," Meela said. "Right now, though, you have some more talking to do."

The man wiggled around within the ropes once again. It was another desperate attempt to get them to loosen. As before, he had no luck. Meela had done her job well. He even hopped the chair up in the air a few times. Finally, he spat at the ground in frustration. "When my team and I first saw you three, we had been sent out from home in search of the compass. We had been told that one of you was possibly in possession of it."

How could they know? Jake thought to himself. The only people who were aware of his disc's special properties were sitting in this room, at least as far as he knew.

"They should have sent more men," Meela said, bluntly.

"Where does the compass lead?" Jake asked.

"Don't you know already?" the man said.

Meela, Tom and Jake just stared back at him, nonresponsive.

"Do you seriously mean to tell me that you are flying blind with that thing?" the man continued. "The Chancellor would get a good laugh out of that if he ever found out."

"Do you know or not?"

A small chuckle came from the man's throat. "You are so stupid. You have no idea what you are dealing with here. Even if I did tell you, your tiny brains wouldn't even be able to comprehend it!"

"Try me," Meela said.

The man hesitated for a moment, looking as if he were willing to take on another blast from Meela's weapon if need be. Then his shoulders slumped. Clearly he had rethought his options.

"Fine, I'll tell you," the man said. "Damned bit of good it will do you, though. It leads to paradise, our ancestral home. This is the place where all of us under these domes used to live. The one place my kind was told we could never ever return to!"

"What do you mean?" Tom asked.

"Centuries ago, my people were left to die while the rest of humanity was saved from destruction. When these perfect little worlds were made, my people were not allowed in any of them. Apparently, we were deemed unworthy for some reason."

"Wait," Jake said, "if you weren't allowed in any of them, then how come you said you came from your own dome?"

"The Omega Order represents only a small fraction of our original ancestral group. Long ago, a handful of those ancestors were able to sneak into one of the domes as it was being populated. The vast majority of the people who live there aren't even aware of our existence! We hide in plain sight. Only those who bear the mark belong to the order."

Jake looked at the strange upside-down "U" on the uniform's shoulder once more.

"Those who exist among us and do not bear the mark are ignorant of the truth," the man continued, "and ignorance can be a wonderful tool."

Jake felt a sting at the comment, remembering his conversation with Meela, only moments before the soldier had awoken.

"So," Meela said, "your mission is to find the compass and bring it back to this, this *Chancellor* of yours and then your road back to paradise is set?"

"Legend says that when paradise is at last discovered, the one who finds it will control all of the domed worlds that exist in all of creation. When the Omega Order reaches that destination, all of you will feel the same sting of death that my people felt, all those years ago. Finally, justice will be served. You want to torture me some more? Fine. You want to KILL me? Fine. None of it will matter. Even if I die, the Omega Order will find you and destroy you. We have you outnumbered and outmatched. Your fate is set."

CHAPTER 19

"Knowing and doing are not the same."

-The Book of the Founders

The rock exploded into a shower of dust and debris. Jake lowered the weapon, a grimace on his face. He checked the sight once again. Everything seemed to be calibrated the way Meela had instructed, so how had he missed? He felt a hand on his left shoulder. He turned from the puzzle in front of him to see Tom. Where had he come from? The man had a strange talent of popping up out of thin air.

"Nice shot!" Tom said.

"It would have been if I were attempting to hit that particular rock," Jake said. "I was actually aiming for the one to the left of it."

"Oh, sorry."

"It's alright. I just... I'm not sure I'm ever going to get this. The hunting and tracking lessons were fine. I feel alright about what Meela taught us about using stealth in order to avoid detection, but these laser weapons? I'm not used to shooting things with any weapon, let alone these things. You, at least have had experience hunting with that bow of yours for a while before we ever came here."

"It's not as similar as you might think. It was still an adjustment for me."

"Oh, come off it, Tom. You've bested me in every aspect of this training. If there were some kind of official accreditation process, you'd have your license by now and you know it."

"Sheesh, jump all over a guy for trying to cheer his buddy up."

"Sorry, I'm just so damn frustrated. It seems that every step of the way on this journey of ours I have messed something up or have not been prepared. I... I..."

"You wonder why the Overseer ever picked you in the first place."

"Well, *yeah!* Sometimes I think he picked me because I happened to be in possession of the device at that particular moment, that's it. I'm not anything special at all, really. I worry that this whole venture is going to end in failure because someone more qualified than I wasn't selected."

"Jake, I'll just say one thing. Sometimes the qualities that make a person a good choice for something like this are more than just an ability to fire a laser weapon correctly."

"Yeah, but they don't hurt."

"True, so keep practicing."

Jake frowned and brought up the weapon once again. He looked through the tiny sight attached to the top of the gun, doing his best to line up the small plus sign and his intended target. He took a few deep breaths and concentrated on keeping perfectly still. His thoughts shifted to memories of Meela hitting her marks with this very same weapon while running, while riding a hover bike, while leaping high up into the air...

How in the Founders' names can she do that when I can't even hit a rock fifty meters away, without moving whatsoever?

Jake let his own internal logic shake those thoughts away. It was useless to worry about such things. It was like someone who had never run a day in his life comparing himself to a professional marathon runner. It would only end in frustration. He returned his concentration to the rock and exhaled slowly. He squeezed the trigger ("don't PULL it, just SQUEEZE it!" Meela had said). A bright blue beam of energy struck the front face of the rock and blew it into thousands of tiny particles, flying in all directions.

"Ha ha!" Tom shouted. "I knew you could do it!"

Jake smiled as he lowered the weapon to his side.

"So, how are things coming, gentlemen?"

Both Jake and Tom turned to see Meela, striding up to join them and stopping when she reached Tom's side.

"Jake is making progress," Tom said.

"Good!" Meela replied. "Just remember to be patient. These things take time."

"Yeah, yeah, I know," Jake said.

"So how is our Omega friend doing?" Tom asked.

"Fine for now," Meela said, "I gave him another shot of the tranquilizer."

"Do you think hitting him with that so often is safe?" Jake asked.

"I could give a damn if it is safe," Meela responded, "but if I am going to be up here on the surface with you two, he goes back to sleep. I don't ever want him to be awake unless I am down there with him."

"What are we going to do with him?" Tom asked. "I mean, we can't keep him here indefinitely."

"And we are NOT killing him," Jake added.

"Why not?" Meela said, incredulously. "What has he done that gives him the right to live?"

"The fact that he is a human being gives him the right to live!" Jake shouted back. "You may have no qualms about killing, but I do."

"You let this miserable son of a bitch live and it will be nothing but trouble, mark my words!" Meela said.

"Maybe, maybe not," Jake replied, "but we are not killing him!"

"We can't send him back to the Omega Order," Tom said. "I think we can all agree on that."

"So we can't kill him, we can't send him home, and we can't keep him here," Meela said. "Gentlemen, I think what you have created here is what's called a paradox. The no-win scenario."

"Maybe not," Jake said. "I've been thinking about this and I might have an idea. Meela, you said before that you have witnessed some of the other domes that the Omega Order have visited while searching for the other devices. Do you know, perhaps, which ones they have left completely?"

"I'm not sure I understand what you are asking," Meela said.

"What I mean is the Omega Order has lots of devices in their possession now, maybe even over a dozen. That means they have visited over a dozen different domed worlds and have stolen a device from each. Once that device was taken, they move on, with no need to return to that dome ever again."

"Right. Well, at least that seems to be the case for now."

"So, if there is no chance of the Omega Order returning any time soon, why not dump this guy inside one of them?"

"Right!" Tom said. "Without his own device to get back out again, he would essentially be trapped!"

"There would be no way for him to get back in touch with his Omega buddies to tell them about us," Jake said.

"I suppose," Meela replied, "but it is an awful lot of extra running around when it could be a lot easier to shoot the bastard in the head right now. He was about to do no less to us."

"And that is why we can't do the same to him," Jake said. "We are not like them. We do not simply execute someone just because they disagree with us. This is exactly why keeping the compass out of their hands is so important."

"Fine," Meela said, "we'll do it your way. But we are taking an awful risk to simply satisfy your *morals*. He stays here until I feel you two are ready to handle yourselves in a firefight."

"Understood," Tom said.

With that, Meela walked back to the tunnel and let herself back down again.

"Remember those qualities I was talking about earlier, Jake?" Tom said once Meela was gone.

"Yeah?" Jake replied.

"There they are," Tom said and smiled. "Come on, keep blowing up more of your rocks. The sooner you get the hang of this, the sooner we can be on our way."

A day later, Jake was an expert at obliterating any rogue boulders or rocks that might pose a threat to them. The next step, of course, was to hit something that wasn't sitting still. Meela's first exercise was a simple one. She had with her a large bucket filled with dozens of small, green rubber balls. Jake didn't recognize them, but figured they were probably used in some game that didn't exist in Magella. Either way, they weren't going to be used for their original purpose this day.

"I am going to throw these up in the air one at a time," Meela said. "Your job is to shoot them before they hit the ground. And for my sake, please don't aim too low."

Tom, who had already passed the moving target drill, was standing beside Meela, as if he were just another instructor. "You can do it, Jake," he said, "just anticipate where the ball is going to be."

Jake felt like the dumb kid in school, for whom the rest of the class was patiently waiting.

We found all of the right answers already, Jake, why don't you? he heard the voices say in his head.

There had been almost forty tosses before Jake was able to make one of the cursed little balls go away. It was exhilarating and frustrating at the same time. An hour or so after that, though, he was picking them off three or four in a row. By late afternoon, he had hit a streak of fourteen destroyed balls without one having hit the ground. By late the next day, he was running down a set path while shooting at the little green spheres. More than half of them had been ripped apart into tiny pieces of green rubber.

At the end of his last run, Meela was there to greet him. Without really thinking about what he was doing, he threw his arms around her and spun her around in the air. As she twirled, she let out a soft fit of laughter. Founders be praised, the woman had actually *laughed*. Once Jake had set her back down on the ground the two of them both had silly grins plastered on their faces. They quickly locked eyes and then just as quickly averted each other's gaze, both a little embarrassed.

The following morning, only one more test remained.

"This is going to be a crash course in hover bike driving," Meela said as they stood outside of the small cave where the two hover bikes had been stashed.

"A *what* course?!?" Jake exclaimed.

"Sorry, a figure of speech you are probably not familiar with," Meela said. "It just means a quick lesson."

Jake looked at Tom, who just shrugged.

Meela led them inside the cave. It reminded Jake of Morzellano's mine, but on a much, much, smaller scale. They traveled down the main passage as it curved to the left before it dead-ended. There, leaning against the wall, were the two hover bikes they had stolen. One appeared to have been tinkered with. A few small parts lay littered across the floor. Jake wondered if perhaps it might be important to have some of those still have attached to the bike, but he kept his mouth closed. As little as he knew about piloting these contraptions, he knew even less about how they were put together.

"While you two were having fun shooting things," Meela said, "I spent some time working on the bike that had been shot. It still doesn't run as well as its counterpart, but I think it is serviceable. Come on, let's get these outside."

Meela reached over and lifted one of the bikes to an upright position.

"Unless you want to drag one of these through the dirt behind me," Meela said, "I suggest you follow my lead. You two can use the good one. I don't mind taking my fixer-upper."

She pressed a large red button on one of the handles her bike. The sound of the engine coming to life filled every centimeter of the tight, enclosed space. Jake ended up covering his ears with his hands. Fresh clouds of black smoke began to pour out of a small tube sticking out the back of the bike. For a moment, Jake thought for sure the thing was going to explode, killing them all, but it lifted itself up into the air and hung there, about half a meter off of the ground.

"I knew it would work!" Meela said as she began pushing the bike in the direction of the cave's mouth.

Jake reached down and activated the other bike. There wasn't as much smoke and it wasn't quite as loud, but it had the same affect as Meela's. Soon all three of them were outside of the cavern, two transports hovering beside them, ready to be used.

Unlike his early obstacles with shooting things, Jake had much more success with the hover bike. Jake had ridden a (What? Normal? Regular? Wheels-only?) bike to work every day when he had worked for Morzellano and he found that although he had no actual traction with the ground this time around, the skills from one were easily transferrable to the other.

Tom was not too far behind, either. He had obviously spent a number of hours on a wheels-to-the-ground bicycle in Magella as well, even though Jake had never seen him do so in person. It made Jake feel better that he was taking to something quicker than Tom, if only by a small fraction.

The two men took turns riding the "not fixer-upper" bike around the terrain near Meela's home. Meela stayed continuously on her own bike, shouting instructions and pointing out errors. Thankfully, there were no accidents or serious injuries. However, there were quite a few close calls. Most of the time, Jake or Tom would be smart enough to jump off before any major incidents could occur. The bike would then naturally slow down on its own or bounce harmlessly off of some obstruction and then just sit there hovering, waiting for its next rider.

The hardest part was what Meela had called the "accelerator". Back in Magella, Jake's acceleration had always come from his feet, pumping hard on pedals. These bikes, however, needed only a slight twist of the handles and the rider would be shot forward at speeds far exceeding anything he had even come close to hitting back home. The jump in speed was so sudden that both Jake and Tom had to take a number of attempts before they wouldn't fall off (or half-fall off, as was the case with Tom on a number of occasions).

By midday, the two were zipping around hills and rocks like pros. Jake even attempted to launch himself and his bike from a slight incline. The bike's trajectory was higher and farther than he had originally planned, but he still managed to stick the landing without completely losing control. He had to remind himself of the effects that the lower gravity had on riding a vehicle such as this. Learning to walk in this new world had been one thing. This was quite another. By the time they had to stop for the day, Jake was actually disappointed. He would have been quite content to fly around well into the night if Meela had let him.

As the group was leaving the cave after replacing the bikes, Meela said, "I think we are ready, you two."

"Ready to leave?" Jake asked.

"I think so," Meela replied. "There is still plenty of room for improvement, but I know you two are on a time crunch here, and I don't want to make you wait any longer than is absolutely necessary. Just remember one thing once you leave: greater numbers equals greater danger. If you see a lot of enemies on the horizon, run. Don't do something stupid like trying to be a hero, ok? You'll just end up dead."

Jake nodded intently.

"Are you sure you don't want to come with us?" Tom asked. "Your skills sure could come in handy."

"No," Meela said, "my place is here. Thanks for the offer, though."

"Well, even so, we sure do appreciate your help, Meela," Jake said.

"Just don't embarrass me by getting yourselves killed the minute we get rid of our Omega detainee downstairs," Meela said.

"So, did you find a suitable dome in which to, um, *deposit* him?" Tom asked.

"I believe so," Meela said, "and I did as you requested. It is located almost directly northwest of here."

"Good," Tom said.

"Daisy and I can help take him there," Meela said. "You two can keep the hover bikes when we are done. I am sure they will be of good use to you in saving time on your trip. Once we get this guy safely secured inside of the dome, then we'll part ways," Meela said.

"Understood," Jake said. "Thank you, Meela."

They locked eyes once more.

"Stop thanking me before I change my mind!" Meela said, waving her hand in a dismissive gesture to break the spell. Jake could see her trying to hide a small grin on her face.

For the first time since he had met Meela, Jake realized that he was actually going to miss her, and it wasn't just because of her skills with laser weapons and hover bikes.

Chapter 20

"When you are ready, the Founders will come and fulfill their gracious promise to bring you back home once more."

-*The Book of the Founders*

The following morning, the four companions prepared to leave. One, not at all by choice. Meela, Tom and Jake had all agreed that it would be best not to tell their Omega captive of their plans. Jake and Tom had held tight to each of his arms as Meela had undone his bindings. She had considered knocking him out once more, but then decided that pulling about one hundred kilograms of dead weight up a ten meter hole was not in anyone's best interest, including the dead weight itself. The Omega soldier was actually more amenable than they had anticipated. Perhaps it was because he was leaving and to him, *anywhere* had to be better than where he been the past few days.

When everyone was up on the surface, Meela bound the Omega soldier's wrists and helped him up onto Daisy's back. The megacat had had issues in the past with strangers riding her, but this was something different. She roared in protest and even attempted to bite the nuisance off of her back, but was unable to reach him with her jaws. Meela quickly worked to subdue the poor beast. She rubbed vigorously under Daisy's chin. The cat began to breathe slower and eventually she even raised her nose up into the air and squeezed her eyelids closed, clearly enjoying herself.

"There," Meela said, "that's better."

While Meela stayed along side Daisy with an eye on her rider, Jake and Tom fetched the two hover bikes from the cave. Once they were back, Meela climbed aboard Daisy behind the Omega soldier. He turned to look back from his sitting position to eye Meela suspiciously. She just smiled back, a devilish grin on her face.

Every member of the party, other than their unwilling captive, was outfitted with a pack of supplies, each of which included a device. Daisy also continued to carry her own device, snapped on tightly to her collar. As usual, Jake held on to the compass, the "special" device amongst the four. He felt good that they were finally moving once more, heading towards their final destination. Whatever it held for them, he still wasn't all that sure. Meela, Tom and Jake also each had their own laser weapon, complete with holsters wrapped around their waists. For the first time, Jake didn't feel as if he might accidentally blow his foot off with the damned thing.

"Everybody ready?" Meela asked.

Tom and Jake answered in the affirmative. The Omega soldier stayed silent. Out came the scowl once more.

"Good!" Meela said. With that, she produced her laser weapon and shot the Omega soldier right in the back. He slumped forward instantly.

"What did you do that for?!?" Jake shouted.

"Don't look so shocked," Meela said. "All I did was put him under again. He's sleeping just like a baby. He should be used to it by now."

"I really wish you'd stop doing that," Jake grumbled.

"I'm not going to risk him jumping off and running away on us or something," Meela said. "He's the reason we are on this trek of yours, right?"

"I guess so."

"Besides, you aren't the one that now has to keep his limp body from falling off Daisy."

"True enough." Jake felt a little better now. Fine, he was Meela's problem, then.

The three transports, two mechanical, one animal, took off to the northwest, just as Meela had described. Daisy started at a slow trot, so Tom and Jake had to be sensitive with their accelerators not to get too far ahead. Not long after, they had found a nice cruising speed. Their destination was still a mystery to Jake and Tom. Meela had been very specific about its location, but when pressed about what the world inside was actually like, she had acted rather cagey. Meela had said that it would probably take them most of the day to get there, which included a few stops to eat and allow Daisy to rest.

At one particular stop, Jake sat next to Meela on the dusty ground. She was shoveling some beans out of a small can. Tom was a few yards away, keeping an eye on the Omega soldier who had been laid (none too delicately, Jake thought) on the ground. The black-clad soldier looked as if he were dead, sprawled haphazardly on the ground with limbs splayed out in all directions. The fact that he was laying face down didn't help the image much. Tom had checked, though: he was still breathing fine. Daisy was happily chewing on a small piece of raw meat, a "thank-you" for her hard work thus far.

"So, Meela," Jake said, opening his own can of beans, "have you thought of a good place to leave this guy once we get there?"

"Not really," Meela said, not even looking in Jake's direction, still chewing on her own beans.

"Well, I've been thinking and it would probably be a good idea to have something in mind before we get there. The last thing we want to do is bring attention to ourselves, right?"

"We'll be fine."

"You said you've been here before?"

"Can you just trust me? I know what I'm doing."

"Right," Jake said as he got back up to go eat his beans somewhere else.

Later that day, as they were traveling at a walking speed for Daisy, Jake motioned from his speeder to get Tom's attention. As they had been all day, the two of them were riding behind Meela, letting her lead the way. Jake gave Tom a "come here" motion with his hand as he pulled back on the throttle. Tom got the message and pulled back as well. Soon, the two were about five Daisy-lengths behind Meela. Jake pulled over close to Tom so that their two bikes were nearly touching one another.

"Tom," Jake said, "I've got a bad feeling about this."

"What do you mean?" Tom said.

"You've had to have noticed it, too."

"What?"

"The fact that Meela hasn't exactly been forthcoming about this place where we are headed."

"True, I guess, but maybe its just because we aren't really staying there all that long. I mean, it is just a drop-off point for our extra baggage up there. Zip in quick, dump him off, and then zip back out again, easy as pie."

"What does pie have to do with anything?"

"Nevermind."

"I don't know, Tom. I think she is hiding something from us."

"It's just your imagination, Jake, I'm sure."

"Hmm. Maybe."

"If she was trying to deceive us, why now? Why this? Why *train us,* for that matter?"

"Yeah… I guess."

"Come on, let's catch up before she gets suspicious."

Jake did as he was told, slowly rotating his hand forward causing his bike to pick up speed. As he did so, he noticed a familiar sparkle in the distance in front of them. It was the light of the sun, now getting low in the sky, bouncing off of the surface of a dome. Jake increased his speed even more so that he was now riding alongside Meela.

"Is that it?" Jake asked.

"Yup," Meela said, "we should be there in a few hours."

"Good, I'm exhausted," Tom said, pulling up along the other side of the megacat on which Meela was riding.

Daisy turned to look in Tom's direction as he spoke. Jake couldn't see her face, but he had to bet that the look said something like, "are you kidding me, man?"

When they were close enough to begin seeing what lay on the ground inside this new dome, the sun was beginning its color changing sequence. A few light oranges began to paint the world around them. The first feature of this new world that Jake noticed was the water. He had never seen so much of it! It was hard to tell at his current distance, but he had to guess that a sizable portion of the ground beneath this particular dome was just one gigantic lake. That didn't leave as much livable land for the dome's inhabitants, at least when compared to the other domed worlds they had visited.

If you think Magella *is going to have population problems soon,* Jake thought to himself, *think about* this *place.*

Where there wasn't water, there appeared to be many structures with sharp points, directed straight up into the sky. It reminded Jake of his old Starseeker temple, but in this case there were dozens, maybe even hundreds, of them. Some were tall, others much shorter, but they all had the same basic design. As they got closer, he could see that even the smaller, more modest buildings had at least one spike or a pole of some kind, all pointing directly skyward. As the larger buildings now came into a clearer view, he saw that they not only had a single spike, but many smaller spikes as well, mostly attached to the sides of the structures.

"Meela?" Jake asked, pointing. "What are those?"

"Superstitious nonsense," Meela replied. "Come on, this way."

Meela gave Daisy a slight tug to the right and the cat immediately changed directions. Jake and Tom followed, unsure as to why they were now heading away from the dome looming before them. Jake's only thought was that Meela must have thought of a specific destination and was leading them around to it. One thing was sure, though: whatever *was* going on in Meela's head, she was staying tight-lipped about it with him and Tom.

The group trudged steadily along, the dome beside them now ever-so-slowly rotating to reveal more of what lay inside. The lake Jake had first noticed was growing in size before his eyes. Parts of it even ran up against the side of the dome itself. More of the spikey buildings also appeared in all shapes and sizes. There were a few sections of wooded areas right along the dome's barrier that Jake felt would be perfect for their mission, but on they went, passing the foliage and trees within the dome.

Right about the time Jake was building up his courage to ask Meela just what the hell was going on, Daisy turned to her left and began making straight for the dome's barrier. The area before them didn't seem all that different to Jake than a lot of the other places they had already seen inside this particular dome, although it was near the shore of the lake they had seen. Or was this a different lake? Jake wasn't sure now. There were a few small buildings scattered about the lush, green countryside. Oh, how Jake had missed that color. He never really knew to what extent until he saw it spread so beautifully before him.

It didn't take long to see that they would be entering the dome near a small village, most likely a fishing town. Jake assumed that most of the places in this world were probably fishing towns. A few small boats could be seen along the edge of the lake, either attached to docks, or in some cases, anchored a few dozen meters from shore. The sun was nearly behind the horizon now. Fishing for the day was apparently over.

As they approached the barrier itself, he began to scan the area for any human activity. It was mostly deserted, save for a few individuals far in the distance, walking in and out of a few small shacks. He realized for a moment that those shacks might actually be their homes. It made his apartment back in Magella not seem quite so bad anymore. By the time the sun had set completely, Jake felt that it was dark enough that they were fairly safe to enter and not be noticed by anyone. Those who had been outside of their homes seemed to have turned in for the evening.

Without a word spoken, the group passed into the dome. Jake clenched his teeth when everyone and everything with them (including the hover bikes) glowed a bright blue. If a nosy fisherman had been peeking out of his window at the exact right instant, they might be in big trouble. As soon as they entered, Jake was struck by the smell of grass, trees and even a slight fishy/salty smell that had to be coming from the lake. As they covered more distance from the dome's edge, the blue glow quickly faded. Now, time to get rid of their unwanted companion. He was still snoozing happily. Meela had given him another shot in his right buttock just to be on the safe side about an hour earlier.

"Alright, Meela," Jake said, "where are we putting him?"

"Just a little farther," she said in a whisper.

Jake sighed. Daisy continued to pad across the grassy fields before them, curving along with the lakeshore. There were far fewer trees than Jake would have liked. Meela did her best to steer Daisy near any that happened to appear, but they were spending far too much time out in the open for Jake's taste. They were bordering on certainty that some local would see them. How exactly were they going to explain the megacat and two hover bikes? Not to mention the Omega soldier on Daisy's back?

According to Meela, these people had already encountered the Omega Order before, when they had invaded to look for their dome's device. Based on his own experiences with the Omega Order, Jake had to believe that the current residents would not react positively if they thought those same people had once again entered their home. Why hadn't they just ditched their captive back by the wooded area? A quick entrance and a quick exit, right?

"Meela, what in the Founders' names are you doing?" Jake asked, raising his voice above a whisper. The only response he received was a look of such anger that it would have evoked shrieks of terror from a small child.

As they continued, many of the structures around them began to appear abandoned. Some simply had windows and doors boarded up. Others looked as if they had sustained a significant amount of damage. There were a few that had doors and windows smashed in. More than a few had entire walls missing with rubble strewn all over ground. Further in, the carnage just grew worse. It looked as if a war had been fought here and no one had bothered to clean up the damage. It went on for kilometers. Jake looked at Meela. Her head stayed fixed in the direction they were headed.

There was clearly something else going on here. What had happened here? There was no need to go this far into the dome. Jake wondered what would happen if he just turned his bike around right then and there, making a break for it. Tom would probably follow him, leaving Meela there all alone to deal with the situation she had created for herself. Although he looked back behind him many times,

Jake never did follow through on this idea. His mind kept stubbornly repeating...

Stick to the plan, stick to the plan, stick to the plan...

Yeah, but WHAT plan?

Then, finally, they stopped.

They were sitting in the front yard of a very modest old house. Not as small as some of the fishermen's shacks Jake had seen earlier, although it was difficult to be sure since the entire building had been destroyed. The outer shell was still intact, but the roof was completely gone. Nearly every centimeter of the structure's outer surface was scorched black. A few streaks of the original wood color could be seen, but that was about it. Nearly every window was cracked, broken or completely missing.

Looking through the damaged window frames, even in the darkness of night, Jake could clearly see what remained of the building's interior: ashes. A few shapes indicated what had once been: a table, a few chairs, perhaps even a picture frame or two. The walls inside had been burned to such an extent that large pieces had crumbled away, making it almost possible to see the entire layout of the home, just from looking through the window.

Meela leapt down from Daisy and approached the door, leaving the Omega soldier to just sit there, face planted down into the back of Daisy's neck. The megacat shook her head side-to-side at the annoyance. The Omega soldier, still bound and still very much asleep, slowly slid off of her back and to the side. Thankfully, his fall was cushioned somewhat by a gnarly old bush.

Tom and Jake hardly noticed the man's fall. Both were concentrating on Meela, who was kneeling down by the door, head hanging low. She reached one hand up and pressed it flat against the black wood before her. Her entire body began to shake. Jake hopped off of his bike and approached as she turned back to him, face filled with tears. As soon as she saw Jake coming her way, she sprang back up to her feet and tried to wipe the tears away from her eyes. It didn't work out too well.

"What is this place?" Jake asked.

"I couldn't help myself..." Meela mumbled.

"Huh?" Jake said.

"I know what this is," Jake heard a voice behind him say. He looked and saw Tom, now off of his bike as well, making his way towards them. "This is not just any dome. This is not just any house. This is Meela's home."

Chapter 21

"Children are the Founders' greatest blessing in this world.
The task of every parent is to keep them safe from harm."

-*The Book of the Founders*

"Is Tom right?" Jake asked. "Is this where you grew up?"

Meela didn't say a word but simply nodded, still trying to compose herself. She took a few deep breaths and tried to look out and away from the two men standing in front of her, as if to somehow disconnect herself from the events that were playing out in that moment. She closed her eyes tight. Another single tear pushed its way out from between her eyelids and rolled down and around her cheek, finally coming to rest at the corner of her mouth.

Jake walked partway around the house and stopped. He looked out at the lake that was less than a kilometer away. At that time of day it was completely dark, save for the little bit of light from the brothers Phor and Dor up above that danced upon its waves. A few lights could be seen further down the shoreline from people's homes or perhaps torches set outside. Directly across the lake stood the mighty behemoth, the all-too-familiar clear barrier, arching its way slowly up into the sky. He looked back at Meela.

"This must be the lake in which you found the device, isn't it?"

"Yes, this is it," Meela said, now walking to join Jake for a better view. "I spent months out there on the water during my childhood. I wanted nothing more than to get as far away from this old place as I could."

"What happened here?" Jake asked, looking back at the charred remains that had once been Meela's home.

"What do you think happened?" Meela said.

"The Omega Order," Tom replied.

"They did this?" Jake asked. "But how do you know?"

"Because I saw them do it." Meela said.

"What?" Jake said.

"It was a couple of years ago, not long after they first appeared. This was one of the first domes that they entered. We are not all that far from their dome, you know. They came in here in search of the very device I now hold. Of course at the time, I had no idea that was what they were after, but I knew what they were capable of. By that time I had seen their form of 'diplomacy' with other people and knew what was about to happen.

"They entered this dome in almost the exact same spot in which we just entered it, did you know that? By some twist of fate, they were headed right for my old village. Odd that they knew right where they were going, isn't it? As you know, I found my device in that lake, not too far from here.

"I had watched them for days as they approached the dome from out in the sandy desert. I watched as they set up camp on the eve of their invasion. I watched as they made their advance. I watched as the carnage began. I watched as my people were murdered. I stood by and did nothing. And you know what? I didn't feel the least bit guilty about it. Do you know what I *did* feel? Justified. Satisfied. I was perfectly fine with the events playing out before me. I felt as though they deserved it. And why not? Hadn't they left me to die as well? My own parents were only too willing to sacrifice their little girl for their damned gods.

"I watched with a smug sense of self-satisfaction as they all got what was coming to them. I thought that after they got their payback that I would finally be rid of the hurt... that I could finally have a night when I wasn't waking up every few hours, haunted by their cold, unfeeling faces, ready to watch me die. I thought all of that would go away... but it didn't. Well, at least not in the way I expected. Now, I had new sounds and images to haunt me: that of their screams and horrified expressions as they were cut down, one after another."

The tears came again. Jake wasn't sure what to do. He had very little experience with the opposite sex, let alone under such emotional turmoil. The best he could manage was to very softly rub his hand around in little circles on Meela's back. He half expected her to whip around and break his wrist for being so bold, but she made no attempt to stop him.

"Meela, you have to know that there was nothing you could have done, even if you had tried to intervene," Tom said.

"Maybe," Meela said, "but I didn't even try. Believe me, I've gotten really good at playing the 'what if' game in my mind over all of this. In my heart, I know that I could have done something."

"You'd probably be dead," Tom said.

"Maybe that would be better," Meela said. "It doesn't matter anymore, though. It's over and done with."

"So, why are we here?" Jake asked.

Tom gave Jake a look as if to say, "why the hell did you ask that?"

"This is the first time I've been back here since the massacre," Meela said. "I don't know why I wanted to come, really. I just had to see for myself, up close."

"To see what happened to your family," Tom said.

"I guess I've always known in my heart that they were dead, but somehow I needed to know for sure," Meela said. "And I want you to know that this is indeed the closest dome for the two of you and your journey. When I checked my maps to find a suitable drop-off point for our Omega pal over there, this dome was it. I couldn't believe it when I saw it, but this was it. I even tried to find alternatives to use instead, but they were all much too far away. You two would have been suspicious from the start. I had to accept the fact that I was going to be headed back home.

"While we traveled here, I told myself I wasn't going to do it. I wasn't going to come to this place. I told myself that we would just move in quickly, get rid of him and get out again just as quick as we could. Once we got closer, though, it got harder and harder to not see the ruins up close. By the time I saw the lake again, I knew there was no way I was turning back. I felt somehow drawn here, as if it was my destiny. That probably sounds ridiculous."

"No, not really," Jake said, smiling slightly.

"Look, I know we have a mission to accomplish here, so I will try to be quick, but would it be alright if you two just gave me a few minutes?" Meela asked.

"Of course," Tom said, "take your time Meela."

"Thank you," she said.

As Meela trudged around to the far side of the burned-out house, Jake and Tom stayed put with Daisy and the Omega soldier, still snoozing in the bushes. After an hour or so, Jake was beginning to get restless. He looked over at Tom, who was now actually asleep as well. Daisy also appeared to be resting comfortably. He rose from his sitting position, and began to make his way around the house the same way that Meela had traveled, careful not to make too much noise and disrupt either Meela or their sleeping companions.

Jake found that he didn't have to travel far when he came upon Meela. She was in what remained of the backyard of the house. Much of the plant life in the backyard was as scorched as the house itself. Through the grass great long strips of black pointed their way out away from the house and towards the lake beyond. Meela was bent down with her knees in the black dirt, crouched in front of a handful of small stone slabs sticking out of the ground. The light from the twins Phor and Dor illuminated the top of each slab and pulled a thin shadow away from Meela, in Jake's direction.

Jake heard Meela whisper two words: "I'm sorry."

When it had become clear that he had overstayed his welcome, Jake turned to leave. As he did so, he saw Meela rise to her feet in the corner of his eye. Damn, too late. She had most likely seen him. He turned back.

"Hey there," Meela said.

"I'm sorry," Jake said, "I'll go."

"No, no, it's alright."

Jake approached her, feeling a bit embarrassed now. As he did so, he saw that there was lettering etched into the stone slabs. It was hard to make out, but it appeared to be names, one for each piece of stone. There were four in total... one for each parent and one for each sister. At least now she knew.

"One of the survivors from the village must have buried them here," Meela said, still staring down at the stone markers as Jake got close. "I just wish I knew exactly what happened. Did they fight back? Did they surrender and get killed anyway?"

"If you really wanted, I suppose you could ask someone around here," Jake said, stepping behind Meela to get a better look.

"No, they'd recognize me for sure. I may be a lot older now, but I'm willing to bet that they'd be able make out the face of Gilea and

Rand's daughter in a second. And then they'd have all kinds of questions. Questions I don't want to answer."

"I suppose you're right," Jake said. "What if-"

Jake saw that Meela had turned around to face him now, her hand covering his mouth. Her eyes locked on his, then quickly darted down to the ground. She paused a moment, then they tentatively glanced back up. Without a word spoken, she turned back to face the lake and pulled him in close behind her. She wrapped his arms around her waist. Her head fell to the side, resting against his upper arm. Jake didn't say anything, allowing Meela to pull their embrace in even tighter. There they stood for several minutes, feeling one another's heartbeats, one another's inhales and exhales. The twin's light continued to sparkle on the surface of the great lake before them. Jake let their light dance in his eyes, letting the warmth of the woman in his arms fill him up.

Meela then slowly turned to face Jake once again, keeping his arms tight about her waist as she did so. She bent her head back slightly to look up into his eyes. Her hands found the sides of his face and brought it down to meet hers. Their lips touched, lightly at first, and then with increasing pressure. Jake closed his eyes. He felt as if his heart might explode, it was beating so quickly. The softness and wetness of Meela's lips on his was intoxicating. When their lips finally separated, he wanted nothing more than for them to touch again, even if only for a moment.

Both Meela and Jake slowly opened their eyes. Neither said a word to one another. Neither needed to. Meela tucked her head into Jake's chest and brought him in closer. He held her for several more minutes, now gently rubbing her back, more confidently this time, slowly up and down, up and down. He lowered his head down to the top of her head. He could smell her hair. It smelled of dirt and sweat. It was the sweetest smell of his life.

Meela and Jake lingered a little longer, gazing out at the lake before rejoining Tom, Daisy and their Omega prisoner back by the front of the house. All three were still fast asleep. Jake kicked Tom in the foot to wake him. It took a couple of tries before Tom's eyes finally opened. He groggily got to his feet and eyed Jake and Meela.

"Ready to go?" Tom asked, his eyes blinking wide several times. Stretching his arms, he let out a none-too-subtle yawn.

"Yes, we're ready," Meela said.

"Good," Tom said, "I was worried that I was going to fall asleep for a second there."

"So, what should we do with him?" Jake asked, kicking again. This time it was the man in the bushes.

"Should we just leave him here?" Tom asked. "Let him wake up with a mouthful of prickers?"

"Works for me," Jake said.

"If it is all the same to you two," Meela said, "I'd rather not leave him at this particular address."

"Ah, gotcha," Tom said.

"We can drop him off a little further down the road on our way out," Meela said. "Shouldn't be a problem."

"Works for me," Jake said, as he grabbed the Omega soldier's left arm and began dragging him out from the bush, pulling out all manner of sticks and tiny leaves along with him.

Soon, they were ready to get moving once more. Daisy hadn't been particularly happy upon being awoken from her catnap, but within a matter of seconds it was as if she had never been asleep in the first place. Cats were funny creatures that way. The team loaded her up with much of their gear, as well as the Omega soldier, hopefully for the last time. Tom and Jake turned on their hover bikes, but stayed off of them, content to float them across the ground in an effort to reduce the amount of noise the group made. Meela walked along side Daisy, only to make sure the cat's Omega rider didn't fall off.

As the group slowly made their way farther and farther away from Meela's destroyed childhood home, Jake couldn't help but look back several times. He wondered to himself what life must have been like for her, all those years ago. He wondered how a pair of supposedly loving parents could willingly condemn their daughter to death. What must have driven them to make that decision?

Their faith, that's what.

Jake had to stop himself for a moment. Where had that come from? Was it right, though? Was that what blind faith reduced people to? Would he do the same if his faith required it? No, surely not. He couldn't murder someone, no matter what the justification. But, was that only because his particular brand of faith condemned murder as wrong? What if it didn't? Was he really just another... what had Meela called it... pawn? He had to believe that the answer was no, but wasn't that what this whole quest was about? Wasn't he blindly following what the Overseer had told him to do? Was paradise really out there, or was he just being *used* for a more nefarious outcome?

"Stop it, Jake!" Jake said to himself, soft enough that he was sure not even Tom had heard him. He looked up and noticed that Daisy had stopped. Good, perhaps they were finally ready to be rid of the Omega soldier once and for all.

"We have a problem," Meela said.

Or not.

"What is it?" Tom asked.

"Look!" Meela said, and pointed straight down the road, towards their exit point from the dome.

At first, Jake saw nothing, just the dirt path they were on, surrounded by a few groupings of trees. But as his eyes traced back and forth, they caught what Meela was getting at. Right along the base of the dome he saw a handful of tiny objects, each glowing light blue. They started out quite faint, then grew in intensity, and then once again fading away to nothing. Jake counted as each one lit up. There had to be over twenty of them. Even though this dome had supposedly been left by them almost two years ago, here they were and coming right for Jake and his friends.

The Omega Order had found them.

Chapter 22

"Force is the swiftest form of justice."

-The Book of the Founders

"**G**et off the road!" Meela hissed, already pushing Daisy off the side, down an embankment and into some light brush. As she did so, the unconscious captive unceremoniously fell off once more and rolled down the embankment, coming to rest in yet another bush. They made no attempt whatsoever to help him. Given their current circumstances, that bush was as good a place as any to leave him. He was no longer their problem. They had all kinds of new ones now.

"How the hell did *they* get here?" Tom said as he scrambled to join Meela.

"Did they follow us?" Jake asked, last to meet up with the group.

"We were here quite a while," Tom said. "It seems strange that they would wait this long."

"They didn't follow us," Meela said. "I would have seen them."

"Maybe you missed-" Jake started.

"I would have *seen* them," Meela repeated.

"Then what?" Tom asked.

All eyes turned to the Omega soldier, laying with an arm and part of a leg enveloped in a small piece of shrubbery.

"Don't you see?" Meela said. "He *wanted* to get captured! It was his plan all along! He must have had some sort of tracking device!"

"Tracking device?" Jake asked.

"It's a locator tool," Tom said. "You place it on an individual and then another piece of equipment can be used by someone else to find that locator."

"How in the Founders' names did you know *that?*" Jake asked.

"I think I heard Meela talking about them the other day." Tom said.

Meela gave a dubious look at that comment.

"Whatever," Tom said. "Listen, we need to do something and fast. It is time to think outside of the box here, people."

"Box? What box?" Jake said. "Tom, you are really starting to weird me out."

"It just means we need to come up with a new idea!" Tom snapped, clearly frustrated.

"Well if you are right about that tracking device, then we need to get as far away from this guy as possible," Jake said, gesturing to the limb-infested bush next to them.

"He led them all straight to us," Tom said.

"Yeah, well not anymore," Meela said. "Get on your bikes. My new idea is to make a break for it- NOW."

With that, Meela climbed aboard Daisy. The megacat seemed MUCH happier with the switch in riders, contorting her head around to rub the side of her face against Meela's leg. Daisy's tail then shot straight up and she hopped forward, ready to move. Jake and Tom took the hint and had to scramble to get up onto their hover bikes. By the time they were ready to hit their respective accelerators, Daisy had already taken off, bounding through the tall grass in front of them.

Tom looked down at the Omega soldier, lying on the ground. "Gonna miss you, pal," he said.

"No, you're not," Jake said.

"No, I'm not," Tom agreed, laughing.

The two men revved up their bikes and were soon off, trying desperately to keep up with Meela and her feline companion. As they moved, Jake looked back to where they had seen the Omega Order soldiers enter the dome. It was still dark out, so it was difficult to make out much of anything. He thought that perhaps he saw some movement coming closer. He just hoped that he, Meela and Tom were still far enough away not to catch the attention of the invading Omega group. The sun would begin to rise in less than an hour, and Jake hoped that in that time, they would be far enough away not to be noticed.

He was wrong.

Only a few minutes later, the all-too-familiar blue bolts of energy flew in their direction. They missed wildly, but it was enough to confirm Jake's fears: they had been spotted. As the first few rays of the morning sun began to spill out from the horizon, Jake was able to get a better view of their attackers. Some were on foot, but many others were riding bikes identical to his. There was even a much larger vessel that he could now see, rumbling along behind the rest. Floating about a meter above the ground and slowly making its way forward like some overgrown elephant, it was big enough to hold perhaps a dozen or more men. Jake prayed to the Founders that that wasn't the case.

As the trio of humans and their megacat continued to move, it became apparent that they were losing ground. Jake hated to admit it, but it was because of Daisy. She was a fast cat for sure, but Jake knew full well that the hover bikes could go much faster than her for a much longer period of time. It wasn't her fault. She was running just as fast as her massive black legs could move her. He knew what they needed to do but he didn't like it. He pulled his hover bike up along

side of Meela and signaled her to stop. The look on her face told him
he was crazy, but she did as requested.

"Look," Jake said, "we can't outrun them. We need another plan."

"We need to split up," Tom said.

"No!" Meela shouted. "We stick together!"

"No, Meela," Jake said, "Tom's right. He and I can cover more
ground than you. Perhaps we can pull most of them off of your trail."

"Eh, fine," Meela said, begrudgingly.

"Ok, Jake," Tom said, "I'll follow you."

"No," Jake replied, "we're splitting up too."

By this point, Meela and Daisy had already left, heading towards
the great lake.

Smart, Jake thought to himself, *you are the swimmer in the group, Meela.*

"Jake, we can't!" Tom protested.

"Tom, we don't have time for this!" Jake said. "You know as well
as I do that we will have greater success if we split them up. Greater
numbers equals greater danger, remember? I'll keep going the same
direction we have been up until now. You just find somewhere else to
go. Hopefully we can keep most of them away from Meela and Daisy.
Now get going!"

Tom did as he was told, but frowned while doing so. He turned
his bike towards the interior of the dome and took off. Within seconds he was gone; all that remained was a small trail of light grey
smoke. Jake thought about his next move. The edge of the dome was
a few kilometers away yet, but if he moved quickly, he might be able
to get there before the Omega troops did.

As he sped towards the barrier and the barren outside world beyond it, Jake looked back to see how the group of Omega troops were
reacting to the new situation. As expected, several of them where
beginning to splinter off in various directions. The bloated hovering
contraption stayed put, unmoving, as if attempting to establish some

kind of base camp. It looked like about six of them were following Jake, each on his own hover bike. It was difficult for Jake to tell how many had followed Tom or Meela, with the distance growing between him and them so rapidly. It did look like some members of the group had indeed elected to stay back with the larger ship, though. That made Jake feel better. Not much, but a little.

The edge of the dome was getting close now. Within a few seconds he would be back outside of it again. There was a chance (though not a good one) that nobody in his group of pursuers had a device with them to get through the great barrier. It was worth a shot at least. Jake surveyed the landscape outside. It was actually quite uneven. Good. There would be plenty of places in which to hide. He was about to find out just how good he really was at driving one of these contraptions.

Jake shot through the dome's barrier and immediately looked behind him. The six other bikes were much closer now. The driver in front even took a few shots at him as they approached. The blasts of blue energy bounced harmlessly off of the dome's interior surface. So, the blasts from those weapons couldn't penetrate the dome even if humans and other objects still could. He felt a tiny bit of relief at this revelation. All the same, he continued to push the accelerator forward as far as it would go. The first four bikes in the train of pursuers made it through with no difficulty, but the same could not be said for the last two.

The impacts were so quick in succession that it looked more like only one had occurred. The explosion (or explosions, though it was impossible to tell the difference) was enormous. Flames spread out in all directions along the inside shell of the dome, blooming like some fiery flower. Within seconds, the flames had retreated back and all that was left were two small, charred clumps laying on the ground, billowing smoke up into the sky within the clear wall.

Perfect, so no device of your own, eh? Jake said to himself. *You just made my job a lot easier, fellas.*

Jake continued to move on his ride, now arcing to the left to head towards a much more rocky and uneven portion of the reddish terrain. The four remaining bikes followed, now all of them firing in his direction. Most of the shots missed, but one grazed his arm. He gritted his teeth in pain, but did not shout out. He figured it was high time he returned the favor. He removed his laser weapon from its holster and fired back, over his shoulder. The shot landed nowhere near their targets, but at least it had caused the others to stop firing momentarily.

His bike dipped down as it entered the rocky area, and he began to zig and zag, side to side, trying his best to throw large rock formations in front of his pursuers at the last possible instant. It didn't seem as though they were falling for it. A few more shots were fired and Jake found himself having to cover his head as a cascade of debris fell on top of him. The showering of rocks was large enough to be painful, but small enough not to disrupt his bike's trajectory. But, his plan wasn't working out too well. If anything, the four men behind him were even closer now than they had been before.

"Time to think outside of the box!" Jake said, remembering his friend's words from earlier.

Jake spied a rather large rock formation directly ahead. He twisted the accelerator forward as far as it would go. His bike leapt forward with such a jolt that he nearly fell off of it. The lead bike behind him matched his speed almost instantly.

Perfect, stay right there, buddy.

As the rock formation grew in size, he checked behind him once more. The other bike was nearly on him now. More shots were fired.

One grazed his bike's controls but did no serious damage. He looked forward again. Almost there...

Seconds later, his bike made impact with the side of the rock wall, but he was no longer aboard. The instant before it had made contact, he had pulled his feet up onto the seat and pushed off as hard as his legs could handle. The next instant, his feet found purchase on the top of the rock formation. It was nearly the same moment when the second bike had impacted the wall. Its rider, however, had not been as forward-thinking as Jake.

Yet another gigantic fireball erupted. Jake quickly bent down and was able to partially shield himself from the blast. The heat was overwhelming, but it quickly dissipated. He ventured a quick peek down below. Two hover bikes had clearly been destroyed, their black carcasses littering the ground in all directions. Smoke was billowing up so quickly and so violently that he had to look away as it was already beginning to irritate his eyes.

If he had continued looking for a mere second more, he might have been able to see the secondary impact as it happened, although he heard and felt in through the rocky ground. There was a distinctive *CHINK* sound and then he saw another one of the hover bikes, spinning out of control, out beyond the base of his rocky perch. The bike had a sizable piece of metal flapping along behind it, attached only by wire or perhaps the fuel line.

The bike eventually plowed itself into the ground, throwing its driver far, far into the air. The driver's impact with the ground was head-first. Jake looked for a long while and saw no movement from the man lying there in a very unnatural position, looking an awful lot like an ostrich checking its nest. The bike itself had tumbled end-over-end a couple of times and then was laid to rest on the ground, now covered with red sand. No explosion this time.

While Jake was amazed that his desperate trick had worked and four enemies had now been reduced to two, the realization that he no longer had a ride slowly began to sink in. He hadn't exactly thought this far ahead.

Great, what are you going to do now? he asked himself.

Before he had too much time to think about the answer to that thought, the small plot of land on which he was crouched began exploding all around him.

"Dammit! Dammit! Dammit!" Jake swore as he pointed his own weapon over the edge and began firing indiscriminately.

As expected, the other shots stopped, if for only a brief moment. He ventured a quick look. One of the bikes was stopped, its rider standing beside it and crouching down low, looking for a moment to take another shot in Jake's direction. He didn't see the second one right away, but then he caught it in his peripheral vision. This one was a little ways away, circling around, most likely preparing to take a second run at Jake's position.

He had to be quick.

Jake trained the sights of his laser weapon on the stationary attacker, his bike partially concealing him with only his shoulders and head visible.

Steady, Jake said to himself. *Remember what Meela said, just breathe out and squeeze that trigger, nice and easy.*

Jake squeezed…

…and missed.

His shot hit part of the bike in front of the soldier, creating a small burst of sparks and smoke, but the man himself was unharmed. Multiple shots came right back at Jake, forcing him to duck down once again. A red cloud of dust filled his vision and filled his mouth, causing him to cough repeatedly. Once the cloud cleared somewhat, he noticed that part of his perch was now missing. One of his legs had been left dangling over the edge, but he tucked it in as quickly as possible. He now had barely enough room to keep both feet planted on the ground. Keeping his head covered and trying to look the opposite direction from the man firing at him, he noticed another soldier riding a hover bike, still a ways away, but speeding towards him.

In the few seconds that followed, Jake made a decision. It was probably a stupid one, but he was getting desperate. Any moment now he was going to be blasted to bits. He reached into his pocket and found the device. Without even looking down, he wedged it carefully between two rocks that made up the top of the structure on which he was perched. He looked back down at the soldier approaching him. He was much closer now.

He had to time this just right.

Jake, you idiot, you're not going to make this jump.

Jake snarled at himself for even thinking such things

Shut up, you, of course I am.

The man on the bike was really moving now, his weapon up and ready to fire. Jake counted silently in his head as the bike got closer and closer.

Ten...

Nine...

Eight...

Seven...

Six...

Suddenly, a blue beam shot out from the rider's weapon, missing Jake's head by less than a couple centimeters. The second shot impacted just below his feet, causing the rest of the ground beneath him to give way.

FiveFourThreeTwoOne!

As the rocks fell, he not only leapt down, but also out, away from the rocky structure as best he could. He found his target, alright, but not quite in the manner in which he had planned.

Jake landed directly on the head of the bike's operator, ass-first. The pain he felt in his crotch was excruciating. Distracted somewhat by the bombs going off between his legs, it took him a moment to realize that he was sliding down behind the man on the bike. He grabbed out for anything that his hand might be able to find and ended up getting a tenuous grip on the edge of the bike's seat. His feet were dangling down onto the ground now, kicking up red dust all around them as the bike continued to move forward.

The bike started to pull down and to the left, from the added weight of Jake's body hanging precariously from its side. Trying desperately not to let go, he reached up with his free hand and grabbed the Omega soldier (still seated with his hands on the controls, but clearly dazed) by the belt. As Jake attempted to pull himself up, the man started to fall to his side, the bike listing to the left even more.

Eventually, Jake had gathered enough strength to pull himself up so that he was seated behind the bike's driver, who had avoided toppling off of the thing completely. The timing couldn't have been better, as Jake noticed a small bump in the road streak by that clearly would have smashed his kneecaps into tiny little pieces. Now up where he could get a better view of things, he saw that his other attacker, the one that had been crouched behind his parked bike, was right in their flight path, standing straight ahead, mouth agape.

There wasn't much the poor man could do. The bike that carried Jake and the still half-conscious Omega soldier smashed right into his chest. As the wildly changing trajectory of the hover bike advanced on, Jake felt a spray of warm liquid slap his face. What was left behind the bike, however, no longer resembled much of a man. The ground and the bike he had been standing next to only moments before were now painted red. Not the orangish-red of the surrounding dusty landscape, but a deep, dark, gruesome red.

As soon as he had seen what had happened, Jake had to look away. His stomach began to turn over and ache terribly. It almost felt worse than his boys down below, who were still on the slow march to recovery. His last meal threatened to make its way onto the man seated in front of him, but it only progressed as far as the back of his throat. Not that he would have cared too much if he had barfed all over the fellow. He was now the only one remaining.

The driver had now come back to reality. The hand reaching back for Jake's throat told him that much. Jake twisted around, trying to avoid the clamping jabs of the black-gloved hand. He put in a few punches to the man's back, but he had to be careful. The last thing he wanted was for the man to get knocked out again, or fall off the bike for that matter. Just a few more meters and they would be there.

Two things happened simultaneously that told Jake they had reached their arrival point. First, the driver's hands stopped reaching back for Jake's neck. Instead, they were now reaching for their own. Second, Jake could feel his skin begin to prickle. It was subtle at first, but soon it was as if a thousand knives were being thrust through every last millimeter of his body. The instant he had felt the affects taking place, Jake had taken a quick, deep breath. Now he was slowly exhaling, letting only tiny amounts of air back out at a time. He only had a few moments at best if this was going to work.

He could see the veins begin to pop out along the back of the neck of the Omega soldier. The skin began to turn a light orange, then red, then purple. Jake assumed the same was happening to him (perhaps at a slightly slower pace), but he dared not look to see. Stars slowly began to appear in his vision as the bike the two men were riding began heading down into the ground. Quickly, he reached forward and grabbed the controls, trying as best as he could from his position to pull the bike back up. As he did so, he yanked the controls to the left, hard. The Omega soldier in front of him, now completely oblivious to anything other than the fact that he could no longer breathe, fell easily off the bike, tumbling a couple of times when he hit the ground.

The stars were brighter now, nearly filling Jake's vision completely. In one wild instant, he thought perhaps the Founders were invading his living body, flying down from their heavenly homes and whisking him away to the afterlife. His ears began to ring loudly. Was that the sound of the Founders' holy song, proclaiming their glory as they brought another of their beloved creations home?

No! Jake said to himself. *You are not dead yet. Concentrate! You can do this!*

With what tiny amount of strength was left inside of him, he pulled hard on his arm, sliding his body forward little by little into the seat of the hover bike. All the while he had to make sure it was kept upright and continued to turn to the left. Finally, after what seemed like hours had passed (which in his heart he knew had only been a few dozen seconds at most), he had the bike facing back in the direction from which it had come. He hit the accelerator.

About an hour later, when Jake had had enough time to suck in the rich, beautiful oxygen-filled air all around him, he attempted to stand. He had been lying on the ground, limbs outstretched in all directions, hover bike still on and hovering dutifully right beside him. He looked up to the top of the rock formation on which he had originally been hiding. He took a few additional deep breaths (oooh, that felt good!) and jumped back up to the top. The landing was a little bit harder to stick this time with the additional rubble, but he found his balance quick enough. He glanced around the tiny area, far up above the red, dusty ground below. He had been a little concerned when much of the structure had been blasted to pieces by enemy laser fire, but luck had been with him. It didn't take him long to find it.

There was Jake's device, the Overseer's compass, the hope for all mankind, still lodged innocently between two large, flat rocks.

Chapter 23

"Compassion is the most righteous form of justice."

-The Book of the Founders

With the compass now safely stored back in his pants pocket, Jake knew that his next move was to locate Meela and Tom. If the Founders were with them, perhaps they were both safe and sound as well. Jake thought about that statement for a moment. He supposed he was safe, for now, but sound? Maybe not. His lungs still burned every time he took a breath. He had to believe that eventually the feeling would go away, but he also had to accept the possibility that his little stunt may have caused irreparable damage to his body. Had it been worth it? He was still alive, so logic told him yes, but he couldn't help wondering if there couldn't have been a better way.

Now with his feet back on solid ground, Jake found the hover bike, still hanging there like a dog ready to take a run with his master, almost eager. He hopped aboard and pointed it back towards the area of the dome where his friends had parted. He didn't have much else to go on. Hopefully he would pick up on somebody's trail and not get ambushed by half a dozen Omega troops in the process. As he started his journey back, he passed by both the burned up wreckage of a hover bike and its owner as well as the bloodied remains of the bowled over soldier who had been nearly turned inside-out when nailed by the high speed bike. As before, he had to look away; he couldn't bear to see up close what kind of carnage he had caused.

When he was farther out, he came upon a body that he *did* want to look at more closely. He couldn't quite explain why he had to stop and peer at the man laying on the ground, hands still clutched around his puffy neck, but he did. He knew full well that his friends may need his help and that it would only upset him, but he stopped, regardless.

Just a quick look, he told himself.

The body was still in its complete Omega Order body suit, save for the helmet. That had come off long before the man had asphyxiated, probably in the thrashings and contortions in the final seconds of his life. Jake wondered what must have been going through the man's mind in those last few moments. He wondered if it really had to have ended with his death.

It was kill or be killed.

The idea was logical enough. Still, it didn't sit well in the back of Jake's mind. The whole purpose for coming out here with Meela had been because he was unwilling to kill another human being. Now six were dead because of him in only a matter of minutes. Some had been blown to bits, one had his insides sprayed all over the ground and this one... this one may have been the worst of them all.

Jake looked at the man's face. A look of confusion and anger was now forever painted there. It looked as if his entire head had ballooned out, causing his skin to crack and peel under the pressure. Tiny little rivers of red worked their way across his forehead, cheeks and neck. The skin tone was still purple, but perhaps less deep in color now. His eyes were the worst part, though, bulging out of their sockets like a pair of small cucumbers, as if they were trying to escape his skull.

I had no choice. It was them or me.

Meela had warned Jake that this is what life would be like out here, outside of the domes. There was no protection, no safety net. If you wanted to survive, you needed to be willing to make the hard choices. Perhaps she had been right. If they had just shot the Omega soldier they had captured, would that have been the only fatality? In the end, would that have been better? It certainly would have been easier. No, he had to stop this train of thought dead in its tracks. He had remembered what he had told Meela, down in her cave of a home only a few days ago:

We don't kill. That is what makes us different from them.

Maybe he had to clarify that statement now. Perhaps it should be "we don't kill unless we have to." Jake had to assume there would be times when he would "have to" yet to come. Some might even happen in the next few minutes. Was the Overseer's mission worth the deaths of all of these people, even if they were willing to kill Jake themselves? He was on a mission to save lives... millions of lives, if the Overseer was to be believed. What were a few murderous thugs when compared with those millions? The math was simple. The ugliness he felt deep inside was far more complex.

Climbing back onto his hover bike and speeding away, he left the body behind him. He didn't look back.

As he approached the dome's great barrier, he happened to see something out of the corner of his eye that could only be associated with the Omega Order. There were two people standing in the distance, so far away that they looked almost like ants. They were outside of the dome, their dark shapes contrasting starkly with the light red backdrop behind them. It was clear they were in possession of their own device, otherwise how could they be surviving on the outside of the barrier? He whipped the controls of his bike sharply to the right and found himself riding along the edge of the dome, which was racing past him only a meter or two to his left. The ants in front of him slowly began to morph into humanoids.

Jake had an idea. He turned his bike's controls so that he slowly began to drift to the left. As expected, his body began to glow blue as it got closer to the dome's surface. Soon, he made contact with it. Of course, "contact" wasn't exactly the right word because he really didn't feel the dome as he entered, unless you counted the slightly fuzzy sensation in his belly. For a surreal moment, Jake noticed that he was flying within the thick, clear structure itself. To his right were reds, greys and oranges. To his left were greens, blues and browns. It was striking just how different the two worlds were to one another, especially when presented in this strange profile presentation.

Soon, Jake pulled further to the left and was wholly and completely inside of the dome's protection once more. He eyed his targets. As expected, when he was close to being detected, the two Omega soldiers fired in his direction. Their shots could very easily have hit Jake, if it weren't for the dome's surface that was now between him and them. He smiled.

I'm beating you at your own game, fellas.

Only a few seconds later, a couple of shots of blue energy flew past his head. Jake jolted the bike to the side in his surprise. He had to quickly compensate to avoid crashing into a small stump jutting out from the ground.

"What the hell?" Jake heard himself say.

Was there someone else inside the dome now, flanking him from the side? No, the shots had come from in front of him. Jake looked directly ahead. The two men he had seen earlier had simply run a few dozen steps so that they were now inside the dome, just like him. They fired again. This time, Jake turned the controls just in time for him to exit the dome and enter the world outside once more. The shots bounced off of the interior dome wall. As before, his stomach twitched and tingled. He wondered how many more times he would have to do this and if his body was up for it. In the end, though, he figured that if he could survive near asphyxiation, a few stomach fuzzies shouldn't be too much of an issue.

Jake was getting very close now and in moments he would be upon them. The two Omega soldiers looked as if they were staying put for the moment, not attempting to run back outside. Jake pulled his weapon from its holster and set it up on top of the bike's controls with his right hand, now steering with only his left. The two soldiers had their weapons out as well. He could clearly see the ends of the weapons, pointing directly at him.

Remember what Meela said. Take some deep breaths, and just squeeze.

Jake ran so close to the dome's edge that he began the familiar color-changing sequence. When he was only a few meters away from the two men, he jerked the controls to the left hard, but only for an instant. He was still outside. The weapons of both men went off, hitting the dome's interior and bouncing away harmlessly. Then, just as he saw the two men pass to his left, he pulled the controls hard to the left once more, this time holding them there. His bike swooped back inside, turning sharply as it did so.

As it passed through the mysterious clear shield, his bike was already facing nearly the exact opposite direction that he had just been heading... and there were his two targets: standing right in front of him, still facing the other way. One of the two men began to turn, albeit slowly. He squeezed off four shots. Every single one found its mark, two for each man. Both men collapsed to the ground instantly. He pulled his bike to a halt and checked his weapon's setting.

SUBDUE.

Not unless we have to, he repeated to himself.

He got down from the bike's seat and approached the two bodies on the ground. They were obviously in possession of another device and it would be silly to leave without taking it. It was like some sort of weird game where they were keeping score by who had the larger number of these strange, metallic discs. The Omega Order was still clearly winning, but the home team was closing the gap.

He quickly found the all-too-familiar pouch on the first body. It was empty. He checked the second man's pouch. There were black burn marks all over it. One section right in the center of its circular shape looked as if it had been burned away. He opened what was left of the pouch and produced the device from inside. It, too, was scorched with streaks of black, but not nearly as bad as its carrying case. That wasn't the worst of it, though. Almost in the exact center of the disc's flat side was a small hole, big enough to insert one's thumb up to the first knuckle.

So, I guess these things aren't quite as indestructible as we first thought, at least as far as these laser weapons are concerned, Jake thought to himself, filing the data away for future reference.

Jake reminded himself to tell Meela and Tom about this when he had a chance. An accidental shot to their prized compass and their merry little adventure would be over. The thought of his two friends got his mind back to the more immediate task at hand: he needed to find them as soon as possible, and hopefully still alive. He pocketed the damaged device and hopped back aboard his bike.

With nowhere else to go, he made for the great lake, which was now only a kilometer away. Meela had been heading in that direction when they had split up. Perhaps if he were lucky, she and even Daisy would still be there, or at least somewhere close by. Still staying near the dome's surface, Jake made for the shoreline. One never knew if that hover bike trick he had just pulled off might be needed again in the future.

On his way, Jake saw for the first time the indigenous residents of the world they had entered. A lot of them peered out of windows or stood in doorframes, ready to take cover if the action ever got too close to home. Some looked upset. Most looked scared. For many, it appeared as though they had just awoken and had stumbled outside to see what the commotion was. They were still dressed in their nightclothes, which covered only the most private of areas for both the men and women. Not much else was needed on a morning that was already quite hot, he noticed.

It had been daytime now for a few hours and anyone who lived in this particular area of Coustea had most likely witnessed some of the violence that had taken place that morning. He wondered just how well the people here had recognized the members of the Omega Order that were now back, although for a different purpose. He wondered if he might be mistaken for an Omega himself. As far as these people knew, the Omegas were the only ones who were able to enter the dome from the outside world.

Well, there were also the Demockadles, of course.

In a moment of shock, Jake realized that the Omega Order had essentially proven these people's beliefs to be true. How else would one describe them? To the people of Coustea there probably was no difference between the Omega Order and demons. The Omega Order had forced their way in, killing and destroying whatever got in their way, and then when their efforts to find a device had been unsuccessful, they had left without so much as a goodbye.

In fact, Jake had to assume that the carnage in this particular world had been especially devastating, given the fact that the Omega Order never did find what they were looking for. How much destruction had been enough until they had finally given up? It had to have been more than just Meela's village. How long had it lasted? At any point, Meela could have told them the truth and saved quite a few lives. It would have meant her own death for sure, but still…

There was more here than a few family members for Meela to feel guilty for, Jake realized, there was an entire civilization.

When he made it to the lakeshore and dismounted his bike, there wasn't much to see. All of the boats remained anchored or docked. Not a good day for fishing today, apparently. There wasn't any movement whatsoever as far as he could tell, other than the gentle lapping of the waves near his feet. The skies were eerily calm, too. It looked as if even the birds had decided to take a day off. But the local people he had passed on his way here? They had been frightened. They had seen *something*, right? It couldn't have just been his little adventures, which were now several kilometers behind him. No, they had seen enough to make them fearful for their lives and it had happened close by.

"Stop right there!"

Damn, too little too late.

Jake turned around to find the source of the voice. As he had expected, it was a person clad in the all-too-familiar Omega Order get-up, complete with the white upside-down "U" on the shoulder. A weapon was pointed directly at his head. He could tell from here that it was set to KILL. They were always set to KILL.

"Now, slowly place your weapon on the ground."

Jake did as he was told.

"Good. Now, it is time to give me the compass. Don't mess with me, boy. I know who you are. If I have to I will just kill you and take it myself. For some reason the Chancellor wants you alive, so if possible, I'd like to avoid that unpleasantness. But don't test me. Our primary mission is that compass and that supersedes all other commands, including keeping you alive."

Jake had never hoped to see his friends more than he had in that moment.

Just then, he heard a rustling of leaves to his right. He wasn't sure but he thought that perhaps he heard some kind of rumble, too? It reminded him of when he and Tom had been near starving and their stomachs were pleading with them for food. He looked to his right, trying to find the source of the sound but there was nothing. Either whatever had made the sound was now gone or his exhausted brain was once again playing tricks on him.

Right as he was about to turn his attention back to the Omega soldier before him, he happened to spy an eyeball, hanging there amongst a number of large bushes with long green leaves. Its shape was not of a human, its pupil a thin, black strip, bulging slightly towards the middle. The strip swam in a sea of bright yellow, which was now slowly getting smaller.

Another rumble.

Everything after that happened in a blur. One second there was a large, long-leafed bush sitting nonchalantly next to them. The next, a megacat was pouncing forth, jaws opened wide. Jake ducked instinctively, but he was never in any real danger. The black cat's jaws flew over top of him and found the shoulder of the man standing behind him. The man was knocked to the ground, but managed to get his blood-soaked shoulder free from the beast's grip. He staggered to his feet, but was knocked back down again.

A few seconds later, it was all over.

Jake heard another rustle of leaves and soon saw a familiar face appear.

"Meela!" he said.

"Hey, there," Meela said with a slight grin on her face.

Without really thinking too much about what he was doing, Jake grabbed Meela by the back of the head and brought her in for a quick kiss. She seemed to protest slightly at first, but soon gave in and even kissed back. When the two of them parted, Meela had a slightly concerned look on her face. He felt an immediate pang of guilt. Perhaps this wasn't the time or place for public displays of affection. It wasn't as if he had had a whole lot of experience in that area.

"Jake," Meela said, placing one hand on his shoulder and looking straight into his eyes, "we need to get moving. I know where Tom is."

"Where?" Jake asked.

"The Omega Order," Meela replied. "They have him."

Chapter 24

"Value the time you have with your loved ones, for you will never know how much of that time still remains."

-*The Book of the Founders*

Jake did his best to keep Meela in view and not fall too far behind as he piloted his hover bike. It was difficult to navigate through the extremely tall grass that lay beyond the lake. Meela was once again on Daisy's back directing the creature towards their destination. That destination was both their hope and their despair. Hope that they might be able to rescue their friend. Despair that he might already be dead. Or worse, that not only was he already dead, but they were flying right into a trap.

About fifteen minutes later, Jake spied the same large ship he, Meela and Tom had noticed earlier, when the Omega Order troops had first entered the dome. From this distance it was no bigger than his fist, but it was no less ominous. Its bulging brownish-orange shape contrasted sharply with the greenery all around it. It looked like a pregnant, foul creature ready to give birth to Founders only knew what. He could see three other Omega soldiers milling about outside of it. Was that all that was left? Perhaps some were also hiding inside that puke-colored monstrosity. He saw no sign of Tom.

Meela and Daisy slowed to a trot and then stopped completely just as they were about to hit a tree line that was only a few meters away from the remaining Omega soldiers. Jake stopped his hover bike and switched it off, hoping he was far enough away that nobody had heard him. From what he could see of the Omega soldiers through the overlapping greenery, they hadn't. Or at least they were pretending as if they hadn't.

Jake tip-toed his way up to where Meela and Daisy were hiding. Every brush with forest life that he made seemed to make some kind of noise. He cringed, admonishing himself for any potential danger he might put them into due to his less than stealthy trek through the forest. When he came upon Meela and Daisy, both were crouched down low, eyeing the scene. He did the same. Meela said nothing, but tapped him on the shoulder and pointed straight ahead. He had to move to the side slightly to get a better view. There were the three Omega soldiers, standing outside of the, what had Meela said they called it? A transport vessel?

One of the Omegas was standing and facing away from them, laser weapon in hand, but in more of a sentry position than attack mode. The second was facing their general direction, but his eyes were locked on to something above or perhaps behind them. In his hand was not a laser weapon, but a pole of some kind. It reached all of the way to the ground and was blackish-grey in color. Its smooth surface ended when it reached the grip, which was at about shoulder height. Above the grip was a sharp blade that extended up into a pointy tip about half a meter above the Omega's head. The third soldier was leaning up against the transport vessel itself, head down. For all Jake knew, he might actually be asleep.

Meela made a series of gestures pointing to each of the Omega soldiers, and then back at each of them, including Daisy. Jake thought he got what she was trying to say. Meela would get the one with the laser weapon, Daisy would get pole man and he would get Mr. Sleepy. He had to wonder if Daisy had any clue what Meela was talking about, but then to his surprise, she seemed to sit up a bit and get into an attack-like posture. Her hind quarters raised into the air and her tail began whipping back and forth like an energized snake.

Jake took a deep breath and pulled his weapon from its holster. Meela did the same. She then gave him a long nod and turned to aim. He mirrored her movements and looked through his weapon's sight, trying to find the lazy member of the Omega trio. In his current position, he saw that there were a few branches in his way. The last thing he needed was to hit one of those and not his intended target. He shifted to his right, and then heard the most gut-wrenching sound he could have thought of in that moment: the load SNAP of a twig on the ground that he had just stepped on. All three Omega soldiers' heads popped up and looked in the direction of the sound instantly.

They had been spotted.

"Go, go!" Meela shouted.

Meela fired. Jake fired. Daisy catapulted from her attack position. Everything happened simultaneously, and within only a few seconds it was done.

Meela was the most fortunate of the three of them. Her shot struck home, right in the center of her target's chest. The man's body flew back, both hands flinging upward. The man's hand that was holding his weapon actually fired it as he fell. Three or four blasts sailed into the woods, narrowly missing Meela. The man landed square on his back in a puff of dust, not moving whatsoever as he struck the ground.

Jake wasn't quite as fortunate. His shot only hit the arm of Mr. Sleepy. Well, not Mr. Sleepy anymore. It was also the wrong arm. The other, non-injured arm still held firm to his laser weapon. That one swiveled around and fired, but before Jake had even known about the fate of his shot, he had the good instinct (or perhaps training) to fall flat to the ground. The shot passed above his head. He could hear it but not see it because his face was now buried deep into a pile of dirt. The sound had been quite loud.

Daisy was the least fortunate. Her pole-wielding prey was ready for her. As soon as she had made her presence known by leaping from behind the greenery, the Omega soldier did two things in extremely quick succession. First, he struck the butt of the pole down against the ground hard. This action activated some kind of blue energy output surrounding the bladed portion of the weapon. Tiny blue streaks of lightning danced all around the blade, like a mini thunderstorm. Second, he crouched down to the ground and thrust the tip of the blade up and out.

Still in mid-air, Daisy had no time to adjust. Her belly fell directly into the tip of the weapon. It ripped through her insides with almost no effort whatsoever, and soon the pointed end could be seen protruding out of her back, just missing her spine. The bolts of blue lighting hovered at the weapon's tip, but then they lashed out, jumping and rolling all over the megacat's body like a sick fireworks display. As the lightning storm ended, the soldier thrust the weapon out from the beast's belly.

Daisy lay there, completely limp and unmoving. Jake could hear Meela's voice but could not make out any of the words. Everything seemed to go hazy... fuzzy. It was hard to make out anything visually or audibly with any real sense of clarity. He thought perhaps he saw a few more blasts discharged from weapons, but it was impossible to tell whether or not they had come from Meela's or one of the Omega's. They certainly hadn't come from his.

Moments later a familiar voice shook Jake from his dream-like state.

"Jake! Meela! Please stop!"

It was Tom.

"Please, stop shooting!" Tom continued. "They are going to kill me!"

Jake looked around. Meela was still next to him, sitting there on all fours, face streaked with dirt and wet, eyes rimmed in bright red. He wanted nothing more than to pull her close and hold her tight, but that was not possible. There were at least two remaining Omega soldiers out there right now and they had the upper hand. He wondered if they could see him or Meela. He supposed not. If that were true, they'd probably already be dead by now.

He peered through the brush and saw everything he needed to know. There were three Omega soldiers in front of them, although one was clearly no longer a concern, laying flat on his back. The one with the pole (the one that had gutted Meela's dearest companion) was now holding Tom gruffly by the upper arm with his non-pole wielding hand. The third Omega soldier had his weapon sticking directly into Tom's back. It must have been digging in quite deep, too, considering how much Tom was squirming around.

Jake stood up. The Omegas would have a clear shot now, but he didn't care about that anymore. It went against everything his gut told him he should be doing in that moment, but he slowly stepped forward, one foot at a time until he was completely free of the forest's protection. This was not a surrender, however. His weapon was up and ready to fire, pointed in the direction of the Omega soldier currently threatening Tom's life. He stopped about a meter away from the three men.

Daisy's body was just a few steps to Jake's left. She was lying on her side, her belly facing Jake. He could still see the puncture wound. Blood was slowly draining out of it like a sadistic sink, collecting into a large pool that was continually growing, heading in his direction. In a few minutes if he stayed put, his shoes would be stained red. Her face hung there, eyes looking skyward as if hoping for some divine intervention that would never come. Her mouth was slowly opening and closing, displaying the jaws that had on so many occasions been a terror to her enemies. Now they were useless. Her breaths were long and labored.

"Good, now we come to it," the Omega soldier holding the laser weapon to Tom's back said. He used his free hand to remove his helmet. When it plopped to the ground, Jake saw a familiar face. It was hard to forget that salt and pepper hair, that grisly face, those scars.

"It's nice to see you again, Jake," he said. "Although I must admit, it is under much different circumstances than the two of us have been used to. Where's your girlfriend?"

"She's dead!" Jake lied. "Your friend got her just before he died."

"That warms my heart," the man said. "She always was such an annoying bitch. I only wish it was me that had gotten to pull the trigger. Oh well. One down, one to go!"

"Let him go!" Jake growled.

"I don't think so, at least not yet. You've lost one of your friends today, but if you are smart you can still save the other. Look Jake, you know what we are after here. If you want your friend to live, the answer is simple. Give us the compass."

"Don't do it!" Tom yelled.

"Shut up, you!" the man said, kicking the back of one of Tom's legs. Tom fell to the ground, but was just as quickly yanked back up again by his pole-wielding captor. His feet scrambled around on the ground, but they finally found purchase, hanging his body a little lower to the ground than before. Jake could see the look in Tom's eyes. It was a look of desperation, even defeat. It wasn't a look he was used to seeing from Tom. Had Tom given up?

"If I give you the compass," Jake said, "do you promise not to harm him?"

"Is that not what I just said?" Salt and Pepper hair said, now seeming to grow impatient.

"Jake…" Tom mumbled. His head lowered to face the ground.

"Fine," Jake said, "I'll give it to you."

"That's a smart boy," Salt and Pepper said with a smile.

Jake reached into his pocket and pulled out the small, metallic disc. He eyed it for a moment and then looked back up at the two Omega soldiers before him. He lifted the thing up so that it was held at eye level. The eyes of the unmasked man before him seemed to grow twice as large.

"How do we do this?" Jake asked.

"Feel free to give it a good toss," Salt and Pepper said.

"Ok…" Jake said and gave his wrist a flick, releasing the device into the air.

It landed right at Tom's feet.

"Oops," Jake said.

Salt and Pepper contorted his face into his all-too-familiar scowl. Very carefully, he bent down towards the ground, attempting to keep the point of his weapon attached to Tom's back. Keeping his eyes trained directly on Jake, Salt and Pepper found the disc that was lying on the ground with his free hand and grabbed it. He then began the same slow dance, rising back up to a standing position.

Salt and Pepper's partner leaned over slightly for a better look at the new object. "Wait a minute!" he said. "This one looks different from ours, doesn't it?"

"Of course it does," Salt and Pepper barked, "this one is the compass. It is not *supposed* to look like the others!"

"Yeah, but it sure doesn't *look* like a compass!"

"Don't worry, the Chancellor will know how to operate it. All we need to do is get it to him."

"Are you sure it works like the others? Because when Shail and Grot left they had our only-"

"Of course it does! How do you think this little twerp and his friend made it outside of their dome in the first place?"

"Oh, right."

"Come on, let's go. We have what we need. The Chancellor will be pleased to see us when we return. We have finally succeeded where so many have failed. He will surely have a great reward in store for us."

"What about Tom?" Jake said.

"Oh right, our arrangement," Salt and Pepper said. "You know, I think the Chancellor will probably be even more pleased if we not only return with the compass but if we report that all of you are dead as well."

"WHAT?!?" Jake screamed. "I thought the Chancellor wanted me taken alive!"

"Is that what one of the others told you? Yes, it's true, Jake. The Chancellor did request that if at all possible, we bring you back with the compass. But you know what? What the Chancellor doesn't know won't hurt him. He may want you alive, but after what I've been through, I don't."

"You bastard..."

"Sorry to break our little 'gentlemen's arrangement', Jake. If you ever took the time to actually get to know me, you'd know that I am in no way, shape or form a gentleman."

Jake took a step forward. That was all the farther he got. The weapon discharged and everything after that seemed to slow down. Jake saw Tom's eyes open wide as his chest opened up from the inside and several streaks of blue came pouring out. Tom's face had turned from one of shock to one of confusion. He fell forward and his head turned slightly to the side, as if in an attempt to turn around and figure out what had happened behind him. His torso hit the ground with a plop, his near-perfect blonde hair flapping up amidst the cloud of dust.

"NOOO!!!!" Jake screamed, too stunned to do much of anything else.

Then he heard the voice in his head, *Jake, you are going to be next if you don't do something!*

His reaction was nearly too late. He raised his weapon and fired… and fired…and fired. He didn't know how many shots he squeezed off or where they all went exactly, but he hoped it would be enough to cover his escape. He made for the forest. A few more laser blasts came sailing his way as he ran. He fired back over his shoulder in return, once again not really looking to see where his shots had gone. He nearly tripped over a downed tree branch as he entered the brush.

Once he had cover around him, he ventured a quick peek at the two men behind him. One was on the ground. He had actually hit one! Salt and Pepper was gone. No pursuit. He guessed the man didn't want to push his luck, especially given the fact that he had a prize for his Chancellor in hand. The transport vessel boomed a deep tone and then seemed to belch itself to life. For something so big and lumbering, it lifted up off of the ground and started moving fairly quickly. It wouldn't ever beat a hover bike in a race, but it would surely beat any man running on foot.

Jake turned and saw Meela laying there, not a meter away. She was still on all fours, but now the rest of her body seemed slumped to the ground more, like someone who has completely given up on doing any more push-ups. She was frozen there. It was strange. He placed a hand on her back. She jumped as soon as he had felt the fabric of her jacket. He pulled back instantly.

"It's me, Meela," he said. "It's Jake."

Her head turned slowly to the side as if to confirm this information. When she saw that it was indeed Jake, every muscle in her body relaxed. She moved slowly, but eventually she was able to turn her body over and form it into a sitting position on the ground.

"Jake, I'm so sorry," she said. "After they stabbed Daisy, I just... just... froze. I can't explain it. I should have been there to help you. If I had been... maybe Tom..."

So she knew. Jake had to admit to himself that maybe she was right. Maybe Tom would be alive right now if she had intervened. Perhaps that transport ship wouldn't be barreling its way toward the dome's barrier, either, but he had to put those thoughts out of his mind. What was done was done and there was nothing anyone could do about it anymore. Things had not gone to plan. And now... now, they each had a friend who was gone from their lives forever.

CHAPTER 25

*"Put your trust in the Founders, but
put more trust in yourself."*

-The Book of the Founders

Jake and Meela exited the protection of the forest. There was no need to hide anymore. Their last remaining enemy had left them and was now far away, making steady progress towards the world outside of the domes. In minutes, the transport vessel would be through the great barrier.

Meela had very quickly found a spot on the ground near Daisy's head. She sat with her legs crossed and began slowly stroking the fur atop the megacat's large head. The beast was still breathing, but now only in a few shallow gasps. Fresh tears began to flow from Meela's face and landed in the large pool of blood that had now stopped growing. With little splashes they plopped in and mixed with the blood, appearing lighter in shade for a moment... but only for a moment.

Turning from her dying companion, Meela looked up at Jake, who was simply standing there, staring at Tom's body, dumbstruck. Should he turn him over? Should he lay his hands upon him, much like Meela was doing with Daisy? Should try to say some kind of eulogy? He didn't know what to do so he chose to do nothing instead. The shock of Tom's death froze him still as if he had been killed himself. After a brief moment, his eyes slowly floated up to see the transport ship continue to make its departure. Meela attempted to look for the ship herself, craning her neck this way and that.

"Should we go after him?" Meela asked. "We still have one hover bike."

Jake said nothing, but continued to watch. The transport vessel was at the border now. It began the familiar change in color to blue, but this time it flashed and flickered, like someone opening and closing their eyelids in quick succession. He could clearly see half the ship was outside of the dome and the other half was still inside. Another flash, this time with greater intensity. The ship slowed to a halt, running aground. Then came one more bright, blue flash that lit up the entire sky. Even a few tendrils of blue energy shot up from it, reminding him of the weapon used to stab Daisy.

Then, came the explosions.

There was one on either side of the dome's surface. Once the initial fireball had subsided, Jake could see that the transport ship had been ripped cleanly in two. The section that had intersected the clear barrier itself was... well, just *gone*. Gone to where? He had no idea. What remained were two smoking piles of debris, one inside the dome, the other outside the dome, and although he couldn't see it, he knew they also included a corpse belonging an Omega Order soldier.

Meela sprang up from her seated position. She stood in disbelief, her red, tear-soaked eyes wide. After a moment, she turned back to Jake.

"What the hell just happened?" she asked.

Jake just smiled and reached into his pocket. Out came the compass, complete with its two sets of red numbers. One read "3,221.92" and the other continued its lazy progression towards zero:

7,456,322....
7,456,321....
7,456,320....

"The compass? You still have it?" Meela said.

"You don't think I was about to give it to those assholes, do you?" Jake said.

"But, how…"

"What I gave them was a decoy, I guess you could say. It was a different device, one that had a hole blasted in it," Jake said, still surveying the wreckage. "I guess it must have malfunctioned."

"Wow!" Meela said, turning back to view what was left of the massive vessel.

"I knew that the only people who had ever actually seen the compass were you, me and Tom," Jake explained. "I took a chance that the Omega Order had no idea what the compass actually looked like; how it was different from the other devices."

"That was a pretty big chance," Meela said.

"What choice did I have? I had to do something. I just wish they hadn't shot Tom."

Jake looked over at his friend again, lying there with his face in the dirt. Tom had always been the optimist in the group, always telling Jake that everything would be all right. Was it some sort of sick irony that Tom was the one to end up with a shot to the back? How was that fair? "Life under the dome never is fair," Tom had once said. Apparently, that dome didn't have to just be Magella. Tom had always been there to encourage him and keep him pressing forward, ever since they had left Magella. That was a moment that seemed like a lifetime ago now. How could he go on without his friend by his side? He felt cold and vulnerable without Tom, like a man who was halfway home and realized as the rain began to fall that he had forgotten his umbrella.

At the same time, Jake knew that thanks to his friend, he was now a different man, a changed man. The scared little boy was gone. A confident, strong man now stood.

Jake walked over for a better look at his friend. From this position, Jake could clearly see where the shot of energy had entered Tom's back. Dried blood surrounded the hole that was about as wide as the weapon that had been used to create it. Jake looked down and closed his eyes. A single tear found its way down his right cheek.

"Tom... oh Tom..." he said.

He heard footsteps approaching and looked up. It was Meela, of course. She bent down for a closer look, as well. This time it was Meela's hand that got to rub Jake's back. His eyes closed once more, squeezing out a couple fresh tears.

"Jake, I'm so sorry," was all Meela could manage.

I'm sorry, you're sorry, everybody's sorry, Jake thought. *What else is there to say but 'I'm sorry'? What CAN someone say in a situation like this? 'Everything will be all right' might be a close contender, but that would be a lie, wouldn't it? Everything would absolutely NOT be all right.*

"Um, Jake?" Meela said. "Did you notice this?"

Jake allowed his eyes to begrudgingly open once more. The longer he had been here, the more he came to realize that he wanted to be someplace, *anyplace,* else. He knew in his heart that they would probably have to take this body with them somehow and give him a proper burial, or send-off, or whatever. He wasn't even sure what Tom would have wanted done in the event of his death. He knew full well that the man wasn't particularly religious to begin with. With his eyes open now and looking back down at his friend and his mortal wound, all he could think was, *what could I have done differently? How could I have avoided this fate for you, my friend?*

Then, he finally saw what Meela was getting at, looking deeper into the wound. There was plenty of blood, and scorched flesh, yes, but there was something else there as well. It was what looked like a bunch of strands of... well, Jake wasn't exactly sure. They were mostly golden in color, but others looked to be more silver. Some were severed from the blast, no doubt, but others were still intact, running from one unknown place inside Tom's body to another. Then one of them sparked. It actually sparked!

"Wha... what am I looking at?" Jake asked.

"It isn't anything I've ever seen before," Meela said.

"What is he?" Jake said, now standing up and taking a few steps away from Tom's body, as if it were some kind of disgusting monster. "He's not human... WHAT IS HE?!?"

"Your guardian," came a gargled voice below them.

Both Meela and Jake instantly looked down at Tom. His body still lay there, motionless. Had it been a trick? Had it all been in Jake's mind? The look on Meela's face told him it wasn't just his imagination. She had heard it too. Jake carefully bent back down near Tom's body and grabbed his right arm with both hands. Meela got the idea very quickly and did the same thing.

"One, two, three..." Jake said.

With that, the two of them pulled on Tom's arm and were able to turn over his body. Jake immediately looked at Tom's face. His eyes were open and they were looking directly in Jake's direction. Jake had never believed in ghosts or the notion of being haunted ever in his life, but in that moment, he decided he could be a believer.

Jake didn't know whether to be happy, relieved, shocked, betrayed, mad or all of them at once. In the end, he chose to simply be thankful that his friend was alive. He would have time to deal with all of the other questions swirling around in his head in time, he hoped. Tom was not only alive, but he was now propping himself up on his elbows and sitting up. More blood flowed from his open wound as he readjusted his body, cringing as he did so. Jake couldn't believe it. Tom was acting more like he had just stubbed his toe rather than having his chest blasted open.

"Tom, I don't even know where to begin," Jake said. "How are you still alive? What's with those strange wires inside you? Who- what are you... *really?*"

"All wonderful questions," Tom replied with his trademark grin.

Jake wasn't impressed this time, "all right cut the crap. Come clean, Tom."

"Well, let's just say you've seen things you weren't exactly sup- posed to see... at least not yet. It is unfortunate, yes, but it shouldn't affect our mission too significantly. There are certain portions of the plan that just need to be moved up, that's all."

"Stop speaking in riddles!" Meela shouted. "Tell us what is really going on here!"

"Well, I'll tell you what I can," Tom said. "This may frustrate you, Jake, but there is a lot to this quest that even I don't know."

Jake did his best to understand, but it didn't show very well. "Ok, fine, Tom. What can you tell me?"

"What I have to, considering the circumstances," Tom said. "As you can see, my inner anatomy isn't exactly the same as yours. I am not human. You may not even consider me 'alive', depending on your definition. I am called a 'synthetic human'. I am made to resemble human beings, but I am not one myself. I am a human replica created by other human beings."

"Impossible," Meela said, "no human has the knowhow or capa- bility to create an exact replica of themselves, not the least of which one as sophisticated as you."

"From your life experience, I can see why you feel that way," Tom said, "but I am not lying to you. As I said, there are some things that really should have waited until later, but our current circumstances have made that impossible."

"Why were you created?" Jake asked.

"Long ago, during the great war, we synthetic humans were created as infiltration devices." Tom said.

"What war?" Meela asked.

"The war between the Omega Order and the Founders." Tom explained. "It was long before these domes were created. The Omega Order was much larger back then. What we have seen here is just a small fraction of their original force."

"Wait," Jake said, "you are speaking of the Founders like they were actual people... like us."

Tom took a long breath. "Jake, they *were* actual people, like us."

No.

No, that couldn't be. Jake had spent countless hours praying to the Founders, seeking their guidance, asking for their help. He refused to believe that he had just been praying to nothing. He had felt their influence in his life. He had felt their presence when he looked up at them hanging in the night sky. That *was* them... wasn't it? Tom was lying. He had to be. That was the only explanation. He was some kind of spy, some kind of evil agent, sent to seed mistrust and lies. What he was saying couldn't be the truth. Jake could not, would not, believe it. One simple statement couldn't be enough to shatter a lifetime of belief.

"You're wrong." Jake finally said.

"Jake, I realize just how difficult this must be to hear and believe me, I didn't want to say anything to you until later, when you might be better prepared to hear it." Tom said.

"Are you trying to tell me that everything I have believed in has been a lie? That it has all been a load of crap? Is that what you are saying?"

Tom sat up a tad bit higher and looked Jake right in the face. His eyes burned with a level of intensity that Jake had never seen in Tom before. "Jake, I want you to listen very carefully to what I am going to say next because it is very important. The Founders ARE real. Your faith in them was not misplaced. All of the important aspects of what you believe are true. Only the details have changed."

"Only the details?" Jake said, almost mockingly.

"Yes, all of the important facts still remain. The Founders still saved the human race from destruction by the creation of these domed worlds. They just did so by their own ingenuity and skill, not by some divine magic."

"And the stars up in the sky? Are you telling me that they are not the Founders, either?"

"I'm sorry, Jake, but no, they are not."

Everybody's sorry.

"What are they then?"

"They are suns, just like our own, just incredibly far away."

"What?" Meela cut in.

"Ugh, look, as I mentioned, some of this stuff might be hard for you to understand right now," Tom said. "Over time, perhaps, it will get better."

"Ok, Tom," Jake said, "we'll stop with the metaphysical questions for now. You said you *used* to be an infiltration device. Is that what you are now? I guess what I'd really like to know is, what do you want? What is your purpose? Why are you here?"

"I'm here to guide and protect you, Jake," Tom said. "That compass you carry is more important than you could possibly imagine."

Jake looked down at the device that was still in his hands. He had almost forgotten about it amidst all of the chaos that had occurred recently. It felt warm in his grasp. The little blue light still pointed the same direction. The numbers on it continued to count down...

7,455,707...
7,455,706...
7,455,705...

"What happens when the numbers stop?" Jake asked.

"I don't know," Tom replied.

"Bullshit!" Meela yelled, grabbing Tom by the collar with both hands.

Tom wasn't phased. He didn't even flinch. "I said I don't know."
Meela let go, reluctantly.

"What do you mean you don't know?" Jake asked.

"I only know what I'm supposed to know, just like you only know what you are supposed to know," Tom said.

"No more goddam riddles!" Jake said, forcefully.

"My brain is different from yours, Jake," Tom said. "An incredible amount of information can be stored in it, far more than any human's. However, information can also be extracted. There may have been experiences in my past that I can now no longer recall. Do you know what my first memory is, Jake?"

"What?"

"The knowledge that I needed to find you and help you complete this quest. I had all of the necessary details: where to find you, what your name was, what you looked like, where to find the device for your dome..."

"It wasn't originally in Morzellano's mine, was it?"

"Actually, it is still there."

"What do you mean?"

"The compass, this special device, has been with me the entire time, since the beginning. Magella's device is still there, in Magella. It's actually closer to Hope City than New Salem, if you want to know the truth."

"So again, you lied to me."

"Only because I had to. Jake, I do apologize for the deception. I know it must be difficult to feel as though you can trust me now, but understand, it was for a good reason."

"And why is that?"

"The conscript, YOU, had to choose for themselves to take this journey. I am here to help, not force someone into a role they did not want."

"Are you saying that there were others?"

"If you decided not to, yes. But understand, Jake, you were our, um, number one draft pick."

"What the hell does that mean?"

"It means you were our first choice, Jake. You always have been."

"But why, Tom? Why? I've told you this before. I am not special."

"Are you sure?" Tom said with a smile.

"There are plenty of others far better suited for this than me," Jake continued.

"I overheard you saying something to Meela earlier," Tom said. "Correct me if I get any of the details wrong, ok? You were explaining to her that as a ploy to save us, you gave that Omega Order trooper a different device, one that had a hole blasted in it, correct?"

"Yes, that's true."

"And how, pray tell, did that device get its hole?"

"I had shot it with my laser weapon."

"Right, and what setting was that laser weapon set to?"

"Subdue."

"Of course it was. Did you know, Jake, that the only way one can damage these devices is shooting them with a bolt of energy with a power frequency that can only be achieved by a setting of 'subdue' on these weapons?"

"How do you know that?"

"You see all of this advanced technology the Omega Order uses? These *transport vessels,* these *laser weapons,* these *hover bikes?* Where do you think it comes from?"

"Them, I assumed."

"They do know enough to fix and maintain these items, that is true, but they did not invent them. These in actuality are relics from the days of the Great War. I was created by those who also created all of these wonderful inventions. So, I know for a fact that only a shot at 'subdue' could disable one of the devices. Just a fun twist of irony made possible by their creators. Jake, there are more important things than skill with a weapon or strength and stamina. Your compassion, your love of life, even the life of a terrible enemy, kept you from setting that laser weapon to kill. And look, it was that action in the end that saved you!"

Jake looked back at the ruined remains of the transport vessel, still pumping thick, black smoke out into the sky. A small crowd of people had begun gathering around it now. "But I ended up killing them!"

"Not on purpose. You had no idea that would happen, Jake. Sometimes death is the only option. It doesn't matter who you are or what you believe. There are times when there are no other choices left but the death of your enemy if you wish to survive yourself. You, however, will always look for those other choices first. This is just one of the many things that makes you so special, Jake. Perhaps in time you will discover the others."

Jake had to pause for a moment. It was a lot to take in. Hearing he was responsible for saving the entire human race had been a big shock to his system at the time. This new shock was much bigger. If Tom was right (and Jake had a pretty good feeling that he *was*), Jake's entire world had been flipped on its head and was now completely different.

Or was it?

It wasn't as if the mountains had been ripped from their foundations and replaced by flat, grassland. It wasn't as if all of the lakes in the world had suddenly dried up. It wasn't as if all of the domes had suddenly disappeared into the ground. Everything and everyone was still there. Nothing was different, *really*. Maybe Tom was right after all. Only the details had changed.

Jake's destiny still lay before him. Paradise and salvation for his people was still out there, waiting to be found. It was up to him to find it, if he still believed. If he still had faith. Jake's faith had brought him this far. Perhaps his faith could take him the rest of the way, too. It was just a new faith, a *revised* faith. He just had to have the courage to accept it, to accept the fact that perhaps he didn't have all of the answers. Nor should he, now that he thought about it. This was a journey after all, not some static point where he could stay put, knowing everything there was to know about his one little area of the world.

More was out there… more to discover, more to challenge him. Was he ready? Could he take that next step?

Jake extended his hand out to his friend.

"Come on, Tom," he said. "Let's get you fixed up."